Cover Copy

There can be only one…for both of them.

Year 1210, Scottish Highlands.

Annella, the fae-blooded daughter of a warrior, holds the spirit-walker ability. With her fae skill, she has only one goal, to find the man who captured her father and brother and seek retribution. The last thing she expects though is to connect within her dreams with an infuriatingly rugged Highlander of shifter blood who lives over eight-hundred years in the future. Her destiny is set, to free her nearest and dearest, although to find them she must now enlist the aid of the warrior from the future. He's the best tracker there is, and also her best chance at finding them.

Highland warrior shifter Alec Matheson meets the most intriguing lass who visits him in his dreams, a woman who also poses the greatest challenge. His soul bound mate has come to him during her greatest time of need, and now he must travel back through time to aid her. His lithe, golden-haired enchantress wears lad's clothing and is swift with the sword and trained in all manner of warfare. She is also nothing like he expects, yet everything he has ever desired.

Now, he must make certain they both survive her perilous mission, for seeking retribution could ensure their death, or unite their spirited souls. Let the battle for love begin.

Books by Joanne Wadsworth

The Matheson Brothers Series
Highlander's Desire, Book One
Highlander's Passion, Book Two
Highlander's Seduction, Book Three
Highlander's Kiss, Book Four
Highlander's Heart, Book Five
Highlander's Sword, Book Six
Highlander's Bride, Book Seven
Highlander's Caress, Book Eight
Highlander's Touch, Book Nine
Highlander's Shifter, Book Ten
Highlander's Claim, Book Eleven
Highlander's Courage, Book Twelve
Highlander's Mermaid, Book Thirteen

Highlander Heat Series
Highlander's Castle, Book One
Highlander's Magic, Book Two
Highlander's Charm, Book Three
Highlander's Guardian, Book Four
Highlander's Faerie, Book Five
Highlander's Champion, Book Six
Highlander's Captive (Short Story)

Billionaire Bodyguards Series
Billionaire Bodyguard Attraction, Book One
Billionaire Bodyguard Boss, Book Two
Billionaire Bodyguard Fling, Book Three

Books by Joanne Wadsworth

Regency Brides Series
The Duke's Bride, Book One
The Earl's Bride, Book Two
The Wartime Bride, Book Three
The Earl's Secret Bride, Book Four
The Prince's Bride, Book Five
Her Pirate Prince, Book Six

Princesses of Myth Series
Protector, Book One
Warrior, Book Two
Hunter (Short Story - Included in Warrior, Book Two)
Enchanter, Book Three
Healer, Book Four
Chaser, Book Five

Highlander's Sword

The Matheson Brothers, Book Six

Joanne Wadsworth

Highlander's Sword
ISBN-13: 978-1-99-003436-7
Copyright © 2015, Joanne Wadsworth
Cover Art by Joanne Wadsworth
First electronic publication: January 2016

Joanne Wadsworth
http://www.joannewadsworth.com

All Rights Are Reserved. No part of this book may be used or reproduced in any manner whatsoever without written permission, except in the case of brief quotations embodied in critical articles and reviews. The unauthorized reproduction or distribution of this copyrighted work is illegal. No part of this book may be scanned, uploaded or distributed via the Internet or any other means, electronic or print, without the author's permission.

AUTHOR'S NOTE:
This book is a work of fiction. The names, characters, places, and incidents are products of the writer's imagination or have been used fictitiously and are not to be construed as real. Any resemblance to persons, living or dead, actual events, locale or organizations is entirely coincidental. The author does not have any control over and does not assume any responsibility for third-party websites or their content.

Published in the United States of America

First digital publication: January 2016
First print publication: January 2016

Gilleoin – The Legend

In the twelfth century, a man named Gilleoin became the first and only known man to hold bear shifter blood, an ability gifted to him by The Most High One. His clan was called Matheson, and when he mated with a woman carrying faerie blood, they created a line shrouded in secrecy, a line that far into the future, now neared extinction…

Cherub – The Fae Angel of Love

Clan Matheson warrior encampment, Scotland, 1210.

In the dead of night, unease consumed Cherub and wouldn't abate as she paced the sandy shoreline of Loch Alsh. The gentle glow of the moon rippled over the rolling waves and across the treetops of the forest rising high behind their warrior encampment. The foamy swell of the surf tumbled in, bubbled over the tips of her riding boots then washed back out. With her hands raised high and the golden ribbons at the cinched waist of her white gown fluttering about her arms, she allowed the very air itself to whisper across her fingertips and bring to her the secrets it held. As an immortal time-walker and the faerie king's daughter, her duty to her fae kind who walked this Earth would always come first, no matter what place or time that drew her toward, and in this moment, untold secrets unraveled around her. So many lost souls. So many of her fae kind needing her aid.

"I can sense your worry. Talk to me, my elusive imp." Kirk, her warrior soul bound mate, stepped in behind her and nuzzled her neck, his body a heavenly heat she wished only to surround herself in.

"No' only do I sense lost souls this night, but I also sense the pain of loss to come, particularly for one of my fae kind. I also fear 'tis a pain I cannae halt." She turned around in his loving embrace, slid her fingers through his silky, black shoulder-length locks. Being this close to him soothed her, always eased her tension when naught else could.

"Tell me whose pain you sense."

"Annella's. She is soul bound to Alec. The two have actually already met even though they reside over eight-hundred years apart." Breathing deep, she pinpointed Annella's current location. She should be right here at their warrior encampment with her father and brother, the young woman an enchanting lass who wore lad's clothing and was swift with the sword and trained in all manner of warfare. Only something had drawn Annella away from their camp and across their land border with clan MacKenzie, their fiercest enemy. Now, Annella had been strung up within the bow of a tree, her worry and fear pummeling through to her. It vibrated with such strength that she'd easily picked up on it, as had Annella's closest kin. "Annella's father and brother both hold the battle skill and have sensed her need for them rising, just as I have. They've set out after her, the bonds between the three incredibly strong."

"How have Annella and Alec already met when you've never taken either through one of your portals?" Confusion marred his brow. "I would have noticed them joining us as we traveled."

"Annella is a spirit-walker and has visited Alec by traveling through the dream realm to him while he sleeps." She rubbed her cheek against Kirk's broad chest. "Annella does no' require one of my portals to reach him."

"Alec has never mentioned Annella to me before. Are you certain they're mated?" Alec came from Ivanson Castle, from the same twenty-first century time as Kirk did.

"Very, although even they are unaware a bond has formed between them. Alec believes Annella is naught but an apparition since she remains only visible to him within his dreams, although once Annella's skill fully evolves, something which is overdue in happening, then she'll be able to travel to him through the dream realm then emerge and solidify her spiritual body. Spirit-walkers use the dream realm to travel to where they wish to go. That is the essence of their gift."

"What of the pain of loss you sense is coming?" He caressed her back, his love flowing down their merged link and surrounding her with its vibrant intensity.

"Duncan MacKenzie has already captured Annella, and Niall and Ronan have gone to her. The battle to come is one I cannae halt, because if I do, then I'll forever alter Annella and Alec's journey to come. The loss I sense is that of Niall and Ronan. They'll be captured and taken, for they too have a journey ahead of them. All I can say is that the mated bond is a very sacred union and I'm no' permitted to breach its creation or completion, no' for any of my fae kind."

"Alec is so very far away."

"Aye, and he is also in denial of their bond, although all mated males long for the chase, and part of their journey is in what they must overcome in order to be with their chosen ones. It builds the foundation for their bond and all that 'twill be. Alec needs to see reason." In the grassy clearing between the shoreline and the forest, a long line of canvas tents dotted the verge and sixty or so warriors sat around the central blazing fire, all except for Annella, her father and brother. "We must wait until things unravel as they should. I will keep my senses open, listening to all the secrets my element brings me."

"So even you don't know all that is about to occur until you're permitted the knowledge?"

"Aye, very much so. The future is interchangeable, always fluctuating and moving. I have no control over it, or at least a very minimal amount."

"I truly don't care for any of our people feeling any pain."

He gripped her tighter around her waist. "Holding back when I know a battle is about to rage isn't easy."

"The same goes for me, but Alec's chase will soon be underway and he must be given the chance to hunt his chosen one as he will be drawn to do."

Never would she abandon her kin during their time of greatest need, but neither would she betray her duty to them either, so for now, she and Kirk would wait, no matter that doing so pained them both.

Chapter 1

Enemy MacKenzie land, Scotland, 1210.

Restrained and tied high in the bow of a tree in the dark of night, Annella Matheson stopped sawing her bound hands together as the forest went eerily quiet all around. 'Twas as if even the small creatures of the night had sought refuge from the warring about to unfold. Certainly, her kin would never allow the enemy to take her.

At the base of the tree she was wedged within, a shadow passed. Duncan MacKenzie. The Chief of MacKenzie's second-born son was every inch a fierce Highland warrior. If only she'd never left her clan's warrior encampment. She wouldn't have done so except for the fearful cry of a child which had drawn her across their border and onto their enemy's land, a child's cry that had come not from a distraught bairn but instead one of Duncan's men. Such trickery and deceit. She should have known better, that the MacKenzies would try such a ploy.

"Captain." A warrior burst into the clearing wearing black breeches and a steel-studded coat, his sword strapped at his side. "Niall Matheson approaches, along with his son. They're moving through the undergrowth, one closely following the other."

"Good. They've come for the lass, just as Muirin's brother saw that they would. The fae sorceress is strong, just as her brother is, their knowledge vast." Hunkered down, Duncan scooped dirt and smothered the flames, his short black hair blazing blue on the ends in the eerie moonlight. Smoke curled into the air, thick and acrid as he glanced at her up high. "Neither your father or brother will escape their capture this night, although sorry I am that I've had to use you in this way, lass. Mayhap in time, you'll come to understand why."

Sorry? He'd just apologized to her? Huh. More trickery. Would he never cease with it?

"What will you do with the lass once we've captured her kin?" The warrior strode to her tree, pressed one palm against the trunk.

"The lass isnae needed, apart from luring her father and brother to me." Duncan pulled a rawhide pouch from his pocket and opened the drawstring, tipped a glittering gold dust into his palm then clenched his fist around it. To the warrior, he muttered. "I'll see to the lass afterward, either ensure her freedom, or mayhap even convince her to come with me. She is a spitfire, a worthy woman to stand at my side, and I'm in need of a wife. She would do rather well, particularly with her spirit-walker skill. Return to your position and make certain the other men are made aware that Niall and Ronan are mine. Neither will escape Muirin's fae magic this night. Both are about to embrace their destiny, something which even their fae princess will likely understand by now. Their coming capture is meant to be, their journey to come one none of us can halt. 'Tis the way of the fae."

How dare he speak as if he knew her fae kind so intimately. She'd certainly never stand willingly at his side, not in any capacity, particularly that of a wife.

"Aye, Captain, then I'll inform the men." The warrior disappeared into the dark, the breeze whispering through the high canopy and rustling the leaves.

"How do you fare up there, lass?"

If she could do more than release a mere mumble through the foul-tasting gag he'd stuffed in her mouth, she'd tell him exactly how she fared. This was madness, all of it. Duncan was her enemy, and if she could, she'd drop down from this tree and slice his head from his shoulders. 'Twould be the best way to ensure his mad ramblings ceased. He certainly needed to be taught a lesson, that no one imprisoned one of the fae.

Argh, if only she could get down. She'd been taught the arts of warfare at Father's hand and should have been better prepared for this attack and containment.

Duncan lifted his massive two-handed claymore free of the baldric across his back and swung it in a wide arc as he limbered up and prepared for the battle to come, for there surely would be one. Father and Ronan held the fae battle skill and would fight for her freedom.

She narrowed her gaze on Duncan's blade, the MacKenzie clan motto blazing upon it. *Luceo non uro*, "I shine not burn." All their enemy ever did was burn, destroying lives as they so shamelessly stole in their ferocious battle to take it all. Clan Matheson had never raised arms against the MacKenzies, unless they'd been forced to defend themselves first.

No more burning for Duncan. Even though restrained, she'd find a way to warn her kin of exactly what awaited them on this forested hilltop. With her eyes closed, she calmed her mind and allowed her thoughts to settle until slowly, the dark finally encroached and she glided toward the dream realm. With her spiritual body separating itself from her physical body, she gladly soared free, her true form slumping within the bow and her head drooping to one side. She'd need to hurry. Danger always lurked when she left her physical form unattended.

No more than a wisp of white, she swept away on the breeze then dipped down toward the forest trail and weaved through the undergrowth, her senses on full alert as she searched for the two men who'd always come for her, always stand by her side.

A rustle tinkered to her left, and she breezed in underneath a thick scrub and swirled to a halt. Father lay on his belly under the bush, Ronan beside him. Father moved first, crawled through to the other side and crouched in his belted kilt and leather jerkin. Chin lifted, he breathed deep, his fae battle skill gifting him with added sleuth and strength during any mission.

Gently, she wound her misty form around him and tried to solidify some part of her ethereal form. How frustrating. Still naught came forth. Surely her skill would evolve soon and she could be far more present at her kin's side. In Father's ear, she whispered, "I'm so sorry. Duncan MacKenzie set a trap and I fell for the ploy. He intends to use me to draw you and Ronan to him then contain you both. He insists your coming capture is meant to be, that your journey to come is one that none of us can halt."

"Duncan and his twin brother have never gotten involved in the fighting between our clans afore, not like their father and younger brother, Jeremiah, have. Although now, he's clearly taken you and declared exactly where he stands, which is firmly on his father's side." He swept his hand out, his fingers lightly and affectionately grazing her misty form. "How many men await us?"

"Close to a dozen warriors, and one of his men has already reported your arrival. They're everywhere, Duncan's trap now set. He also holds a fae sorceress's magic, a glittering golden dust in one hand."

"I know of no fae sorceress. Certainly there is none within our village."

"He called her Muirin."

"Then I'll take additional care, although no one holds my daughter against her will, or uses her as bait to capture either me or Ronan. If Duncan wishes a battle, then he'll have one." Firm determination slashed Father's face, the silver flare on one side of his blond-haired head catching the moonlight as he bent and motioned to Ronan with a flick of his hand.

Ronan snuck in beside Father, both men an imposing sight. They held their position and scanned each direction, the canopy thick overhead and the bitter scent of smoke from the doused fire drifting toward them.

Slowly, succinctly, Father palmed his dirk, his gaze narrowed on the trail leading to the rise. Keeping to the shadows, they both crept and she breezed in beside them, all wispy-white as she kissed her brother's cheek. "You'll find me bound and gagged in the bow of the tree at the top of the hill."

"I'll be there soon, little sister. Wait for me."

"I shall." Her brother had stood at her side her entire life and she didn't doubt he would as well this night, and even though she detested leaving them both, she swept upward toward the treetops and whisked back before taking a deep breath and settling inside her physical body. Her heart continued to beat with or without her present, her breath moving slowly but surely through her, and now returned, she lifted her head, her fingertips tingling and her worry pounding strong.

Father stepped fully into the clearing and withdrew his sword. "'Tis about time we met, Duncan. You and your twin brother have never raised arms against any of our Matheson warriors afore, although clearly that has now changed."

"This isnae about me raising arms against you, but ensuring a future only a few can foresee." Duncan's voice rumbled low and smoothly through the clearing, his words holding her captive.

"Cease speaking in riddles." Father snorted and stole closer, his blade at the ready.

At the base of her tree, Ronan clamped onto the lower branch and with swift and precise ease, snuck his way upward. Hunkered down next to her, he sliced her bindings free and plucked the gag from her mouth then with one finger to his lips, gestured for her to remain quiet as he motioned for her to follow him back down.

In her green tunic and black breeches, lad's clothing she always wore, she swung nimbly down after Ronan then landed on the ground with nary a noise.

"Your daughter is far too impulsive, yet glad I am that she is. Her capture came with ease." Brow cocked, Duncan opened one hand and the glittery dust in his palm sparkled. "She led you directly to me, exactly as foreseen by Muirin's brother. I'll take you to Muirin soon, allow her to answer any questions you might have."

"You'll take me nowhere. Certainly anyone who raises their blade against me or my kin has just ensured their death." Father edged around the clearing, keeping to the darkest corners as he drew Duncan farther away from her and Ronan's hidden position against the tree.

She remained perfectly still, not wanting to divert Father's attention from the one man who would clearly take every advantage of it if she did.

Ronan gripped her shoulders and lips to her ear, murmured, "You need to swing wide of Duncan's men as you return to the camp. Alert our guard and ensure you find Cherub and Kirk. Cherub can come to our aid far quicker than anyone else can since she can soar directly through the skies."

"I cannae leave you and Father behind."

"Never forget our battle skill, little sister, and consider my request a direct order, as if Father himself issued it." He dropped a kiss on her forehead, slid his sword free of its scabbard. "I love you."

"I love you too." And direct orders couldn't be disobeyed. She waited no longer and took off to secure their aid. Aye, the Fae Angel of Love commanded the *air* element, could halt the wind or send it churning if she so desired. She could also cloak her form and become unseen to others. Cherub could whip up a storm and unleash it on whoever she wished, which right now needed to be Duncan and his men. She wouldn't lose Father and Ronan this night, not as Duncan had boasted.

Sprinting, she bounded along the forested trail and once certain she'd gone wide enough to divert Duncan's men, veered back on course toward their warrior encampment a mere mile distant.

The ground blurred, the trees whizzing by. Branches scraped her arms and cheeks but slowed her down not one bit, not when Father and Ronan's fierce battle cry rang out.

Their fight for freedom had begun.

* * * *

Over eight-hundred years in the future and standing at the edge of a forested meadow under the misty moonlight near Ivanson Castle, Alec Matheson swiped another massive log from the pile and thumped it on top of the chopping block. His inner bear raged at him, clawing under his skin, his insistent demand to fight flaring strongly through him. Never had his beast been this on edge, as if something were happening of great import.

"Calm down," he snarled at his other half. "There'll be no freedom for you when you're in this kind of a mood."

Teeth gritted, he swung his axe high and slammed it down on the round head of wood. The thumping *thwack* boomed all around as he drove his axe into the block over and over, until he'd near shredded the wood into a mass of splintered pieces.

One shoulder lifted, he wiped his sweaty brow with his cotton-ribbed blue t-shirt then tossed the slivers of wood into the wheelbarrow. Another massive log in hand, he slung it onto the block, gripped his axe and sliced the wood clear in two, the chopping block underneath it as well.

Grrr. He hadn't meant to do that.

Hell, he really needed to shake off this foul mood, this frustration and anxiety too.

Eyes closed, he tried desperately hard to find some form of control.

Slow breath in. Slow breath out.

Memories surged, of his mysteriously annoying sprite who'd visited him each night this past month in his dreams. Huh. Thoughts of her right now wouldn't calm either him or his beast in the least.

"You believe I'm a ghost, Alec? No more than a spiritual apparition?"

Her question had echoed hauntingly around him as he'd slept, and as usual his bear had thrashed to get closer to her in his dreams, even though impossible. Dreams were dreams, not a reality. *"Of course you're an apparition, made up within my own mind in my desperate need for some company, someone both me and my bear can't harm. That's what you are. A desire for me to feel normal."*

"I can sense your other half who you continually try to keep tamped down." Her spirit had warmed him deep within, as it always did each time he dreamed of her. *"His soul too reaches out to mine, his need for company clear to see."*

"Again, you're just a dream, a figment of my imagination. You should leave. I've certainly had enough of this annoying conversation tonight." He'd thumped his pillow, burrowed his head deeper into it. *"Maybe tomorrow I'll be in a better mood, although that wasn't a request for you to return."*

"You're rarely in a better mood, no matter how many times I return." A giggle escaped her, wound its way around his heart and made him ache for her to take some kind of form and be real.

"Go away, pest. Isn't there someone else you can annoy this night?"

"Well, you arena the only one who I visit within the dream realm. Father and Ronan are fun to annoy when they slumber."

"Then go and pester them. I'm sure they'd appreciate your

company more than me right now."

"You really are in a terrible mood, far more than usual." Her presence began to fade, her voice drifting away. *"I wish you sweet dreams, Alec. Rest well, my mighty bear. I shall grant you the uninterrupted sleep you seek this night."*

"Damn it, wait." He'd demanded her return, yet she hadn't come back. She'd wisped away and a dark cloud of loneliness had saturated him. His mysteriously annoying sprite had gone and he'd never been more frustrated. What was it about her that so intrigued him?

With a shake of his head, he cleared his thoughts, propped his axe against the trunk of the closest pine tree and checked his wristwatch. Two-thirty in the morning. He'd have to be up in three and a half hours for training with his fellow warriors. He tapped the hilt of his ever-present claymore belted at his side. The mighty two-handed sword had been passed down throughout the generations, from father to son until it had reached his hands, although never would he hand it down to his own son, not when he had no desire for a soul bound mate as his fellow kinsmen did. Shackling a woman to him in such an intimate way would only ever end in her death. His beast was too fierce, unruly, and completely unapproachable.

With a roll of his shoulders, he heaved the wheelbarrow up by the handles and weaved through the trees. He left the gritty, pine-needle covered trail behind and emerged next to the woodshed, stacked the wood and tipped the barrow against the side then strode through the postern gate and into the bailey. From the center well, he lifted the swinging pail and flipped the water inside over his head. It sluiced down his chest and back. So invigorating. He jogged to the front door, bounded inside and upstairs, opened his chamber door at the end of the passageway on the third floor and walked inside. Soggy shirt stripped off, he tossed it into the corner wicker basket as he made his private bathroom then flicked on the overhead light.

Boots toed off and faded jeans unzipped, he shoved the worn denim down his legs and opened the glass shower door before flicking the lever on. Water sprayed and once it had heated and steam swirled, he stepped inside the cubicle and soaped himself clean. So often he wondered what his ghostly apparition looked like, what her name was. He'd never ask her though. That would only feed into her insistence she was real. Real, his ass. Although since it didn't hurt trying to imagine her, he'd have her all curvy with golden tresses that swayed beguilingly to her pert backside. Aye, and her eyes, they'd be a mesmerizing blue. Her breasts. Full and heavy in his hands with succulent nipples he could lave attention on. Now, that would be a dream.

He scrubbed his hair, rinsed the shampoo out and shut the water off. From the vanity cupboard, he nabbed a thick white towel, dried himself then shaved his jaw and combed his hair. Done, he tossed his towel over the heated rail and stomped to his king-size bed, slipped between the crisp white bedsheets and head on his pillow, counted the wooden slats in the ceiling above as moonlight slivered through his window and flickered over each slat. The third plank across held a knot and he followed each of the ring marks around it as he tried to clear his mind and focus only on sleep.

Slowly, he drifted, sheer exhaustion taking him under.

"I cannae stay long this night, Alec." Her voice floated within his mind, filled with pain, her sudden arrival and clear anguish gripping his heart and fisting it tight. *"Father and Ronan have been taken by our clan's enemy and I needed to speak to you afore I no longer could."*

"What's happened?" Hell. Nothing had happened. She wasn't real and he shouldn't be encouraging her in this clearly impossible conversation. He shouldn't be encouraging himself either. Dreaming about what she'd looked like as he'd showered had clearly set the stage for him thinking of her the moment he'd

fallen asleep.

"*'Tis all my fault. I allowed myself to get caught by our enemy and Father and Ronan came to my rescue. Ronan sent me back to camp for aid and when I reached my fellow warriors, we returned to where I'd been held but all we found was a pool of blood and glittering golden dust smeared through it. Duncan MacKenzie has stolen them away from me and if I lose them, then I'll lose a piece of myself. I must find them.*"

"*Where are you? I'll come and—*" Wait, still a figment of his imagination. There was no woman. No trouble. No father and brother now captured by the enemy. "*Go away.*"

"*I'm sorry. I didnae mean to disturb you this night and lay all my problems at your feet.*" Her tears fell, dripped through the insubstantial white of her essence and splashed his face. He swiped one thumb across his cheek and touched the tip to his tongue. The taste of salt and sorrow gripped him hard. How the hell could he now taste her tears?

"*Don't cry. Please don't cry.*" He fumbled to grasp ahold of her then nabbed her hand as it appeared like an ethereal vision from within his dreams. She had such small, tiny fingers, swallowed almost whole within his tight hold. "*Show me the rest of you.*"

"*I am of fae blood, Alec, and hold the spirit-walker skill, one that is right now evolving. That is how I've come to you in your dreams this past month. I am no' an apparition as you believe. I truly am real and always have been. While you rest, so do I, then I travel to you. I seek you out because there is something about you that draws me toward you, night after night, and this night I needed to be with you more than I ever have afore. The loss of my kin engulfs me.*"

His own pain intensified as hers swirled in and around him.

Another tear fell, one that trickled over his lower lip and then her face emerged and he touched his fingers to her wet cheeks and her eyes squeezed so tightly shut. "*If you're truly real then show all of yourself to me."*

"One moment." She blinked her eyes open. Incredible. She had stunning blue eyes with sparks of gold glittering at the edges, an otherworldly gaze he got lost in.

Gently, he cupped her cheeks in his hands, traced over dimples showing either side of her pouty pink lips then swept one thumb along the smattering of freckles on her nose. Her long golden tresses swept forward over her shoulder and brushed his bare chest as she floated above him. *"Are you truly real?"*

She touched her nose to his, then the rest of her body took form, her upper body clothed in a green tunic, her lower limbs encased in black breeches. She lowered herself onto him, her weight slight but most definitely there. "Now I'm really here."

Her voice no longer echoed within his mind but all around. How the hell had his ghostly apparition just taken actual form? He pulled back, tried to shove his eyes open only they were already open and he no longer dreamed.

"I can see your confusion, Alec. I'm one of the fae, can travel through the dream realm due to my spirit-walker skill and as I said my skill has now fully evolved. I am right here with you, have crossed centuries to be by your side."

"This is impossible." He had to be going nuts.

"I've heard you speak of Cherub and Kirk afore. Cherub travels through time within portals she opens. I can travel through the dream realm in a similar way, although only with my spiritual form."

"How do you know Cherub and Kirk?" The Fae Angel of Love was mated to Kirk, one of his own clansmen, and even though he didn't know Cherub all that well, he knew Kirk as if he were his own brother.

"Cherub is my princess, a guardian of our people and is of fae blood, just as I am. She and Kirk have offered me their aid in finding my kin, but first I thought to do so through the dream realm, only I've found naught other than you at rest."

He stroked up and down her arms, reveled in her warmth. Right now, his apparition was a flesh and blood woman and he could no longer deny it. "Tell me your name."

"You've never asked me for my name afore."

"I never thought you were real until this very moment. Tell me your name, woman."

"It isnae 'woman.'" She glanced over her shoulder into nothingness then back at him, a regretful frown on her face. "I'm so sorry, but I must go. Cherub calls to me, hastens me from my sleep. She promised to watch over my body while I was gone. I am Annella." She smiled, so enchantingly, then she dissolved and was gone in the blink of an eye, and just as swiftly as she'd come.

"Annella!" He jolted upright in bed, fisted his fur bedcover, his breath heaving from him as he searched his chamber. All remained eerily dark, the moon now hidden behind a thick layer of cloud and no longer spreading its misty glow through his window.

Chapter 2

The ancient House of Clan Matheson, led by Gilleoin, the Chief of Matheson, Scotland, 1210, twenty-four hours later.

Fear and frustration coiled deeply within every muscle of Annella's body as she paced her chamber on the uppermost floor of the north tower of the castle, the midnight sky beyond her window holding not even one glittering star as a storm raged outside, a storm that raged with equal strength deep within her. An entire day had passed since Father and Ronan's capture at Duncan's hands, her search for them within the dream realm ending without sight of either of them. If she found them, then she could discover where they'd been taken and ensure their rescue. 'Twas imperative she did.

"Annella?" A knock sounded. "'Tis Cherub."

"Coming." She jerked the door open and grasped Cherub's hands. "Tell me you bring good news." Cherub and Kirk had promised her they'd travel to the Chief of MacKenzie's keep in case Duncan had taken his captives there, although word was Duncan and his elder twin brother held strongholds of their own somewhere deep within MacKenzie land.

"There is no sign of them at the Chief of MacKenzie's

keep. Tell me again what Duncan said to you.”

“He was adamant that neither Father or Ronan would be able to escape Muirin’s fae magic, that both of them were about to embrace their destiny. He said even you would understand, that their coming capture was meant to be, their journey to come one that none of us can halt.”

“I understand only what I sensed that night. You, Niall, and Ronan have a journey ahead of you. The mated bond is a very sacred union, and one I’m no’ permitted to breach with its creation or completion.”

“What do you mean by mated bond? Neither my father, brother, or I are soul bound to another.”

“Already I’ve said too much, but you’ll come to understand my words soon enough. I take it you’ve caught no glimpse of your father or brother within the dream realm?” Cherub crossed to her window in her crimson gown with its scalloped neckline edged in white lace. She pushed the window open and the wind rushed in, her princess’s need to be surrounded by her air element clear to see.

“I’ve tried, but they dinnae rest and there’s no way for me to reach them until they are permitted some sleep.” All she’d done this past day was try and reach them, and lying abed while they were likely injured and hurt was driving her insane. Fear and worry coiled deeply inside her, had nowhere to go but turn her into a frustrated mess.

“You need to search for Niall and Ronan again as you rest, and dinnae cease doing so until you discover where they are. Return to me when you have done so and we’ll join together to see to their rescue. This is something you cannae do on your own, not with a fae sorceress involved. Do you understand?” Cherub’s impassioned plea touched her heart.

“Of course, and you are right. I willnae act alone, but wait for you and Kirk.” She laid down, the golden canopy above her bed sweeping down each of the four posts. She stroked one finger along the length of her belted sword, the weapon a priceless gift from her father five years past, a sword he'd had fashioned by the armorer to fit her smaller hand. She rolled the cuffs of her royal blue tunic to her elbows and traced over the jeweled hilt of the dirk strapped at her wrist, the weapon one Ronan had won after competing in the Highland Games last spring. He'd handed it to her and said 'twas hers, a gift she too treasured.

"I'll be here watching over you while you're gone." Cherub perched on the bed beside her, patted her hand. "Close your eyes. Seek out the ones closest to your heart, no matter where they are."

"I shall." She breathed deep and turned her gaze on the window and the wind whistling in. The dark clouds in the night sky broke apart and the moon blazed through, although 'twas no golden as it usually shone, but instead a mystical red. A blood moon. A most unusual occurrence and one said to bring spirited souls together when separated. A good omen, or at least it better be.

Eyes squeezed shut, she continued to slow her breathing and all wispy-white, drifted toward the skies and the dream realm beyond. Upward, she soared, her very soul seeking her nearest and dearest. There, a single star twinkled more brightly than any other. Alec's star, his very essence calling to her with the soul-deep strength it always did, although Father and Ronan's essence remained without light, their stars not blazing. Damn it. When would they permitted some rest?

Longing for Alec flared through her and she breezed toward him, floated down and burrowed her head against his firm shoulder, his strength needed so very much. He moved underneath her, his arms wrapping around her as she solidified her ethereal form more fully, just as she'd done the night before. Head up, she soaked in the sight of him. "I've missed you, my mighty bear. Wake up. I need what only you can give me."

"Annella?" His arms bunched tighter around her, his eyes blinking open. He jerked then frowned. "Well, it's about damn time you returned. Where have you been this past day? You left so suddenly and all I've done is worry ever since."

"I've missed you too." She nuzzled his neck, her heart lifting a little from the dreary cold that had consumed her.

"I didn't say I'd missed you." His white bedsheets were all askew as if he'd tossed and turned for hours, his thick black fur bedcover over top having slithered onto the ground.

She rubbed her body against his, their full length touching from head to toe as she lay on top of him. Not a position a lass should likely take with a man who was not her husband, but she truly had missed him and—

"I can feel every single inch of you." Wonder flickered in his golden shifter gaze as he swept his hands over her shoulders and down her sides then caught one of her long locks and twined the length around his finger. "It's incredible. I didn't imagine this last night, and for a moment I thought I might have."

"Nay, I am real, will always be real." She tingled wherever he touched her, his body gloriously firm as she pressed her hands against his broad chest. His skin, all golden and smooth, held a light smattering of dark hair the same midnight-black shade as his head, and enticed her beyond reason. He slept with little covering him and his abs rippled as she edged up a little more and traced each defined ridge, the magical blood moon beyond his window casting its shimmering red glow over them both. "There is a blood moon this night in my time too."

"We shouldn't be touching each other so familiarly."

"Aye, you are right." Never had she done so with a fellow warrior before. She scuttled off his bed, her feet sinking into a thick white fur spread across the entire length of his floor. "Oh my, this is incredible. What do you call this large rug?"

"It's called carpet, and what's incredible is you being here, although now that you are and I know you're well, you need to leave." He shoved his bare feet to the floor, hauled the bedsheet with him and hooked it around his waist.

"I can return the way I came, but I'm no' ready to leave yet." She stepped up to him, speared her fingers through his shoulder-length hair, her heart and soul exalting in the silky feel. "I dinnae mean to touch you so boldly, but I can still cannae quite believe I'm here."

"Yours must be a coveted fae skill."

"It can be, yet also not. My mother held the same skill as I do and unfortunately once we evolve and can solidify our spiritual form as I've now done, we can also become terribly reliant on doing so. There is no need for sleep, to eat or any other such thing in this form, which means if we arena careful, we can disregard what our true body needs and fully ascend."

"Fully ascend?" He arched a brow. "As in…"

"Full ascension is when we pass from this Earth. My mother did so and now resides beyond the veil. I was only five at the time, far too young to lose her." She lowered her hands, sighed and paced his chamber. "Now I'm about to lose my father and brother too if I cannae find them within the dream realm and discover exactly where Duncan MacKenzie has taken them. I wouldnae put it past Duncan to keep them awake. He knows of my skill and what I can do, which means he also knows I can reach them in the dream realm to ensure their rescue as such."

"You're saying you can find them the same way you found me?"

"Aye, their essence shines as brightly as yours does within the dream realm. I've been soaring through the skies this past day as often as I could." She halted in front of him, leaned in and touched her nose to his neck, drew in a deep breath and relaxed as his heavenly fresh aroma surrounded her. "Mmm, you smell like the outdoors. I always imagined you would."

"I've been outside chopping wood."

"I'm only ever at home when I'm outside and as one with

nature." She plucked the sleeve of her blue tunic over top of her black breeches then tapped the sword belted at her side. "I am the daughter of a warrior, one who's been raised at his hand, just as my brother has. I am likely far different to any lass you might have met."

"Quite clearly." Snorting, he frowned something fierce. "I wish you'd told me you knew Cherub and Kirk. Why didn't you ever speak of them?"

"I told you Gilleoin was my chief, that I lived at the House of Clan Matheson farther across the Highlands along the mainland's western shoreline. I certainly didnae mean to deceive you in any way." He'd been resolute, that she was naught more than an apparition and couldn't possibly be real. Which had made him almost impossible to reason with, let alone mention her fae princess to convince him she truly spoke the truth. It had been best just to let him think what he had. Being naught more than an apparition to him, had clearly brought him some form of calm. With a deep breath, she stepped away, wandered toward the wall opposite where his bed sat and stroked one finger across a large square of darkened glass with a silver edge framing it. "What is this?"

"It's called a television."

"And what does a tel-e-vis-ion do?" She stumbled over the foreign word. "Did I say that right?"

"You did, and one watches shows on them." He crossed his arms and planted his feet wide. "And now that I'm well aware you're real, that it's possible for my aggressive other half to bring harm to you, you need to turn around and leave. My bear likes his space, gets a little antsy when others encroach upon it."

"That I've learnt this past month while sharing your dreams with you." She unsheathed her wrist dagger, touched the tip to his chest and arched a brow. "Spirit-walkers arena like others. When in our solidified spiritual form as I currently am, I am untouchable. Neither you or your bear could ever bring harm down upon me."

"I still insist you leave." He lifted the tip of her blade from his chest, leaned in and glared. "Also, don't ever raise a weapon against me again, not unless you wish to fight. My beast loves a good battle and your current move is about to ensure it."

"I dinnae mind a good battle myself." She turned her dagger over and offered it to him hilt first. "And when I say I'm untouchable, I mean it. My solidified spiritual body can withstand any injury. I exist in this form, yet I also dinnae exist. Cut me. See if I bleed and you'll find I speak the truth."

"Don't tempt me."

"Cut me." She thrust her dagger toward him. "Take it."

"No."

"You fear hurting me?"

He extended his hand, his claws slicing out. "I could kill you with one single swipe across your pretty little neck."

"Your bear is close to the surface?"

"More than close." He shoved her against the wall, pinned her hands together over her head against the paneled wood and gritted out, "I don't fear anything, especially a mere slip of a woman like you."

"Never mistake my size as a possible inability to hold strength." She tried to move, but he held her firmly trapped in place, the bedsheet wrapped around his waist sliding dangerously low on one hip. "Hmm, I do believe you fear me, Alec. What if I am indeed untouchable to you in this form? What will that mean to you?"

"You mean nothing to me, other than that you're a pest." He slid her weapon from her fingers, ran the pointy tip gently over her wrist, so whisper soft. "Where do you wish to be cut?"

"Wherever you please." Chin lifted, she met his unwavering gaze with one of her own. "Try to be inventive if you can."

"You have a sassy mouth, whether in wispy form or not." Growly words as he dipped his head to her neck and licked her throbbing pulse point. He sank his teeth into her flesh and heat flared through her body, flushed her cheeks and pooled in her belly, his bite both aggressive yet also delicious.

"How interesting." She arched a challenging brow. "Gilleoin is a shifter, the first of your kind and I'm well aware shifters only bite their mates, the one they're soul bound to. Kirk nibbles away on Cherub as if she were his own to devour. Now you've bitten me. Is it possible we're mated?" That would explain why she'd sought him out time and time again within the dream realm.

"That's true of my kind, but I'll never take a mate. Biting you, means nothing." He slammed her dagger right through her forearm and into the paneled wall behind her then hands on his hips, muttered, "See. You mean nothing to me."

"I see, but so should you." She heaved her dagger free, not a drop of blood gushing forth or even a mark gracing her flesh. With her dagger sheathed, she advanced on him, on the one man who believed himself to be far too aggressive for any woman. "Your chief would never allow you to remain here at Ivanson Castle if he believed you're as harmful to another as you say you are."

"You should take what I did as a warning. Next time I'll harm you without any request to do so. I don't trust my bear and neither should you." He stormed across to his tall corner chest and opened a drawer, rummaged within and pulled out a loose white tunic. Over his head it went, the sheet at his waist loosening and slipping free as he lifted his arms. The sheet fluttered to the floor, his firm buttocks on full display for a mere breath of a moment before the hem of his white tunic slithered down and covered him to mid-thigh. He selected a pair of black leather pants from the next drawer, drew them on and fastened the ties at his waist.

She should truly avert her gaze while he dressed, but she'd grown up amongst warriors and seen far too many of them changing right before her to ever worry overly much about it, although this warrior was far different to any of her fellow kinsmen. This man she couldn't keep her gaze from, didn't have a chance of doing so, had been seeking him out this past month for a very good reason. Aye, her very soul had led her directly to him, night after night. Cherub had said the mated bond was a sacred union that even she wasn't permitted to breach with its creation or completion. Her princess must have known she and Alec were mated. Certainly very little ever escaped Cherub's notice. "We need to speak."

"No, what I need to do is shake off some of this frustration you've gone and lumped on me." He strode past her, nabbed his boots from beside a blue suede settee and tugged them on. Sword belt and weapons strapped in place, he loomed over her. "Please leave. You need to go."

"You too have lumped a great deal of frustration on me now I've found my mate and discovered he resides over eight-hundred years from my true time." Frustration she would shake off the best way she knew how. By training. She opened his chamber door, marched down the passageway with its burgundy and blue runner and strange lighting coming from bright overhead orbs of glass recessed into the ceiling above. She halted at the top of the stairwell and motioned toward the lights. "What are those?"

"Lights." He banged his door shut and thumped down the hallway after her. "And we are definitely not mated. How many times must I tell you that?"

"You are a stubborn one." Surely he must feel the strength of their bond taking form. 'Twas impossible to miss now she'd acknowledged it. She trotted down the stairs and into an open foyer. Two large doors stood propped open with a wedge of wood underneath each and she swept one hand over the beautiful carving of the chief's arms embossed on each door. The chief's arms held two bears as supporters either side, those bears signifying all that their Matheson clan fought for—the survival of a loyal race of shifters—Gilleoin's line. Alec's line as well. Her mate was descended directly from Gilleoin's second-born son, Ivan.

"You are not my mate." Alec swept past her and into the great hall lit only by the odd light as the hallway had been. "Go away, pest."

"My name is Annella, and aye, I am your mate." She allowed her solidified form to dissolve into a swirl of wispy-white then breezed through the great hall and under the thickly paneled doors leading outside. The cool night air brushed over and through her then she reemerged and took her form once more in the inner courtyard.

"I would know if you were my chosen one. The men in my clan always sense who they're soul bound to and I sense nothing with you. Thank heavens." Alec banged the front door shut after himself.

"You bit me." Unable to help herself, she tickled a finger under his chin and smiled. "Which means you know exactly who I am, even though you dinnae wish to acknowledge it."

"Pest doesn't even begin to describe you."

"So says the grumpiest warrior I've ever met."

"Damn it, woman, would you cease touching me." He flicked her finger away, shoved forward and towered over her. "Inside me is a beast who would love nothing more than to tear you from limb to limb, then nibble on your bones until I'd picked them clean."

"You're just mad that you cannae see any mark upon my skin from your bite." She tipped her head to one side and stroked over her neck, right across the spot where he'd bitten her. "You can bite me, thrust a blade into me, but never will you actually be able to harm a hair on my head."

"I could kill you with absolute ease should you be in your true form." He snapped his teeth together, his claws slicing out and in. "My bear is a beast you don't want to tangle with."

"You and your beast clearly need a mysteriously annoying sprite such as me to keep you in line." She reached up on her toes and kissed his chin. "Come train with me. I could use a new opponent other than my brother to battle with. He is far too lenient when we train, yet I doubt you will be, mated bond included."

"I can't wait for you to be gone."

"I must remain for now. We still have much to speak about." She dissolved her form and wisped away across the inner courtyard, streamed up the stairs leading to the top of the battlements and solidified herself on the ramparts overlooking the width and breadth of the moonlit forest. Stunning. This parcel of land was so remote and called to her very heart, as did the man who held the other half of her soul.

* * * *

No one currently frustrated Alec more than the woman who'd had him worried for an entire twenty-four hours with her annoying absence, and then exclaimed she was his mate. Not over his dead body were they soul bound. The fact he'd bitten her was irrelevant. Aye, what he needed to do was send her on her way then ensure she never returned. His path was set, a solitary one that didn't include her.

Up the stairs to the battlements, he bolted then stopped behind the woman who had every hair on his neck rising. He breathed deep, drew in her intriguing fragrance, one that held the golden and glittery enchantment of a night sky teeming with stars. Her scent evoked the dream realm she traveled within, and made his lower region harden with lust. She stared up at the blood moon as if it intrigued her, her long golden tresses fluttering in the breeze and whispering over his arms and chest. Hell, she was so small of stature, the sword belted at her side all that gave any indication she in fact knew how to battle.

Carefully, he spread his hands over her hips, then

determined to prove his point, that she wasn't his chosen one, he muttered, "Those who are soul bound can never harm the other, but all I want to do right now is sink my claws into you and rip you apart. You need to steer well clear of me, to leave and never return."

"Since the night we met"—she turned in his embrace and he retracted his claws for fear he'd actually scratch her—"you've grumped and growled and snapped at me to be gone, but through it all I still sensed within you a deep need to have someone close. I am here if you wish to talk, can provide quite the listening ear if you were but prepared to accept me. We are meant to be together. A bond certainly wouldnae have formed between us otherwise."

"I'm a warrior, born and bred. I fight, draw blood and have no issue doing so." It would take only one wrong move on his part and he could so easily kill her. Why couldn't she see that? "I fight within my clan's specialist team who work high level government cases, and out of all my kin, I'm the one who gets called away from Ivanson Castle the most. My beast isn't just aggressive, he's bloodthirsty, which makes him the perfect assassin when needed to take down the vilest of criminals."

"I've chased a few vile criminals myself." She dissolved into a wisp and swirled around then reemerged behind him with her sword in hand. She tapped the tip of her blade against his belted sword. "Arm yourself and train with me for what remains of this night. I must be fully prepared to fight Duncan MacKenzie when I find him. I cannae lose my coming battle with him if I wish to free my father and brother."

"You shouldn't be fighting anyone on your own, and certainly not a warrior who managed to capture both of your closest kin." He lunged, grasped her sword hand, his fingers sliding through nothing but air as she wisped back farther and reappeared.

"Nay, you willnae catch me out that easily, my mighty

bear."

"I'm not your damn mighty bear."

"Please, that is no way to talk to a woman, and your chosen one at that." With a wink, she wagged a finger at him, her royal blue tunic cinched in at her tiny waist with a golden tasseled belt that swayed to her knees as she moved. Her black breeches, of the softest rawhide, molded her legs and that pert backside of hers, which he really shouldn't have noticed, wiggled as she moved.

"I don't see you as a woman, but as a lethal opponent."

"Then raise your blade."

"Training with me is a very bad idea." Still, he slid his sword free of his scabbard and rocked from foot to foot, his beast always prepared for any form of fighting. Perhaps if he trained with her then she'd realize how dangerous he was, leave then hopefully never come back. It was a plan at least. He'd grump and growl a whole lot more as he battled with her, make sure she understood just how fierce and grizzly he could get. That should scare her away.

"I am my father's daughter, born with a warrior's heart even though graced with my mother's petite form. Never underestimate my ability." Her blue eyes lightened with mischievous determination, the golden sparks blazing bright at the edges. "I will leave once we are done and your temper has calmed. You need me right now just as much as I need you."

"I have a raging temper right now because of you." He'd never be able to calm it.

"Then allow me to un-rage it." She swung and their two blades crashed dead center, steel ringing loud against steel and her full lips lifting so wickedly. "'Tis time to fight, my mighty bear."

"Don't call me that again."

"Aye, you are most definitely my chosen one, whether you wish to acknowledge it or no'. Certainly if I could have chosen who my mate would be, I would have asked for a man such as you. One strong of mind and will, yet a man who also held a heart filled with love for his clan." She twirled and struck again, her second hit harder than he'd expected and he shoved one foot back to brace himself against her next strike. She didn't disappoint. She came at him hard, moving swiftly and gracefully.

Ignoring her last comment, he trained with her, she attacking and him ensuring he defended and nothing more, until sweat glistened on her brow and made her tunic cling to her breasts. Those heavy and full mounds of hers were far too big for her slight form.

"Cease looking at my chest, Alec."

"I wasn't." A lie, but he'd never admit he had been. "Have you ever desired what women desire? Wearing skirts and such?" He caught her next blow and pushed her blade back with his own.

"I have only the one gown hanging in my ambry, but I do enjoy wearing a belted kilt with naught underneath it, just as the men of my clan do."

His hand shook and he scrambled to find a breath. "Your breasts are swaying everywhere, likely knocking you off balance. You should contain or bind them to give yourself better footing when you train."

"I've found my breasts distract my opponent somewhat, which they're clearly doing with you right now. I shall leave them loose beneath my tunic."

"Why on earth would your father teach you how to battle?" She might fight well, but every inch of her was still a woman, a woman who needed to be protected, not tossed into the middle of the battlefield.

"Because he loves me, knows my heart and all I desire." She swept her sword toward his knees and he jumped her low blow then whacked her sword from her hand. It flew over the battlements and landed with a clunk on the gravel beyond the curtain wall where the forest surrounded them. "I realize I'm no' like most women, but I do know how to follow an order, of which my father loves to issue them."

"Then follow this order. Leave this minute and don't return."

"Have you ever desired what other men desire?" She gripped the crenellation, leapt over the side and in a swirl of wispy-white breezed down and landed on the gravelly ground.

"I ordered you to leave."

"Answer my question first." She snatched her sword and smiled at him. "Have you ever wanted a woman to warm your bed?"

"Never." He flung himself over the wall and from one hand-and-foot hold to the next, scaled down the craggy stone and dropped in beside her. "Our shifter kind always waits for our chosen one. Lying with any other woman would never do. I have no desire to lie with you either, in case I hadn't made that clear."

"You made it clear, but you are also currently frustrated by what has occurred and no' thinking straight, so I willnae hold anything you say against you." She pressed one finger to his chest and swirled it down over his abs to his waist, her heated touch warming him from within and making his bear roll around and preen under his skin as he demanded a closer touch.

Teeth snapped together, he tried to tamp down his fierce other half. "Cease touching me."

"Those are tough words, although I can see your deep need for touch shining bright in your eyes." She leaned closer. "What have you to say about that?"

"You're mistaken. The only deep need both me and my bear have right now is to bite you and rip you into shreds." He caught her hand, held it firm against his chest, his bear growling with pleasure and demand for more. Stupid other half.

"Is that really true?" She blew a soft breath across his neck. "Because I sense differently. I can hear both you and your bear and although you both growl quite fiercely, 'tis also a hungry growl. Mayhap if you allowed yourself to get closer to me, both you and your bear might be a little less aggressive."

"Getting closer to you is dangerous." He dropped her hand and stepped back, his back brushing the stone curtain wall behind him. Moving away from her hurt, even if only the few inches he had. What was wrong with him? He should just walk away from her. He should climb the wall he'd just descended, return to his chamber and leave her behind. "I want you to go, to return to your own home and time. You're not welcome here anymore."

"I believe you actually want me to stay." She sheathed her blade, stepped forward and planted her feet right on top of his booted feet then slowly, she curled her arms around his neck, her warm hands brushing over his nape as she raised up onto the tips of her toes. "I've no wish to fully ascend as my mother did and joining with you is my greatest chance of ensuring that does no' happen. For a spirit-walker, we thrive on remaining in our spiritual form as I currently am, which means our physical body deteriorates when we dinnae return within an adequate time."

"If your mother ascended even though wed to your father, then how would joining with me ensure you remained on this Earth?"

"Although my parents shared a great love, they were no' soul bound and unfortunately their love wasnae enough to keep my mother from ascending." She licked his neck, grazed her teeth back and forth over his skin and his bear fairly roared to do the same with her. "Your shifter kind, when you find the one who holds the other half of your soul, mate with only one woman. You've been waiting for me. Admit it."

"I would never lie with any woman, let alone my chosen one."

"Yet your shifter line nears extinction." She sank her teeth into him, as fiercely as any woman did with her chosen one and blood pounded to his cock, made him go fiercely hard.

All he wanted to do was shove her to the ground and take her, to rub his chest across those full breasts of hers, grip her lush backside in his hands then thrust his cock inside her. Hell. He really needed to cease these unhelpful thoughts. Teeth gritted, he slammed his hands against the wall behind him and tried to force his fierce need for her down. "A number of newly mated couples have found each other. Extinction is still a possibility, but it's becoming less so by the day."

Panting, she drew back an inch, the gold sparks in her gaze flaring even brighter. "A shifter's bite excites sexual desire, which is why you only ever mark your chosen ones. That I've learnt from Cherub and Kirk. You marked me first. 'Twas only right I get to mark you in return."

"I still want you to leave." She was strong, feisty, able to stand up to him and state her demands. She was everything he could ever desire in a woman, as well as everything he could never have. "Please, you must go. I don't need a mate, nor do I want one."

"You dinnae wish for children?" She rubbed the pad of her thumb over the mark she'd made on his neck then looked deep into his eyes. "I do. I dream of my children one day running after my brother and swinging from my father's shoulders. I want to hear their laughter, joy and delight."

"Today, I thrust a dagger through your arm. Tomorrow, I might thrust a dagger through your heart."

"That shall never happen." She lifted her arm and rubbed the spot where he'd speared her then slowly, she returned her hands to her sides and looked deep into his eyes. "Do you wish to claim me as your mate, to join with me in all ways?"

"No. Yes. No." He thumped the back of his head against the wall. "No. Definitely no." He thumped his head again for good measure, and primarily to make certain that last answer stuck. "I want you to go."

"Are you certain?" She dipped her head, her brow furrowing deeply.

"Bedding you would only tie you intrinsically to my side, something I'd never do." He grasped her around the waist, spun them and shoved her against the wall. "For the last time, leave, and don't ever look back. Do it. For me."

Chapter 3

Within Ivanson Castle's gatehouse security control room, Cherub switched off the camera mounted to the northern corner of the curtain wall and gave the newly mated pair their privacy as they fought. She'd left one of the maids watching over Annella's body then found Kirk and brought him straight with her through a portal into this time. These two would clearly need their aid, particularly given how stubborn Alec was being. At least Annella had seen that their bond had taken form and now tried to persuade her mate to accept her.

"She's strong, not one to take no for an answer, no matter how many times Alec tells her to leave." Kirk eased into the gray-padded metal chair before the monitor.

"We'll need to bring them together as often as possible." She slid onto Kirk's lap and fluffed her skirts. "Are you ready for the challenge, my tempting bear?"

"Always, although let's not forget that Annella is needed elsewhere, her search for Niall and Ronan taking precedence over all else. We can't retrieve them without her finding their location first, which she needs to find within the dream realm." Kirk buried his nose in her hair and breathed deep.

"We'll be going with her on her journey when she leaves to

find her loved ones, and we'll also be taking Alec with us along the way." 'Twas imperative they did.

"Then we'll need a solid plan if we're to achieve that means." He stroked her bottom through the mountainous folds of her skirts. "You speak to Annella, and I'll work on knocking some sense into Alec. He needs to come around to the mated way of thinking, as soon as possible."

"Be careful when you speak to him. I've never seen one of your shifter kind so against the thought of joining with their chosen one." She wrapped her arms around his neck, rubbed the entire length of her body against his until every inch of her longed for more. "I also wouldnae mind joining with my chosen one right now."

"I wouldn't mind that either, not one bit." With a sly smile, he captured her mouth with his. He kissed her, swept his tongue across hers, their breath mingling as one and his desire pulsing so very hot and needy along their merged link toward her, just as strongly as her desire pummeled back to him. "I need you, right now, my love."

"As I need you." And with the magnificent glow of the magical blood moon beaming through the gatehouse window, she gave herself freely over to the depths of their mated bond and the intense love they shared for each other, a bond she too wished for Alec and Annella to hold as well.

Soon. Very soon. She and Kirk would ensure the two embraced their bond and all that it entailed. She'd make certain of it.

Chapter 4

Annella gasped as Alec shoved her back hard against the castle's outer curtain wall and loomed over her. Her mate clearly intended to remain stubbornly ignorant of their bond, yet even she sensed the soul-deep threads between them weaving tighter together. "Cease asking me to leave."

"I can't ensure your safety unless you're gone."

"There's no need to deny either you or your bear what you want." She hooked one leg around the back of his legs, her arms around his neck and touched her nose to his. "Kiss me."

"Even I struggle to keep my beast leashed."

"Kiss me."

"No." A fierce growl rumbled up from deep inside him. "I've asked you to leave this place and you must."

"I dare you to kiss me." She lifted her mouth to his, licked his lower lip and smiled at the sheer joy of touching him so freely. More. She needed more.

"You clearly have no self-preservation." He rubbed his body against hers, seized her lips and kissed her with such a wild abandon. Moaning, he probed her mouth with his tongue then growled and dove deeper, his warm and fresh pine scent surrounding and saturating her.

Her mate certainly knew how to kiss. She wriggled against him and a surge of heat flared through her body and pooled in her core, right between her thighs where his manhood jabbed into her. "I like how you kiss," she murmured against his lips.

"I like how you respond." He stroked down her back and over her hips, nipped her lower lip then nibbled along her jaw. With dedicated attention, he trailed scorching kisses across her skin until he reached the sensitive hollow where her neck and shoulder met, where her pulse pounded the strongest. There, he halted, drew her flesh deep between his lips and released a low rumble. "The urge to bite you again is strong. Say aye. This time I willnae do so unless you give me your agreement."

"Bite me, however and wherever you please." She swayed forward and he captured her mouth in a deliciously fierce kiss, his big body so heavily muscled and gloriously powerful. His heat made her melt against him and she reveled in the moment, her very soul crying out for his.

She sucked his lower lip into her mouth and nipped it, welcomed the hunger roaring through her and his incredibly delectable taste. Never would she experience this kind of raw intimacy with another, only her soul bound mate. He was destined to be hers, just as she was destined to be his, that's if he was prepared to take the risk and accept their bond. She leaned into him and his breath whispered softly across her tongue, an incredibly sensuous caress that had her deepening their kiss to capture more of his fierce essence. His very soul had shone within the dream realm, his star so brightly lit and drawing her directly toward him, time and time again.

"We have to stop." He caressed her sides, roamed down and scooped her bottom then ground his hips into hers. He plundered her mouth once more, so deeply, so wildly, and she gripped his shoulders and rubbed against the hard length of his erection almost spearing through his leather pants.

"Bite me again, Alec."

"Is this truly what you want?" With her trapped against the wall, he ripped her tunic ties open along the deep V at the front and exposed both her breasts. He lifted one free of the ravaged neckline and grazed his teeth along the upper swell until she arched into his touch. "You truly want a man who'd tear your clothes from you and not care where he did so?"

"You are my mate, the man who holds the other half of my soul. You could tear my clothes from me wherever you pleased and I'd gladly allow it."

"I'm a beast you need to be running in the other direction from." He squeezed her breast, plumped her nipple up then sucked it deep inside his mouth.

A scorching heat shimmered through her and she yanked his billowy white tunic away from his neck on the other side where she'd first marked him then latched onto his skin. She bit him again and his bear growled and thrashed for dominance. She sensed his other half's need as greatly as she sensed her own. "Do it," she whispered in his ear. "Give your bear what he wants. Me."

"He'll hurt you." Fierce longing flared in his eyes as he gazed at her neck then he pressed his lips to her flesh and bit down.

Arousal hit her hard, swift and with fierce intensity. She clutched his shoulders, her nails digging into his flesh then he switched to the other side of her neck, sank his teeth into the hollow where her heartbeat pounded the hardest then grazed down her body and nipped all around her breasts, dotting bites all over and naught could have satisfied her very soul more. She sighed with delight, her skin so flushed even though not one of his bites had marked her flesh.

"Are you all right?" He pulled back, his golden shifter eyes ablaze with passion.

"I am perfectly fine." She cupped his face in her hands, tenderly ran her thumbs over his lips. She wanted to kiss him all over again except something pulled at her. Her heart skipped a beat and her breath came harder. Something was wrong, her physical body demanding her return. Gasping, she clutched her chest.

"What's wrong?"

"I must leave. I'm so sorry."

"Don't be sorry." He stepped away from her, brushed his hands against his sides. "I never wanted you to stay, remember? Nothing would please me more than if you left."

All she wanted to do was remain right here, to convince him that they needed to be together. Giving up went against her nature.

"No more last chances, Annella. Go. I can't wait to be rid of you."

"You're lying, and hurting us both by doing so." Yet go she would, before something happened to her true body and she could no longer return to her physical self. She dissolved her form, pain spearing through her as she shimmered away through the endless dark of the dream realm, her heart throbbing at his decree. His words hurt, which only cemented her belief. Those who were soul bound should never be separated, not even by the two within the bond.

* * * *

Alec slammed one fist into the curtain wall, his knuckles bleeding as he scraped skin off. Annella's leaving tore at him, made his bear roar and thrash for her return. He kicked off his boots, unstrapped his weapons and shucked his shirt and pants against the wall then in a myriad of bright lights, made the Change.

His bear ripped from him and he heaved up onto his hind legs and howled.

It was best this way, that she leave, that she understood he didn't want her.

Into the depths of the forest, he loped, sought refuge from

both himself and the one woman he'd fervently denied belonged to him this past month, even though deep down inside he'd known she held the other half of his soul. Hell, his need for her had grown with each nightly visit she'd paid, his desire for her eating away at him and now that he'd had a taste of her and bitten her as their shifter kind did, that need would only continue to grow and gnaw at him. He'd have to work hard to set those emotions aside, of which he would. He'd make damn sure he did. Her safety depended on it.

He lumbered on, until he reached a fast flowing river and his beast finally calmed a little. He reared up against a towering tree, dug his paws into the trunk then slashed down to the base. Again and again, he released his frustration and pain on the only thing that could handle his fierce temper. The tree would survive his fury whereas his mate would perish should he ever unleash his anger on her.

Long minutes passed until shards of bark dangled from the trunk or lay piled on the ground. Exhausted, he dropped back onto all fours and plodded through a patch of grass as the sun rose higher in the sky and sunbeams streamed through the thick canopy overhead. It was time to return, to move on with his duty of protecting and guarding his clan, and to ensure he never gave into the woman who'd come to him in his dreams once more.

Lumbering back along the trail, he tried to leave the storm of his emotions behind, although more simply roared to glaring life. He'd never forget Annella, but so too, he'd never willingly accept her or their bond.

Certainly from this moment forth, whenever he laid his head down to rest at night, he'd make certain she never found her way back to him again. Plodding along, he broke free of the trail and ambled toward his belongings. He shifted, dressed, strapped his weapons on then with his resolve set firmly in place, strode through the main gate then veered across the bailey to the side entrance. He'd speak to his chief, ensure he informed him of all that had happened, of his decision and choice to move forward alone.

Outside his chief's solar door on the lower floor, he rapped and called out, "It's Alec."

"Come in." Michael Matheson, Kirk's father, was a loyal, honorable, and strong chief.

He opened the door and stepped inside, his chief's wise counsel over the years always invaluable. When Michael heard of his bond with Annella taking form, even he would agree he'd made the right decision in sending her away and ensuring he never exposed her to his beast again. Her protection came first, even from himself.

"Kirk's here, Alec, with some interesting news." In tan trousers and a navy button-down shirt, Michael rose from behind his chunky oak desk and dropped his pen on top of the papers he'd been perusing. He walked around and perched on the front edge of his desk, crossed his arms and eyed him. "And with interesting news you need to listen to. He's informed me of your bond taking form with Annella. You have my heartfelt congratulations."

"Then you need to take those heartfelt congratulations right back." He needed his chief to stand behind his decision, not go against it.

"You have my heartfelt congratulations too." Kirk stood before the window in his belted plaid and tunic, the sun glinting off the sword belted at his side and the daggers sheathed at his wrists. "Annella's a fierce warrior, yet also holds a heart of gold and a deep love for her clan, much the same as you do."

"How long have you known about our bond taking form?" Not much ever got past Cherub and Kirk, but he'd ensure they both understood his position.

"Cherub informed me the night Annella's father and brother were taken that you two were soul bound and that things were about to get difficult."

"I'm not accepting the bond, for the obvious reasons."

"She's a spirit-walker." Kirk crossed to him. "And you're the only one who can ensure she remains on this Earth now her skill has fully evolved. Those spirit-walkers who remain unmated always ascend when there is no one close enough to them to hold them to the here and now. She needs you, just as much as you need her."

"She'll ascend a damn sight faster if we ever joined together. Her death at my hands would occur within only a matter of time."

"When we are mated to another, the one who holds the other half of our soul becomes ours to protect and care for. We can never harm them. It's impossible." Kirk grasped his shoulder. "You likely don't wish to hear what else I have to say, but you need to listen all the same. Cherub's duty is to ensure each mated pair find each other, no matter what time they live within, and since the day Cherub and I completed our bond, her duty too became mine. Sending Annella away from you right now isn't the right move, and I can't stress that enough."

"She's safer where she is rather than with me. Where's Cherub?" He wished to speak to the Fae Angel of Love and ensure she understood his position well, that he needed her to keep a close eye on Annella since he no longer could. Keeping his chosen one safe, even though he had no intention of tying her to his side, still flared strongly within him.

"Cherub is with your mate as we speak."

"Good. Make sure she understands my decision. I've no intention of completing the bond and one day harming my chosen one." As appreciative as he was of Kirk's advice, he'd never change his mind. "Her life means more to me than I can ever express, and her safety can only be guaranteed when she's away from me."

"I knew you'd take this stance on the issue, but there is no one who can protect her better than you ever could. You need to trust me on that."

"I stabbed her last night, shoved her own dagger right through her forearm and impaled her to my chamber wall. Should I ever allow my bear his full release, I could shred her to pieces. My bear hungers for her, would maul and mark her and not think twice about it." He gripped Michael's shoulder. "Surely you see I speak the truth, Chief. Tell me you agree with my decision."

"I understand your fears, Alec, but those who are soul bound truly can't harm the other as Kirk has said. You need to have more faith in the bond, and in the woman who has been given to you to cherish and adore. Don't turn her away. Give yourself some time if you must, but she will always feel lost and alone without you."

"My sentiments exactly." Kirk dug his cell phone from his pocket, turned it on. "Even if Annella were in her true form and not her spiritual one as she was last night, you still wouldn't be able to harm her."

"I can't take the risk." Annella deserved to live a life filled with joy and happiness, not in constant fear of what he might or mightn't ever do to her. He dropped down into the blue padded wingback chair next to the unlit fireplace, braced his elbows on his knees and clasped his hands together. "I won't tangle with her again like I did last night."

"She needs your aid in finding her kin, only she hasn't asked you for it yet. Let me show you something." Kirk tapped his cell phone's screen. "I recorded this piece earlier in the week. Occasionally I take a picture or video footage, for memorabilia's sake and such, and this video is of Niall, Ronan, and Annella training at the warrior encampment on the shores of Loch Alsh."

"I don't want to see it." He'd let her go, needed to forget about her and ensure things stayed that way.

"Look, and that's an order." Kirk turned his cell phone toward him.

"Stand still, you menace." Annella's teasing voice swept out from the device and he couldn't help but lift his gaze, her words spoken as if to him even though she faced another. The bright midday sunshine blazed across her beautiful face, her expression awash with vigor and vitality as she swung her sword in the same manner as she'd done with him during their sparring session last night. Her gorgeous golden tresses, contained within a long plait and tied with a red silk ribbon at the end, swayed about her tiny waist, and those plump, pink lips of hers remained open a touch as she swept her tongue out. He wanted to seize her mouth with his, slip his own tongue between her lips and taste the heated treasure of her kisses, to have her clinging to him and completely breathless as he ravaged her all over again.

"You're the menace, little sister." A warrior in his mid to late twenties heaved his blade and Annella met his fierce strike, swords clanging and making his woman jolt back a step under the jarring impact. "Dinnae fall over or else I've won this battle."

"Keep your eyes on your brother, Annella. Ignore his ribbing." A more seasoned warrior with a flare of silver on one side of his blond-haired head, stood atop a boulder along the sandy shoreline where the waters glittered as they rolled in and washed up onto the beach. "Utilize your smaller size, sneak in a blow when Ronan's not paying attention. Aim for his knees. Catch him off balance and disable him. Just however you can, bring him down. Do it, now."

"No' the knees, scamp." Ronan winked at her. "I need my legs in working order so I can kick your mischievous butt when you get too big for your breeches, which is more often the no' these days."

"The knees it is then." Annella laughed, ducked low and swung.

Ronan let out a loud bellow, jumped her underhanded swipe then knocked her blade from her hands with his sword. It went flying and he dropped his weapon and charged, caught her up and tossed her over one shoulder then ran toward the water.

"Nay, let me down, you big brute." Annella's red tunic slid down her back and exposed her creamy skin and the delectable hollow at the base of her spine. Her tan breeches molded every inch of her sweetly curved bottom as she squirmed and thumped her brother. "I'm going to make you pay for this, Ronan Matheson."

"Did you say brute?" Chuckling, Ronan bounded into the water then dove with Annella still clinging to him.

Seconds later, the two burst to the surface and shoved water at each other.

Niall laughed, kicked off his boots and shucked his dark tunic then raced into the waves. He dove and reemerged behind Ronan then with a loud whoop, tackled his son and took him down. Their love burst across the screen, their devotion to each other so very clear to see.

He touched one finger to her tiny image flickering back at him, stroked over her wet braid and flushed face as she jumped onto Ronan's back and tussled with him. "She needs them back." He lifted his gaze to Kirk's. "You and Cherub need to make sure that happens, and if you don't then you'll have me to contend with."

"She needs more than just Niall and Ronan back. She needs you as well, whether you wish to accept that fact or not. In accepting the bond, you won't be tying an innocent woman to your side who could never handle your aggressive bear, not when she's so very strong in her own right. Think on all I've said, because if you but allow it, she could be your very salvation."

He sat back in the chair, Kirk's impassioned plea ringing in his ears. Even if he allowed their bond to take, the risks for her would always be there, and should he make even one wrong move, then he'd be placing her very life on the line. Aye, he'd made the right decision in sending her away. He wouldn't back down on his decision now.

* * * *

All wispy-white, Annella soared through the dream realm the next night in search of Father and Ronan, the cool night air once again rushing around her and the stars blazing bright, although not the stars of her nearest and dearest whom she searched for. Her heart cried out for them, demanded their return. Why hadn't they yet sought their rest? And where was Alec? She circled the place where his star usually glowed so close to her kin's, his essence a bright ray of hope she'd come to crave, only he too remained far from her sight. She huffed, gave up on her search for now and slowly descended, floated back down and returned to her chamber then breathed deep as she settled back inside her physical body.

Eyes open, she stretched in the dark, the candle flickering on top of her bedside table casting its solitary glow over her golden bed curtains and gold and red patchwork bedcover.

"Any luck?" Cherub rose from the red velvet padded chair beside her window, the moon glowing golden and bright over her shoulder and making her sparkly skin shimmer, the trait a physical one held only by the eldest child born within the royal line of the fae. Cherub was her princess and the king's eldest child, born to care for her kind who walked this Earth.

"None whatsoever. Duncan has no' yet permitted them any rest." She wouldn't consider that their essence didn't shine because they no longer lived. Her kin awaited her and she wouldn't contemplate anything else. With her black leather covered knees pulled to her chest, she wrapped her arms around them and rocked on her mattress. "You've searched the Chief of MacKenzie's dungeons on Loch Alsh and they arena there, which means Duncan must have taken them to his own holding, wherever that is."

"The Chief of MacKenzie's land spreads from here all the way to the shores of Loch Broom far to the north. 'Tis a large parcel of land with countless places where Duncan could be keeping them." Cherub paced before the fire, her ruby skirts brushing the polished floorboards. "Since neither of us have found them then we need to set out on foot from where they were taken, which means we'll need the best trackers aiding us on our search. Kirk can certainly track very well with his bear, but in all honesty, Alec is the best within his clan and we need him on our side."

"I told you all about Alec and our battle." She'd admitted all that had happened to Cherub when she'd returned from Alec's time, although it seemed the Fae Angel of Love had already known, watched some of their battle from within Ivanson's security control room before giving them their privacy. "Alec insists his bear is too aggressive, would harm me and even though that's impossible when two are soul bound, he still has no intention of ever choosing me. I fear should I ask him for his aid in our coming mission, he will only turn me down."

"Then you'll need to persuade him otherwise." Cherub swished to Annella's ambry, pushed back the golden curtain and foraged amongst her hanging clothes. She whipped a couple of pairs of breeches and two tunics from within down, then set her belongings on the end of her bed. "I've never known you to back away from a fight, and we certainly need Alec's aid."

"Aye, I'll never back away from a fight, but he seems so resolute, that he'll never allow our bond to take. He also remains awake and in doing so, far from me since I can only visit him once he is at rest."

"Then you simply need to confront him again, and this time face to face in your true form. I shall take you directly to Alec through a portal. He needs to learn no one can deny the mated bond." Cherub arched a brow. "Tell me I'm right."

"You're right." She also wasn't yet willing to give up on her chosen one, not as he'd already chosen to give up on her. Determination flared through her and she swung her feet onto the floor, nabbed her traveling sack from the uppermost shelf of her ambry and stuffed the clothes Cherub had placed on the bed, inside.

"You are a woman of action and I adore that about you." Cherub patted her hand. "Certainly once you have your mate's agreement to join us on our search, we'll ensure our men release their bears so they can track your father and brother's movements. No more will we sit here and idly wait as precious time ticks by."

"That I wholeheartedly agree with." Action was most definitely needed. She pulled on her favorite black leather knee-high boots, tucked the bottom of her pants inside then added a black leather vest over her cream tunic. "I'll take a stronger stance with Alec this time."

"That's exactly what I wanted to hear." Cherub hugged her then walked to the door and glanced over her shoulder. "I willnae be long. I'll return to my chamber and pack, then secure some items of clothing from your father and brother's chambers, things that hold their scent. Our bears will need whatever we can give them in order to track Niall and Ronan as best as they can. We'll head out at first light on the morrow when any tracks will be more viewable. Does that sound like a suitable plan?"

"Absolutely." Alec was the best tracker within his clan and she needed him and his highly skilled ability. She wouldn't rest until she'd procured his agreement. Swiftly, she stuffed her plaid in her sack and added an additional pair of woolen socks. The days were warm but the nights could be cold out in the forest.

In the looking glass propped on her side table, she picked up her comb, brushed her hair and secured her golden locks in a long braid with a blue ribbon tied at the end. With a mint and salt paste, she scrubbed her teeth then splashed water from the basin onto her face. She had a mission ahead of her, both in convincing Alec to aid her in finding her kin, and in accepting her as his chosen one along the way. Aye, she wasn't done with him yet, would fight for their bond and his acceptance of her. She needed him, particularly if she wished to ensure she never ascended as her mother had done. Only a spirit-walker's soul bound mate could keep them tied to this Earth, and she had no desire to leave her loved ones behind, not unless they'd already gone on ahead of her.

"Ready to go?" Cherub walked back inside her chamber, her bag in hand and a white fur cloak draped over her arm, the color a stunning contrast against her velvety, ruby skirts.

"Almost." She opened her keepsake box, picked up her pouch of coins, which was all the savings she had, slipped it inside her pocket and slung her traveling sack over one shoulder. Her heart tightened in anticipation of the battle to come, the fight with her mate one she actually looked forward to. "I must find them, and soon."

"I give you my word that we shall." Cherub extended one arm. "You're to hold on to me while we're traveling through the vortex I open. No letting go, otherwise you'll experience a far rougher journey than what is necessary."

"I understand. This will be a new way for me to make the journey to Alec's time." She'd never traveled through one of Cherub's portals before, the need to do so never arising. With trepidation and excitement flaring strongly through her, she gripped Cherub's offered arm. "This I cannae wait for. I'd like naught more than to catch my mate unawares again. I look forward to tussling with him."

"I doubt this shall be the only time I will ever take you through a portal. I give you my word I'll always be available to take you directly to your mate in this way should you ever have need of it. Ask, and 'twill be done." Cherub swirled her fingers through the air and the wind rose and rushed all about.

A portal opened and holding onto Cherub, she fell away with her princess into the churning abyss. Stars blazed within the dark and lightning flashed. Heart pumping, she gasped at the sheer beauty of moving through both time and space. This was far more spectacular and mesmerizing than when she traveled through the dream realm. What an adventure, and at the end lay all her hopes and dreams, of battling with her chosen one once more, and of finding her loved ones and having them returned to her. She had to secure Alec's aid. Only the best tracker on her side would do, as well as the only man her soul hungered for.

Aye, theirs would be an intriguing battle, one she longed for.

Chapter 5

Annella bumped down with Cherub inside Alec's darkened, moonlit chamber, the air rippling over the blue curtains pushed back either side of his tall window. His room remained similar to when she'd last seen it, his plush black fur cover rumpled on one side of his bed, his sheets all tossed about. She set her traveling sack down on the luxurious white carpet near his wall-mounted television and touched the scarred wood in the paneled wall where he'd impaled her arm to it. He'd thrust the weapon unmercifully fast, but that she'd never hold against him, not when she'd asked him to cut her.

To his window, she wandered and gripped the windowsill. Below in the inner courtyard, all remained quiet and she pushed the window open and caught the slight *thwack* of an axe striking wood somewhere deep within the night-shrouded forest. Tonight, the treetops shone a silvery hue under the golden orb of the moon and she breathed deep, took in Scotland's freshest air and firmed her resolve. She would take on her mate and without any hesitation. "Is that him chopping wood?"

"Let me check with Kirk to be certain. He's on guard along the battlements, will know if that is Alec." Cherub touched her head as she opened her merged link with Kirk. She conversed with her mate then nodded. "Aye, that's your chosen one, out deep in the forest."

"Then I shall go and confront him there." She crossed to the door and together they walked downstairs and outside into the gravelly courtyard.

"Should you need me, call out and I'll come." Cherub hugged her then glanced up at Kirk where he stood in his kilt and white tunic silhouetted with the moon shining bright behind him. "I'll be with my mate should you need me."

"Thank you." With a deep breath, she marched under the raised portcullis then followed the stony pathway sweeping around to the rear of the castle, her hand on the hilt of her ever-present belted sword. The forest rose high beyond a— She stumbled to a stop. Strange contraptions with wheels and shiny coats in a myriad of vivid colors sat side by side within the clearing she'd entered. How unusual. What were these beasts? She trekked toward the first enclosed cart and stroked one finger over the glass window then along the edge of one smooth, painted side. Metal. Incredible. This contraption must be one of this time's conveyances, and with its fortified strength it would surely be able to repel arrows or the strike of a warrior's blade when one sat fully encased within. How clever. Only where were the necessary attachments so the horses could be secured to the front? Frowning, she wandered around the wagon then stuck her nose against the glass window at the front. Inside, luxurious and heavily padded seats took pride of place front and back, along with a small wheel at arm-height before the front seat. What a strange place to put a wheel.

"Those are called vehicles." A giggle echoed toward her from high on the battlements and Cherub leaned over the crenellation with a grin, Kirk standing guard at her back. "Alec's that-away." She pointed toward the worn trail leading through the thick line of pines. "Off you go."

"Of course." She'd inspect these vehicles a little more later.

With a wave, she trod past the conveyances and into the forest, jumped over the odd trailing tree root and toward the resounding hammering of an axe.

In a small clearing surrounded by trees, her chosen one stood, his biceps rippling as he swung his axe down on a log. Wood splintered with the sheer force of his strike, the moonlight shimmering over his bare chest, his skin all sweaty and glistening, his heavy muscles contracting and well-defined abs making her suck in one very necessary breath. Goodness, her man looked completely edible in those black leather pants which clung to his powerful thighs and rode low on his trim hips. Patting her racing heartbeat, she embraced the heady mix of desire and need rolling through her. With one slow but sure step, she moved out from under the trees. "Good evening."

Alec halted mid-strike, his legs planted wide and arms raised high, his axe firm in his powerful grip. He lifted his head, locked gazes with her, his golden shifter eyes blazing bright in the moonlight, then he snarled something wicked. "What the hell are you doing back?"

"'Tis lovely to see you too." She'd stand strong, never allow him to rattle her. Ambling across the lush grass dotted with the odd yellow flower, she halted in front of him.

"I'm not asleep, so either you've infiltrated someone else's dreams to get to me, or you've traveled through one of Cherub's portals."

"Aye, you're such a clever bear. I've come with Cherub and now stand afore you in the flesh." She pulled her collar to the side and angled her neck toward him. Entice him, she would. "If you wish to bite me, this mark will stay. Does that sound tempting?"

"Hardly, and cover yourself up." One narrowed glare as he slammed his axe through the wood. "Why are you here?"

She released her collar, flicked her braid back over her shoulder and walked around him in a slow circle. "Cherub, Kirk, and I will be leaving at first light on the morrow for our enemy's land, to the place where Father and Ronan were captured by Duncan MacKenzie."

"And what has that got to do with me?" Every muscle in his body tensed, his stance rigid as he raised his axe again.

"I've come to ask you a favor." Standing at his back, she ran one finger from hip to hip along the top of his pants. "I still cannae reach Father or Ronan in the dream realm, which means Kirk will need to track their scents from Duncan's campsite. Two trackers would be better than one, particularly since a couple of days have passed since they were taken. I would also like the best tracker there is to be at my side during the hunt. That tracker would be you."

"You can't have me." He lowered the axe headfirst onto the grass, his palm firm around the wooden shaft's end as he slowly turned around and faced her.

"I'm aware of that." She stroked over his broad shoulders, leaned in and blew a warm breath across his damp chest holding a smattering of hair. Touching him in this way soothed her, so very much. "Cherub has searched the Chief of MacKenzie's castle on the shores of Loch Alsh, but there is no sign of Duncan or my kin there, which means Duncan must have taken them either to his own stronghold, of which I've heard about but am unaware of where it is, or some other place. 'Twill no' be an easy task to find them, no' if I cannae find them in the dream realm first."

"You still can't have me."

"Please, Alec. I need your aid and I will do whatever you ask to secure it." With her entire savings in her pocket, she removed her pouch of coins and handed it to him. She would give her entire life if she could to see her kin safely returned to her, as well as all that she was. "That is all I have. Please accept it."

* * * *

An owl hooted in the distance and echoed all around as Alec stared at his mate then the pouch of coins she'd handed him. Hell, he was the worst lout for making her think she needed to offer him actual money to secure his aid. He gripped her hand, gently placed the pouch back in her palm and closed her fingers around it then looking into her eyes, muttered, "You're impossible."

"I need my kin returned to me. I love them, would gladly go to my grave if they've gone from this world, but until I know for certain, I will remain here on this Earth and continue my search for them. Please, say aye. I need your aid in finding them. If this isnae enough, then name your price and I'll try to pay it."

This was his chance to exact the only price he wanted. "If I come, you must give me your word that once your kin are safe again, you'll find another man and wed him."

"What?" Pain and anguish flared in her gaze, her heartache at his demand clear to see. "You hold the other half of my soul, just as I hold the other half of yours. You've just asked of me the one thing I can never give. Accepting another over you is impossible."

"I want you to try."

"Nay." She thrust the pouch at him again. "Take it. I'll find a way to secure more coin."

"Damn it, woman. I won't take your money, no matter how much you give me." He pushed her hand away.

"Then ask me for anything else, only not that I lie with another man and dishonor our bond in such a way." Tears pooled in her eyes and his heart nearly clenched in on itself at seeing her sheer pain. Pain, he'd damn well caused her.

He was such an idiot. He wanted to kick himself. Hurting his chosen one was the last thing he wished to do, and now he'd gone and done it without even laying a hand on her. Idiot. Idiot. Idiot.

"I'm sorry. I shouldn't have asked you to choose another

man over me." He swiped another log from the pile and thumped it on top of the chopping block, her deliciously enchanting fragrance swirling all about and tantalizing him beyond measure. His bear raged at him to take her and his hunger flared with brutal strength inside him. Teeth gritted, he swung his axe and brought it down on the log, drove it into the wood over and over until all that remained was the odd splinter on the block. "I'll come."

"You will?" She grasped his arm, lifted up on her toes and kissed his cheek, the smile on her face one he wanted to memorize and never forget. "Truly?"

"Truly, provided you obey every one of my orders from this moment forth. First, you're to cease touching me."

"Completely?" She frowned, so damn endearingly.

"Completely and utterly."

"You strike a hard bargain."

"Give me your word. No touching." He wouldn't back down on that request.

"What if you were hurt and needed my aid? I would need to touch you." Hunkered down, she picked up the wood he'd chopped and tossed it into the barrow.

"Then touching is only permitted within reason. You're also to call me Captain, not your mighty bear or any other endearment. That'll help you to remember who's leading this trek to find your kin."

"You wish to place boundaries between us, to keep me firmly from you?"

"Exactly."

"We are soul bound, although I shall try to follow your orders, but only those within reason." She gripped the wheelbarrow's handles. "I'll take this load to the woodshed. Is that permissible, Captain?"

"Very. Be gone from my sight until we leave."

"Again, that is an unreasonable request." With a far too

sensual swish of her hips, she disappeared into the trees.

How the hell had she so easily gotten him to accept her request for his aid? He could have sent any one of his kinsmen along with her. Cherub and Kirk would already be at her side on the trek and even though he might be their clan's best tracker, Kirk was still damn good at what he did and could handle any hunt on his own.

Axe in hand, he chopped wood then groaned when she returned. She filled up the wheelbarrow a second time and walked off once more, her long golden tresses pulled tightly back into a braid that swayed all the way to her tiny waist. His fingers itched to wind that braid around his hand, to tug her up against him and keep her pinned in place while he ravaged her mouth with his. She was here, his mate, and in her physical form. He'd never caressed her true flesh and damn it, he longed to.

Thwack. Thwack.

The coming days would be a nightmare as he searched for her kin, and with her in such close reach, he'd need to enforce definite lines between them and ensure she didn't cross even one, which clearly she'd already done and would likely continue to do.

"Are we going to be out here all night chopping firewood?" She set the wheelbarrow down and piled more wood into it, wiped the back of her hand across her glistening forehead. She even sweated beautifully. "I have no' slept much these past few days and wish to be at my most alert during our search."

"Sure. I've finished here. We'll catch some rest." The dark circles under her eyes gave testament to her lack of sleep and as her mate, even though he had no intention of claiming her, everything within him still demanded he see to her care. He scooped up his discarded shirt, tossed it over one shoulder, set the axe on top of the wood in the barrow, gripped the handles and pushed it down the trail. "I'll need to secure you a chamber for the night, although I'll need to wake the chief's wife to do so.

I have no idea which chamber might be free."

"There's no need to wake her. I'm quite happy to sleep in the great hall on my plaid." She walked beside him as he bumped the front wheel over the trailing tree roots. "Or on the plush carpet in your chamber. That too would do quite well for my needs."

He'd never allow his mate to sleep in the great hall where any number of his clansmen—and mostly unmated clansmen—might stumble upon her. "No, you can take my bed and I'll sleep on the settee." He could deal with that.

"Are you certain?"

"It's late. You'll take my bed, and that's an order." He dodged the creeping undergrowth crowding the trail, emerged from the forest and set the barrow down inside the woodshed then marched toward the postern gate as his mate walked beside him and yawned. "You shouldn't have allowed yourself to get this tired, Annella."

"My father and brother would say the same." She stopped next to the center well draped in ivy and picked up the wooden ladle from within the swaying pail and sipped from it. She scooped up a second ladleful and held it out to him. "Are you thirsty, Captain?"

"Sure." He gulped the water then tipped what remained in the pail over his head and shook the drops from his hair, pressed one hand to the small of her back and urged her across the courtyard and up the front step. The vest of soft black leather she wore over her cream tunic matched her black breeches which hugged every inch of her sweetly curved backside, a backside he shouldn't be looking at. He adjusted his suddenly too tight pants, stomped up the stairs and opened his chamber door for her.

"Thank you." She swished inside.

"Don't thank for opening a damn door." Door slammed shut, he flicked on his bedroom light, walked into his bathroom and hit that switch too. Shower lever snapped up, he tossed his shirt into the corner wicker basket and kicked off his boots.

"Oh my, that is the largest looking glass I've ever beheld." She stood in the doorway eying his ceiling-high mirror over the black marble vanity top. "One can almost see their entire self in it."

"We call them mirrors in this time."

"Hmm, mirrors. An apt name." She crossed the bathroom and with one hand resting on the glass shower side, ogled the water streaming from the shower head. "Incredible. What do you call this glassed enclosure?"

"A shower. Water travels through metal pipes within the walls and comes out the spout. You adjust the lever on the wall and set the heat to whatever you'd like. Hot or cold or anywhere else in between. It offers water of any temperature." He motioned toward the door. "Out you go."

"I've never partaken of a shower afore and I wouldnae mind one." Weapons set aside, she tugged off her knee-high boots, pants and vest and standing only in her cream shirt, nodded at him. "You go first. I'll follow."

"You can't shower with me." Hell, she'd stripped off so fast he hadn't had a chance of halting her, had lost his tongue the second she'd pulled the ties on her breeches loose.

"Of course I can. Me and my fellow warriors often bathe together in the loch bordering our warrior encampment. This shower is no different to that, just in a more confined space." She stepped inside under the spray and twirled about. "See, there is plenty of room in here for two."

"You agreed to following my orders."

"Aye, those within reason."

"You're being beyond unreasonable right this second." Still, he stepped inside after her in his pants, heaved the door shut and rattled the glass sides as he did. If other men had bathed with her, then so would he. "Pass me the soap."

"This warm water is glorious." She plucked the bar of soap

off the recessed shelf and built a lather in her hands before handing it to him. Gently, she pressed her hands to his neck, right over the marks she'd given him and rubbed.

"Do you soap your fellow warriors as well?"

"Nay, never, but you're different." She lifted up on her toes and ran more of the bubbles through his hair. "You I'm permitted to touch even though we'll never complete the bond."

"You know why we can't complete the bond." Clearly, she wasn't going to obey his order not to touch, and right now, with her looking so tired, he didn't have the heart to keep reminding her of his request. It may have been a slightly unreasonable one, possibly.

"Aye, because you're a stubborn man with an equally stubborn bear." She plucked the blue silk ribbon from the end of her hair and unraveled her braid, dipped her head back under the spray and softly sighed as the water ran through her locks and down her front.

He didn't dare look down, not when all he could envision was the thin cream cotton of her tunic plastered to her skin. Instead, he grasped her waist and turned her around so she faced the wall then gulped. Her wet shirt clung to her back as well, followed the curvy contours of her bottom and from there the hem hung loose, her gorgeous legs on full display. "Don't move."

Shampoo bottle in hand, he squirted a dollop into his palm then gently worked the bubbles through her wet hair, the silky strands sliding so sensuously through his fingers. He likely shouldn't be doing this, only his idiotic hands were acting of their own accord and he couldn't seem to stop them.

"Mmm, that feels wonderful." She leaned back against him, her head resting on his shoulder as she closed her eyes and tipped her head to one side. Her creamy neck glistened and his teeth ached. All he wanted to do was bite her, to have his mark stamped on her skin for all to see.

He cupped her hips and swung her around. "Tip your head back and wash the bubbles out."

"Aye, Captain." Yawning, she did as he requested, the bubbles swishing down her body and pooling around her tiny toes. "This shower is making me feel all cozy and warm."

Cozy and warm was the last thing he felt. As horny as hell, was. He shoved his head under the water, rinsed his body, turned the lever off and opened the door. From the heated towel rail, he swiped a fluffy white towel and smothered her in it, grabbed one for himself and while wrapping it around his waist and dripping water from the bottom of his pants, stalked to his bedroom. Alone, at least for the moment, he shucked his pants, and from his tall chest of drawers grabbed a clean pair in a dark green and tied the laces at his waist.

"Are you decent?" She peeked around the corner, those sparks of gold rimming her eyes, twinkling. "Oh, you're already far too decent."

"Come in." He dried his hair as she wandered toward her canvas bag propped against the wall, her towel wrapped around her now nude body and her wet tunic in one hand. Her damp hair stuck to her back as she crouched, foraged within her bag and nabbed a dry tunic. "Could you turn around?" She stood and twirled one finger in a motion that mimicked her request. "I would like to change."

"Sure." He did and waited as a wet plop sounded then cotton swished.

"I'm done."

He turned around and nodded. She was presentable, her dry tunic dangling to her about mid-thigh.

"Thank you for the lovely shower. I shall forever remember taking one with you."

"I'll hang your shirt and that towel on the heated rail. Both will be dry in the morning."

"Wonderful." She handed the items across.

"Hit the sack." He motioned toward his bed. "And that's an order. Daybreak is just around the corner and we have a long day of tracking ahead of us."

"'Tis a very large bed you have." She straightened his black fur bedcover and plumped the pillows then shuffled under the sheets and sighed as she wriggled about. "Mmm you have the softest mattress. Are you sure you wish to sleep on the settee? There is plenty of room in your bed for both of us."

"I'm absolutely certain." He hung her shirt up to dry in the bathroom, combed his wet hair, brushed his teeth and snagged his plaid from his wardrobe while she watched him from his bed, which she looked far too enticing within. Her damp hair lay spread across his pillow and the fur cover sat tucked right up under her chin.

"Would you like a pillow?"

"Sure, toss me one." He laid down, his bare feet dangling over the blue suede settee's far armrest then caught the pillow one-handed when she lobbed it to him. "Turn the light switch off. It's right above your head."

"This one?" She pointed to it.

"Aye, it flicks down to go on, and up to go off."

"Oh, I see." She flicked it up and plunged the room into darkness. "I wish you a good night's rest, Captain."

"No talking is permitted once the lights are out."

"But—"

"That's an order. Go to sleep."

* * * *

"All right, all right. You are such a grumpy one." Annella couldn't help but giggle at her feisty mate. He seemed resolute at keeping her at a distance, but since this might be the only chance she had to convince him that doing so wasn't a good idea, and tired or not, she intended to take it. She relaxed back into his mattress and went to open her mouth to speak, only her belly rumbled. "Oh, I'm so sorry. Ignore that."

"When was the last time you ate?" Lowly muttered words.

"I'm no' sure. 'Tis impossible to eat when all one does is worry for their kin, but content I am right in this moment. You have agreed to help me and brought a sense of happiness back to my soul in doing so. Tomorrow, we will track my kin and soon we shall find them. That is all I need for nourishment."

"In my bedside drawer is a chocolate bar. At least eat a piece or two. It'll help curb your hunger until the morning."

"What's a chocolate bar?" She'd never heard of the foreign word before.

"A high energy hit of decadent sweetness. My bear likes chocolate."

"I would like to try it." His bedside drawer beckoned and she opened it and foraged within, the moonlight providing just enough light to see by. She ran one finger over a beautiful, red leather-bound book and a strange looking rectangular device sitting on top of it. The device was as big as her hand yet half as slim. Fascinating. Flattened glass lay on one side while cool metal lay on the other. Curiosity strong, she picked it up. "What's this?"

"A cell phone. Touch the button on the side and it'll light up."

She did and the device flared to life. Oh, good gracious. She squealed, jerked and toppled right out of the bed. On the floor, the device still alight within her fisted grip, she could barely breathe through the shock of what lay before her very eyes. "T-there is a forest contained inside this tiny thing. A small forest, but a forest all the same. How do we get it out?"

"It's just a picture of a forest no matter that it looks strikingly real." Chuckling, he trod across the carpet and held out his hand for it. "Pass it here, sprite."

"You told me to touch the button."

"I did, and it's good to see you have quick reflexes. Cell phones can sometimes break when you drop them. Make sure you never do."

"My reflexes are just fine. You should have warned me about your device, no' told me to touch the button." She slapped his cell phone into his hand and pushed to her feet. "Show me this chocolate bar, and no more surprises."

"One moment." Still chuckling, he pushed another button on the side of his device and it beeped and went dark. He set it down on his bedside table then from his drawer, pulled out a large slab of something wrapped in shiny purple paper with words stamped all over it. From the top row, he snapped off some pieces. "Here you go."

"Are you sure this is 'decadent sweetness?'" Since he appeared in a strangely mischievous mood, she'd best check.

"Taste it and see. I dare you too." A glimmer lit his eyes and she accepted his offering and turned the hard brown thing over in her hands.

"It looks like no food I've ever beheld."

"Once you've eaten chocolate, you'll crave it as badly as I do." He broke off a row for himself, popped a square in his mouth and moaned, his eyes closed and sheer joy flashing across his face.

Taste it she would if it invoked that kind of reaction from him. She reached up and touched her mouth to his, licked across his lower lip and the trace of chocolate smeared along it. Oh my, so good. She urged his lips apart and kissed him, gloried in the taste of both him and the smoothest, sweetest chocolate. 'Twas beyond decadent.

"Annella." He rumbled her name against her lips. "You're not supposed to taste it directly from me."

"More," she whispered and shoved against his chest. The backs of his knees hit the mattress and he toppled back onto the bed and she crawled on top of him, popped one of the squares he'd given her into his mouth then kissed him again, the taste of chocolate and virile man swarming her senses. "This is delicious.

I love your chocolate."

"I'm never going to be able to eat another piece without remembering this damn moment." With his teeth, he bit off another square from his row.

She grinned and hands planted either side of his head, leaned in and licked his lips once more. "Feed me a piece." She opened her mouth and he slid a chunk between her lips and she rolled her tongue around it. "Mmm, so exquisite."

"You're the exquisite one." He flipped her onto her back and over top of her, fed her another piece then buried his head at her neck and razzed his teeth over her skin.

She moaned and rocked underneath him. Would he bite her? She desperately wanted him to. She clutched his shoulders, her nails digging in deep then he sank his teeth into her neck and fierce pleasure coursed through her, wave after wave that she desperately needed more of. "Do that again," she whispered. "Give me more."

"I shouldn't be doing this." He swept around to the other side of her neck, plucked the ties of her V neckline open, his chin bumping the upper swells of her breasts as he nipped her flesh, each of his bites a mark of claim she craved. "Stay still," he whispered, his breath a hot brand against her flesh.

She couldn't, didn't have a chance of doing so. She wrapped her legs around his waist to keep him imprisoned on top of her, speared her fingers through his midnight-black locks as he lifted her breasts free of her tunic. He eased them together and gently sucked one nipple deep inside his mouth, flicked the tip with his tongue and made her moan for more.

"Tell me to stop." He razzed his teeth over her other nipple and heat surged through her, shot straight to her core and pooled between her thighs. He lifted his head, dragged in a deep breath, his gaze swirling with desire. "You smell incredible."

"You should do whatever you please, because this certainly pleases me." She cupped his head in her hands, drew his mouth back to her breasts. "I love the feel of your mouth on mine, your lips touching other parts of me. I want more of it."

"I shouldn't be giving into you like this." He suctioned his mouth around her wet aureole and played the tip to perfection with his clever tongue. "Except I have nearly no willpower when it comes to you."

"You have far too much—oh, good, so good." She cried out as sheer pleasure stormed through her and she rocked her hips against his, the hard length of his leather-clad manhood poking her between her thighs. She wriggled, until the head of his shaft brushed against her entrance. Perfect. He felt so sublime on top of her and she wanted even more, whatever he was prepared to give. "There is something just beyond my reach, but I dinnae know what it is."

"I know what you need." He gripped her thighs, pressed his leg higher into her crotch and urged her to move on him. Pleasure coursed swiftly through her, swept her away on a tide of wonder. Never had she ever known such decadence as this. She was his, whether he wished to claim her or not.

"That feels sublime." A tight need for more built deep inside her. "More, Alec."

"I'm here." He hissed out a breath and gave her even more friction. He eased one hand down her body and underneath the hem of her tunic before sliding his finger along the seam of her womanhood and swirling around her nub. Having him touch her so intimately, felt so very right.

Breathless, she rubbed against him harder, clamped her mouth on the soft skin of his neck and dizzy with need, bit down and marked him just as she desired. He bucked against her, roared and sank his teeth into her neck in return, then with one swipe of his finger across her nub below, white-hot pleasure struck her, ricocheted outward from her core and sent her flying far beyond her body, her mate atop her jerking and groaning as his own pleasure soared through him.

As she slowly came back down, she sucked on his neck and laved his skin. Sweet heaven. She'd just flown to the stars and at her mate's hand no less. He'd saturated her in pleasure, and all she wanted to do was hold onto him and never let him go.

"Are you all right?" Soft words in her ear.

"Very." Panting, she opened her eyes. "I love chocolate."

"So do I, but it appears it's not only decadent, but also dangerous to consume." He popped another square into his mouth then slipped the last piece between her lips, fixed and straightened her tunic then lifted himself from her. He dusted his hands against his sides and gazed somewhere over her head. "We won't be consuming that again. Do you want to use the bathroom first?"

"Aye, I would, please." She pushed to her feet, swayed a little but managed to slip past him and closed the bathroom door after herself. Leaning against the solid wood door, she breathed slowly in and out while in the mirror above the basin, her reflection showed her dreamy, heavy-lidded eyes and mussed hair. Her mate certainly knew how to make her head spin. She craved him, of lying with him without a stitch of clothing between them, of him making love to her and completing their bond. A dream for now, but one she'd work incredibly hard at making a reality. Of course she wasn't like other women and hadn't been since the moment she'd lost her mother and instead donned lad's clothing so she might remain at her father's side, but if Alec could see through those layers and to her true heart, then she'd do all she possibly could to ensure his happiness.

At the vanity, she opened a drawer and removed a comb. She tidied her hair, braided the long length then fetched her ribbon, which lay in a puddle on the floor of his shower where she'd dropped it earlier and secured it at the end. Done, she opened the door and came face to face with her chosen one. "Your turn."

"Thank you." He eased past her and disappeared within.

Back under the covers, she waited and finally he opened the door and in the dark, stomped back to the settee, dropped down and hauled his plaid over his head.

"That," he muttered, "will never happen again."

"That," she murmured, her smile wide, "was a true treat. Thank you, my mighty bear."

Chapter 6

Birds twittered somewhere outside and the dawn's rising sunshine streamed through Alec's window and spilled over Annella's closed eyelids. She wriggled and stretched in bed, her mate's warm and fresh pine scent floating around her. Blinking her eyes open, she flopped onto her side and grinned at her mate as he slept soundly on the blue suede settee, his bare feet protruding over the end of the padded armrest and one forearm flung over his eyes. He must have been exhausted to have slept in such a position.

Black fur cover pushed back, she snuck across to him and knelt on the plush white carpet, cupped his bristly jaw and reveled in the tingles racing across her fingertips. She leaned in and licked his lower lip. This man held the other half of her soul, just as she held the other half of his, their bond one that had crossed the centuries and defied even time itself. She couldn't ignore it, wanted only to keep chipping away at his resolve until he'd fully caved into her. Aye, 'twas a solid plan, one she intended to continue with.

"What are you doing?" He moaned, opened one eye and glared at her.

"I missed you." She touched her lips to his, blew a soft

breath across his tongue then kissed him, captured more of his delicious essence and fairly thrummed at the decadence of him. This felt so very right. All she wanted to do was indulge and never stop.

"Annella." He mumbled her name against her lips. "You can't kiss me like this."

"I think I can." She grasped his shoulders, ran her hands down his sides, over his hips and his dark green leather pants. With a giggle, she pinched his butt then kissed him again.

"You are so annoying, my mysterious sprite." Breaking their kiss, he swung his feet to the floor and stood. "Do you wish to join my clansmen for breakfast in the great hall or for me to bring a tray up here?"

"A tray here please. I still need to travel to the dream realm. I fell into such a deep sleep after our kisses last eve that I didnae have the chance to do so. Will you watch over me while I'm away? I very rarely leave without someone to guard my body and force my return should it be needed."

"Of course. What should I expect?"

"My breathing becomes shallower and my heartbeat slows. Sometimes my skin cools and my lips go a little blue. All you need to worry about though is if I cease breathing altogether. Should that happen then shake me, and dinnae cease doing so until I'm back."

"How long will you be gone?" He gestured for her to lie down on his bed.

"However long is needed, although I will be as quick as I can." She laid down, rested her head back on his soft white pillow as he perched next to her on the luxurious mattress.

"You'll truly return if I shake you?" He picked up her hand, pressed his lips to her palm.

"Aye, for you I would do anything to return." Slowly, she closed her eyes and focused on her breathing. Relaxed, she cleared her mind, then embraced the dark. She drifted deeper into sleep then rose and floated through the darkness. One star twinkled, then another and another. She soared higher, to the place where Father and Ronan's stars usually blazed. All wispy-white, she breezed, yet still there was naught. No Ronan. No Father.

Why? So many days had now passed and she should have been able to find them resting at some point. Mayhap… Nay, she'd never allow herself to consider that they no longer lived. Duncan knew of her skill and simply ensured they didn't rest, or else she'd missed them during the times when they had been able to catch a few winks. That was all.

"Annella!" Alec's voice swamped her. "You're crying. Wake up."

She descended, breathed deep as she settled back inside her physical body and blinked her eyes open. Her mate still sat beside her, her braid now unraveled and one of his hands fisted around the long length. Carefully, he slid his other arm around her back then lifted her up and settled her on his lap, tucked her head under his chin and her cheek against his chest. He held her close, his heartbeat thumping against her ear as he rocked her. "I'm fine, Alec."

"No more crying."

"I couldnae find them and the thought of their death, of them being taken away from me, it hurts, terribly." She wiped her tears away and looked into his eyes. "You have chosen to deny our bond and I fear I will have naught to live for if I ever discover they are truly gone. I would wish only to join them beyond the veil, to leave this Earth behind so I might be with my loved ones once more. Do you understand? Should I ever leave this Earth, then know 'tis because I had no other choice."

"I won't let you leave me, and we'll find them, that I promise you." He pressed a kiss to her forehead. "They wouldn't dare die and leave you alone, not if you only intended to hunt them down beyond the veil."

"Aye, I can be rather persistent when I've set my mind to something."

"So I've noticed." He searched her gaze, such a myriad of emotions swirling within, but most of all, his need for her shone the greatest. "If you ever need a listening ear, then ask Cherub to bring you through one of her portals. I'll always be here."

"Your offer is a good one." Better than any he'd offered her so far.

"I should go and secure us some food." He set her on her feet as he stood then walked out the door and left without a backward glance.

With a long sigh, she collected what she needed from her traveling sack and strolled into the bathroom. She flapped out a pair of tan pants and fastened the ties at her waist, tucked in the hem of her cream tunic and slipped on a buttery-soft tan rawhide vest. Knee-high leather boots back on and sword belt and wrist dagger fastened, she splashed her face with warm water at the basin, plaited her hair once more and returned to the bedroom for her ribbon. The thin strip of blue silk lay on his pillow where he must have tossed it after unraveling her hair. She knotted it around the end to secure her braid in place.

"Here we go." Alec returned with a tray holding two steaming tankards and a plate stacked with bacon slices, eggs, crusty bread, and a bowl of sliced apple set to one side. He placed the tray on the side table tucked in one corner then crossed to his oak chest of drawers, slipped on a black tunic with ties at the V neckline and donned a black leather jerkin, fastened his sword then hid various other weapons around his body.

Comfort settled within her as he did. To not be armed in any way always rattled her, and clearly it did so with him too. He disappeared into the bathroom and she set to work making his bed, plumped his pillows and straightened his sheets before sitting on one of the two wooden backed chairs before the table.

With his jaw shaven and his silky black hair brushing his

shoulders just the way she liked, he emerged, pulled a brown canvas satchel out from under his bed and stuffed clothes from his dresser into it. "Start eating without me."

"Nay, I shall wait." This would be the first breakfast she'd ever share with him and she didn't wish to miss a moment of it.

"I feel like I've forgotten something." Frowning, he glanced about his chamber.

"Might I recommend you pack the rest of your chocolate bar?" She certainly hoped he would.

"You could." He chuckled and shook his head. "Except that might make our trip enter into dangerous territory."

"Pack it. I dare you to do so, or are you scared of me?" She leaned over one of the steaming tankards and breathed in the unusually earthy-sweet aroma within. Its scent reminded her somewhat of the chicory plant with its bright blue flowers. She'd come across it from time to time in the forest. "What is this hot drink called?"

"Coffee. I already added milk and sugar to sweeten it. Take a sip and taste it." He opened his bedside drawer and took out the chocolate bar, slipped it inside his bag and closed the flap before taking the seat opposite her. "You also don't scare me in the least."

"I should." She smiled, her heart lightening. "Thank you for packing the chocolate."

"I didn't pack the chocolate for you."

"Of course you didnae." She picked up the tankard with a pretty motif of a flower on the front and sipped. The hot brew warmed her belly, the taste so different to anything she'd ever tasted before. So many new and exciting things existed in this time, and she couldn't wait to discover all that she could.

"Do you like it?" He sipped from the other tankard then let out a long sigh of contentment.

"I would like anything you brought me."

"Is that right?" He raised a curious brow. "What about a

dead rabbit my bear hunted down and dropped at your feet, blood still dripping from its carcass and between my teeth?"

"Provided you then shifted, skinned and cleaned the rabbit then brushed your teeth, I'd be fine with you doing so." She picked up a fork and stabbed some of the bacon and egg then layered it on top of one of the bread slices. Bread folded over, she picked it up and chewed. "Father calls me his wild child, even though Ronan is far wilder than me, so if you wish to hunt rabbit, then I would gladly join you and your bear when you do."

"There's nothing I can say which is going to deter you is there?" He blew out a long breath then sipped his coffee.

"I adore wearing lad's clothing, climbing trees, roaming the forest, and riding across the grassy moors. I am no' your typical lass, although I have breasts and the body of a woman. I can see to your needs, ensure you want for naught during a coupling."

"I have no issue with you wearing lad's clothing, but what we did last night will never happen again." With a grunt, he slapped some bacon and egg on his own piece of bread, folded it in half and bit into it. "This conversation about coupling also needs to stop."

"I'm slim of build, always on the move and forget to eat at times, would never be a woman who could remain at the hearth, but—" She shook her head, her heart heaving. Aye, if he truly wished a woman who thrived on being safe within his keep's walls, she'd fail him terribly at that.

"Don't. I can see what you're thinking." He grasped her hand across the table, brought her fingers to his lips and kissed each tip. "I find you immensely appealing, would want a woman exactly like you." He pressed her palm against his chest, his gaze softening. "You're nothing like I ever expected, yet everything I could ever desire in a mate. I also find you far too desirable for my liking."

"You hold the strength and the heart of a warrior, your love for your kin shining through You are everything I could ever desire in a mate too."

"You missed the killing part and my beastly bear." He nudged the bowl of apple slices toward her. "Keep eating. You'll need the energy for later in the day."

"Aye, Captain." She scooped up some apple and bit into it. "Can I speak to you of one of my most secret desires?"

"No." He gulped a mouthful of coffee. "Sharing secret desires is absolutely forbidden."

"You dinnae wish to know what I desire doing?" She certainly wished to share her dreams with him.

"No." He gulped another mouthful.

"I shall tell you anyway." She plucked another apple slice from the bowl, leaned across and popped it into his mouth. "I secretly dream of climbing Ben Nevis. 'Tis the highest mountain in all of Scotland and only a few days' journey from my home on the shores of Loch Alsh."

"It's also the highest mountain in all the United Kingdom and first scaled by James Robertson in seventeen-hundred and seventy-one. The plaque says so once you reach the top." He finished his coffee, stood and shoved his chair in. "Ben Nevis is also a popular destination, and if you use the Pony Track from Glen Nevis, you can ascend to the top with far more ease."

"Please, dinnae tell me you have climbed it." Surely, he hadn't. She jumped from her seat, grasped his hands.

"I've climbed it." He dipped his head, touched his lips to her ear. "I do so once a year. My bear needs the hard trek and adventure, as do I."

"Oh my." Jealousy and longing speared through her. "Will you take me the next time—"

"No."

"Wait." She snorted under her breath. "You need to cease saying no to me all the time. My request wasnae a bad one."

"No is a very safe word, particularly around you." He slid one finger under her chin, his gaze locked tight with hers. "We should never have kissed last night, or this morning. I'm sending you the wrong message and I need to cease doing so."

"You are doing no more than showing affection, as those who are mated do." She slid her hands over his chest, rested her cheek against his shoulder and allowed his warmth and strength to surround her. "I adore your kisses, in case you were no' aware."

"As I adore yours, but they truly must stop." He stepped back and she growled under her breath. Her mate needed to see the truth standing right before his eyes, the same truth that lay glaringly obvious to her. Never would he harm her. 'Twas impossible for those who were soul bound to bring harm or pain to the other. Even when he spoke of dismissing all that had grown between them this past month, he still reached out to touch and connect with her. 'Twas clear to see he needed her, just as much as she needed him.

"Go and gather your things. I saw Cherub and Kirk downstairs and they're readying themselves to leave." He motioned toward her bag.

"Aye, we must leave." That she would give him. 'Twas certainly time to begin her search and find her kin. No more could she delay. She collected her bag, folded her belongings inside, slung it over one shoulder and joined him at the door.

"Pass your bag to me."

"I can carry it." She couldn't help but touch one finger to the new mark she'd stamped on his neck. Caressing downward, over his broad shoulder and rigid bicep, she smiled. "I shall carry yours too when your bear needs to track my kin and you wish to remain unhindered by your things."

"My satchel straps around my waist, has magnetic tabs that hold it in place. You don't need to carry my things at all." His shifter eyes heated, his gaze a molten pool of liquid gold as he gazed at her neck and the mark he'd stamped upon her. "I should shift now, let you meet my bear, but I'd rather do so when Kirk is around and he can ensure your safety should something go wrong."

"Your bear could never harm me."

"He's demanding, violent and hostile. I want you to take extreme care when I release him, and I mean that, Annella. If he makes even one wrong move and harms you, then that's it. I'll call off my offer to aid you in your search and find you another of my clansmen to do the job." He twirled her around, flipped her bag off her shoulder and onto his. "Also, when I ask you to hand me something, you do it. That's a direct order."

"Aye, Captain." She giggled, opened the door and gestured for him to go through. "Grumpy bears afore ladies, I believe."

Grumbling, he marched past her and down the burgundy and blue carpet runner then waited for her at the top of the stairs.

She bounded in beside him, pushed him back against the wall and stomped on his booted feet to gain some height, fisted his shirtfront and kissed the man who'd brought desire and love flaring back to glorious and vibrant life within her. "You are mine, just as I am yours."

"I said no more kissing." He took her with him, her feet still balanced on top of his as he stepped to the other side of the hallway and pushed her against the wall. Trapped, he smoothly slid one palm around her nape, dipped his head and sucked her lower lip into his mouth. He rolled his tongue around her lower lip, moved to her upper lip and plumped it between his lips, then he devoured her, his kiss hot and wild and all that she needed, yet also not nearly enough.

"There you two are." Cherub skipped up the stairs in a navy riding habit, her white fur cloak swaying from her shoulders. "Kirk and I have collected some food from the kitchens and have all we need for our coming trip."

Kirk grinned as he strode upstairs in Cherub's wake, the hem of his loose-sleeved white tunic fluttering free underneath his fur-lined jacket, his kilt belted at his waist and two bags in hand, one which must be filled with the promised provisions. "You two appear as if you're getting along quite well."

"She's my mate. What do you expect?" Alec snapped at Kirk as he wrapped an arm around her waist and drew her forward. "I'll need you to supervise my first shift. If my beast hurts her, shoot him."

"You got it." A chuckle from Kirk. "Although it's impossible for us to hurt our chosen ones and you need to remember that."

"Shoot. Gun. Here." Alec pulled a metal weapon with a small barrel from his bag and slapped it into Kirk's hand, a weapon she'd never seen before, although he'd clearly called it a gun, whatever a gun was. Well, it hardly appeared as if it would harm him. 'Twas all smooth edged and without the bite of a blade to it, nor the speared head of an arrow. "The tranquilizer is loaded and you know what to do with it."

"I've got you covered." Kirk slid the gun inside his fur jacket's inner pocket. "Not that I'll need it."

"I've already harmed her, so trust me, you need it."

"You didnae harm me, no' when I asked you to take my dagger and see if I bled." She rubbed her cheek against Alec's wide shoulder, her ability to touch him comforting her so very much. "What does a tranquilizer do?"

"That gun, when aimed and shot at someone, will release a dart holding a sedative. The dose within it is strong enough to bring my beast down, within just a few seconds. I always make sure one of my teammates carries it on any mission we set out on. I'm unpredictable, Annella. I can turn in an instant and you need to take the utmost care around me. I can't stress that enough."

"I understand." She reached up on her toes and kissed his jaw. "I should like you to turn in an instant, and instead of saying you dinnae want me, to instead say you do."

"That's not happening, my annoying sprite."

"Aye, I'm your annoying sprite, and dinnae you forget it." She stepped away from him and hugged Cherub. "Thank you for bringing me here to Alec's time. My chosen one is still adamant we willnae be completing the bond, but I still hold the hope that I might be able to sway his mind."

"You're going to adore the moment you complete the bond. When you two join together in all ways, you'll create the merged link of the mind, one that's inherent in our men's shifter blood. Only then will either of you truly be at peace and Alec's bear more settled. A happy man makes for a happy bear."

"Excuse me. I'm right here," Alec grumbled, yet such hungry hope swirled within his gaze even as he frowned at her.

"Cherub is my princess and so very wise. You'd be foolish if you didnae listen to her from time to time." She poked his chest. "No more arguing. I wish to begin our search and find my kin. Father and Ronan need to be freed, and that is all I can think about right now."

"I wholeheartedly agree." Cherub held out her arms to them both as she glanced at Alec. "You need to take ahold of me. Only those connected to me in some way can travel safely through the portals I open, and if you let go at any point in time, expect a rather rough ride and an equally rough landing." She glanced over her shoulder at Kirk. "Are you ready, my tempting bear?"

"Always, my elusive imp." He slid his arms around her from behind and nipped her ear. "Let's head out."

"We'll find them, somehow and some way." Alec nodded at Annella as he gripped Cherub's arm.

"Aye, we shall. There can be no other way."

"I agree," Cherub bit out with determination then with a swish of her fingers, she opened a portal and the four of them fell away into the dark abyss, all connected as one.

Through time and space, they traveled and a few minutes later arrived on the rise of a forested mountain, one side sweeping downward toward the inner channel of Loch Alsh. A cold wind whipped around and through her, the towering tree she'd been bound and gagged within rising high right beside her. A shiver chased down her spine and she swiftly shook off the uneasy feeling. She had no time for such trepidation.

She swished past Alec and hunkered down next to the fire pit where rocks had been arranged in a circle and the ashes within had all but blown away. Carefully, she touched a finger to a dry pool of blood, now a muddy brown in color. Father's blood. It had been spilt right here, Ronan's likely as well since her brother would never have surrendered with any ease. "This is the place."

"You're not alone." Her chosen one crouched next to her, his big body blocking the worst of the wind. "Never alone."

"Find them, please." She caught his hand, pressed his fingers to the dried blood. "Release your bear and track down our enemy. Duncan MacKenzie must pay for what he's done."

Chapter 7

Hand on the hilt of her belted sword, Annella rose and walked around the abandoned campsite where Duncan MacKenzie had held a bird's eye view of their Matheson warrior encampment with its canvas tents pitched within the grassy clearing edging the loch below this high plateau. Duncan had watched and waited, planned then struck and with the aid of one of the fae no less.

"Alec." Cherub lifted the flap on one of the bags Kirk had carried. "I have an item of clothing from both Niall and Ronan, procured from their chambers. Hopefully you'll be able to find their scent on these pieces."

"Pass the items here." Alec propped the bags he carried against a wide trunk and accepted Father's tartan woolen cap and one of Ronan's great plaids from Cherub. Kirk joined him and the two men sniffed each item.

"I've got both scents." Alec eyed Kirk. "What about you?"

"Their scents are strong, and thankfully we've had no rain these past few days. I wish we could have begun a search from this point sooner, although now that we're here, there'll be no further delay." Kirk handed the items back to Cherub. "Keep these somewhere safe. I'll allow Alec to shift first, ensure all is well when his bear meets Annella for the first time, then shift afterward."

"Let's give them as much privacy as we can." Cherub folded the items back in her bag and tugged Kirk toward the trees. She disappeared within the woods while Kirk waited patiently on guard at the very edge.

"Are you ready?" Alec glanced at her as he kicked off his boots and shoved them in his bag.

"Aye, I look forward to meeting your bear."

"You shouldn't." He stripped off his weapons and slid them into slots on his satchel, removed his leather jerkin and tunic and bagged them, then standing in naught more than his dark green rawhide pants, he nodded. "Last chance to run away and never look back."

"A warrior never runs. Shift." Her pulse raced as the wind rushed up the cliff side and whisked over her, bringing with it the heady freshness of the woods and her mate's delicious outdoorsy scent. She gripped his hips, rubbed her nose against his neck and licked the mark she'd given him. 'Twas important for shifters to ensure their mate held their scent. A bear thing she'd come to understand well from being around Gilleoin and his shifter sons, Kirk and Cherub too.

"The pants have to go. I detest shredding my clothes. Turn around if you need to." He slid one hand down the long length of her braid.

"I've lived amongst warriors who care little for modesty and I'm no' unaware of what a man looks like." She wrapped her arms fully around his waist, drew his scent even deeper into her skin and embedded her own into his flesh. That should help calm his bear during their first meeting and now assured she'd done all she could, she stepped back. "Unclothe yourself, Alec."

"If you feel uneasy at any time then yell out to Kirk. I'll understand." He loosened the ties of his dark green rawhide pants, grasped his waistband and shoved the leather to the forest floor.

She gulped as she took in his beautiful body, all hard and sculpted muscle, all man and all hers, that's if he ever chose to accept their bond and join them together in all ways. Oh, how she wished he would, that just the two of them stood right here and alone in this very place.

"I'm ready," Kirk called out from the far tree line. "Shift as soon as you're ready."

"Don't take your eyes off me," Alec called back then stepped away from her and shifted in a sizzling display of crackling energy and searing light. He was gone, in the blink of an eye, silky black fur sprouting where there'd been only golden skin. His big bear prowled toward her, teeth snapping together and claws digging into the pine-needle covered ground.

She stepped back and knocked her back against the wide trunk of the tree she'd been bound within. "Wait."

Up on his hind legs, he rose then roared and slammed his paws down on the rough bark either side of her head.

She clapped her hands over her ears, his growl thundering all around, his bellow a clear warning, for others to stay far away, that he ruled this forest and no other ever would. "Alec?"

He shoved his muzzle into her neck and sniffed, suddenly rubbed his furry cheek against hers and she grasped the rough bark at her back to hold herself upright.

"I see even your bear likes to be as forceful as you are." He heaved against her and she lost her grip on the trunk, toppled to the ground and hit her head on a protruding tree root. Black dots danced before her eyes. Nay, she wouldn't allow a simple fall to make her lose awareness. She shoved the dark away, grasped the back of her head and gave Alec her fiercest frown. "Stop pushing me around."

He howled, dropped down onto all fours and prodded her with one beefy paw. His strength was immense and he rolled her over onto her belly then sniffed the back of her head.

A trickle of blood oozed between her fingers and he growled again, a low and deadly rumble that had her rolling back over and facing him. She fisted her hands in his silky pelt and gave him a shake. "You didnae hurt me, no' intentionally, you frustrating man."

Nose to the air, he howled again and overwhelmed with a need to reassure him, she pulled him down beside her, only he thumped one heavy foreleg over her waist, shoved his upper body over hers and took a terrifyingly protective position, barely allowing her enough room to draw a decent breath from underneath him.

"Are you all right, Annella?" A yell from Kirk.

"I'm fine. Dinnae come any closer." If Kirk tried to take one step toward Alec and her, her mate might very well attack him. "He's protecting me, ensuring no other can harm me." That she knew to the depths of her soul.

She curled onto her side so she could still breathe under the heavy weight of his body, closed her eyes, calmed her mind and allowed her thoughts to settle. The dark encroached and she glided toward the dream realm, her spiritual body separating from her physical body as she soared free, her physical body underneath Alec's slumping and her heartbeat slowing. With her ethereal form free, she wisped away on the breeze then swept through the canopy and back down and around Alec's bear and her trapped body. She needed him to know she trusted him, fully and completely, that she would never be afraid of either him or his bear. With her spiritual body solidified, she knelt next to him and touched his back before sinking her fingers into his furry pelt. "I'm right here, Alec."

He turned and snapped his teeth at her, his golden shifter gaze narrowing.

"Let me pet you." She stroked him, from his neck to his rump then leaned closer, rubbed her cheek against his cheek and scratched between his ears. "Your bear is big and beautiful and all mine, Alec, just as the man is."

He bumped his muzzle into her belly.

"You wish for another pat?" Heart lifting, her need the same as his, she rubbed his sides, her very soul's desire to be this close to his bear, the same as her desire to be this close to her man as well. They were one and the same, both him and his bear, and hers to care for. She wished to embrace their bond and ensure he never left her, although if she ever wished to make that happen, she'd first need to convince him his beast was never a threat to her, that they would be strongest together rather than they'd ever be apart.

She sat down, crossed her legs and caught his head in her hands and urged him to settle his cheek in her lap. He grizzled but allowed her to tuck him closer then he rolled over and exposed his belly, her physical body no longer cocooned and trapped underneath his. With his paws up, he offered her an expectant look. Aye, he too wanted this moment, to know his bear could be calmed by her, that he'd never harm her as he feared so greatly he would.

"Do you remember the first time I visited you in your dreams?" She caressed his belly, her fingers sliding through his decadently soft fur. With one hearty stretch, he purred, actually purred and she couldn't halt her smile. She spread her hand over his heart, its steady and powerful beat a rhythm she wished to never cease hearing. "We were both completely shocked. Me, because I'd never visited anyone who wasnae direct kin, and you, because no one had ever snuck up on you, even in your sleep. You tried to heave me away from you that very first night, only you couldn't send me away when 'twas I who controlled my very own presence within your mind."

One deeply satisfied rumble vibrated from his chest, the heavenly sound of his content bringing tears to her eyes.

"We are mated, and whether your bear is aggressive or no', I wouldnae wish to be anywhere else than right here with you.

Dinnae send me away again. Accept me and all that I am, just as I wish to accept you."

Lights shimmered in a bright blaze and she toppled onto her back, shoulder to shoulder with her physical body as Alec loomed over both her and her prone form, all man and hard and hot flesh.

"You're my mate, the only woman I've ever been called to protect, the only woman my very soul hungers for." He touched his fingers to the blood at the back of her true body's head. "You bleed right now because of me. How many times should I allow that? Once, twice, three times, or a hundred and three times?"

"You are being unreasonable." She hooked her legs around his waist and unable to keep her gaze from lowering, almost lost her breath as she took in the smattering of dark hair on his chest, which thinned into a teasing line as it trailed down between his defined abs before thickening into dark curls at the apex of his groin. Nestled within those curls his manhood rose thick and strong.

"Cease looking at me like that." He lowered his body down on top of hers, his shaft brushing against her belly, his gaze on hers as he sniffed the air. "Kirk's joined Cherub deeper in the forest. He left when I shifted."

"Even Kirk knows you'd never harm me. So does Cherub. Want me, Alec, the same way that I desperately want you." She stroked down his muscled arms and over his trim hips, lifted up a little and pressed her nose into his neck. His warm and fresh pine scent intoxicated her, sent her senses swirling with desire. Denying the completion of their mated bond was akin to cutting off a piece of herself. "I want the merged link of the mind your shifter kind form with your chosen one when you join together in all ways. I want to be able to speak to you at will, to always be in your thoughts and you in mine."

"You've met my bear." His claws sliced out and back in.

"Aye, and he's a stroppy beast, just as you are. All pushy

and determined to get his way, except I'm no' a biddable lass. My father raised me to be a strong woman, to fight alongside him and Ronan without any issue. So too I wish to fight right alongside you, that is if you'll but allow it."

"I understand what you're asking, but you're also bleeding right now and that's my fault." He glanced at her physical body lying next to her, his need to tend to her flaring strongly in his gaze. "Return, immediately. That's an order."

"Aye, Captain." She dissolved her form, took a deep breath and settled herself back inside her body. Her heartbeat thumped and she gasped, pushed up until she sat, her fingertips tingling and her head aching where she'd hit it.

Alec crouched in behind her, separated her hair at the back of her head and gently touched the area. "The bleeding has stopped and there's only a small puncture wound. It's fairly shallow and doesn't need stitches, but there'll be a bruise."

"Mayhap you could kiss the bruise better for me?" She pulled her braid to one side and offered her neck to him. "Your bite would be even more soothing. I'm sure that will ease any lingering pain that bothers me."

"I can scent Cherub and Kirk again. They're back." In a burst of bright lights, he shifted once more, his big bear standing guard at her back then he growled, nudged her with his muzzle and pushed harder into her back when she didn't move.

"All right, all right." She shoved to her feet, dusted her hands against her tan breeches and flicked his ear with one finger. "I'm moving, you big oaf."

Cherub emerged from the thick tree line with a large, black-pelted bear plodding around the bushes beside her. The two joined them, Cherub's gaze on her. "Is all well?"

"As well as things can be." She flicked Alec's ear again and he snapped his teeth at her. "It appears I like tussling with a bear, intend to forever aggravate and annoy my chosen one."

"There is naught wrong with a little annoyance." Cherub

giggled as she folded Kirk's plaid, white tunic, and fur-lined jacket into his bag. "'Tis time to find Niall and Ronan. Are we all ready?"

"I'm more than ready." She scooped up Alec's discarded pants and stuffed them inside his satchel. "What of you, my mighty bear?"

He grunted, padded to his bag, snatched it between his front paws and with an intriguing flip of it over his back that he'd clearly mastered at some point in time, hooked his bag into place with absolute precision via the magnetized straps he'd spoken of earlier.

Kirk did the same with his bag then the two of them sniffed around the small clearing until Alec snarled and shook his head like a dog when it tussled with a rabbit after it caught it. He lumbered into the forest, sniffing and growling as he led the way and Kirk plodded in beside him.

She grabbed her bag and followed as each of them tracked along one side of the thin trail weaving deeper into the forest and the wilds of MacKenzie land.

Along the leaf-strewn trail edged with low brush, she negotiated trailing tree roots and thick ivy vines draping low over the branches. She moved ahead when needed and slashed at thick foliage with her sword when it clogged the pathway, while all around her the small critters of the forest scurried though the undergrowth as they sensed the presence of the predators within.

Alec prowled and sniffed, the hours slowly passing and the sun crossing from one horizon to the other. The light began to lesson through the thick canopy overhead as evening approached. A whole day of tracking had nearly passed and she'd yet to rest for even a few minutes to see if she could find Father and Ronan within the dream realm. Hopefully, they'd stop soon and she'd have the chance to—

With a menacing growl, Alec halted then veered off the trail and Kirk followed in fast pursuit. She dashed after them, Cherub right beside her.

"What have they found?" she asked Cherub.

"Let me check along my link." Cherub went quiet as she spoke mind to mind with Kirk, then nodded at her. "The scents in this area just doubled. No' only can they make out your father and brother's scents, but now also another party of MacKenzie warriors have joined theirs."

"We must continue on, no matter how many enemy warriors we might encounter."

"I agree."

They picked up their pace as they weaved in and around the scraggly undergrowth until the trees gave way to a small clearing dotted with tiny white flowers and lavender bushes. A wide stream wound through the meadow, water flowing fast past wide gray boulders and sweeping around the bend before disappearing.

Alec plodded along the riverbank, dunked one paw into the water then splashed through the shallows to the other side. Nose buried to the ground, he trod in and around thick clumps of grasses and bushes.

Kirk scoured their side of the river then rose up and slapped his paws down on a large boulder protruding from the river's edge near a set of stepping stones leading from one side to the other. He grunted, over and over and Alec lifted his head, eyed Kirk and grunted in the same manner right back.

"Are they talking to each other?" She grasped Cherub's arm as they waited for their men's next move.

"Aye, bear talk, which I've yet to learn and understand." Cherub went quiet as she conversed mind to mind with Kirk then said, "Niall's scent continues along the bank on our side of the stream here, while Ronan's scent remains strong on the other side. It appears your kin were separated at this point of their journey, both having been taken in different directions."

"Why would Duncan separate them?"

"Kirk and Alec have no idea, although since it'll be dark soon, they'd rather rest here for the night then choose which path we should take in the morning. In the dark, they could so easily miss something of vital importance. We're to make camp here."

"Mayhap I'll be able to find them in the dream realm this eve." Making camp here suited her too. Duncan couldn't keep her loved ones from their sleep forever, and she needed time to search for them. "Did the MacKenzies rest here for the night as well?"

"Nay, they passed straight through, their tracks leading directly on. Kirk and Alec both feel secure in making this the place where we stop for the night."

With a series of grunts, Kirk spoke to Alec again then pushed off the boulder and lumbered into the woods while across the other side of the stream, Alec ambled beyond the tree line. A burst of lights blazed in both directions then both of them reemerged, once again dressed and their satchels looped over their shoulders.

Alec, with his black tunic hanging loose over his dark green pants, his sword belted at his side, halted on the stream bank and nodded at Kirk. "I'll go and set a trap while you start a fire."

"Will do, and by the way, I'm hungry. Bring back plenty of meat." Kirk crossed to Cherub in his belted kilt and fur jacket, pulled her into his arms and kissed her soundly. Against her lips, he murmured, "I'll go fetch us some wood. If you need to wander off, then don't go too far. Stay within calling distance of both Alec and I."

"Be quick and dinnae get lost." Cherub tapped his nose. "I've missed you today, even though we've been together."

"Me too, although I think it's impossible for me to get lost." He pinched her bottom then with a chuckle, disappeared into the brush.

'Twas so wonderful to see the Fae Angel of Love now mated. For over a thousand years she'd tended to her duty, caring for her fae-blooded kind who walked this Earth and now she'd finally found her soul bound mate, even spelled Kirk's very essence to hers so he too had become an immortal as she was. The two would stand at each other's sides for the rest of their lives. 'Twas such a gift to be given a mate and she wished too for what Cherub and Kirk had, a bond so deep that she'd never consider being anywhere but right at her chosen one's side, that he too would desire the same with her.

"Are you all right, Annella?" On the other side of the stream, Alec still stood, hands on his hips and his gaze on her. His beautiful golden shifter eyes blazed with a multitude of emotions. Need. Want. Desire. Untold frustration. 'Twas all there, as if he couldn't get enough of looking at her yet also wished he could look away. The wind tossed his silky black locks about, plastered his tunic to his heavily muscled chest and his rawhide pants to his legs. Her mate would always stand by his clansmen and never allow them to falter. He was a tracker of huge ability and a warrior of immense strength. He'd always be here for her too if she needed him, unable to turn away from her even if he wished to, only she wanted him to want her the same way she wanted him, with all his heart, body, and soul. She wanted far more than he was yet willing to offer, but she'd never halt her drive to secure all she desired.

"Choose me," she murmured under her breath, not nearly loud enough for anyone to hear, yet he straightened as if he'd caught her impassioned plea. She itched to cross the stream and go to him, to burrow her nose in his neck and rest her cheek against the heavy thumping beat of his heart, to know he was hers, for now and for all time.

"Stay close while I go and hunt. Kirk's request of Cherub applies to you as well. We're on the enemy's land, and even as beautiful and serene as it currently is, MacKenzies could still be lurking anywhere."

"That I'll never forget." Mayhap he needed a reminder that

she too could hold her own in the wilds of Scotland. "Go hunt. I'll do the same and see if I can beat you with my catch."

"You're challenging me in a hunt for game?" He grinned, his lips lifting so sinfully.

"Aye, I am and this is a game I know well. First to return with food for the evening meal, wins the game, the winner being permitted to choose their prize."

"A prize within reason." A touch of worry flittered within his tone, which only made her smile sinfully back at him.

"Are you worried I'll win and claim a prize beyond what you can concede to?"

"Hell, yes." He turned and marched back toward the trees, glanced over his shoulder at Cherub. "Stay with her."

"Of course. I'll watch over her, Alec. Never fear that I willnae." Cherub hooked her arm through hers and tugged her into the woods. "Sheesh, men. Our mates can get quite fanatical over our safety at times. Just warning you."

"I appreciate the warning, but I wish for him to get fanatical over me." She gestured toward a tree just off the trail. "I'll tend to my needs first. I'll be but a minute or two."

"Take as long as you need." Off in the other direction, Cherub bounced then snuck behind a thick copse and called out, "I cannae wait to see who wins this challenge."

Neither could she. She rose from behind the bushes then set to work. From a tall pine tree, she collected a ropy length of ivy hanging from one of the lower branches then chose the perfect sapling within the underbrush that would whip up nice and fast when attached to a noose snare. Father and Ronan had taught her how to catch a small creature in various ways, and all with naught but what the forest provided. When out camping, the three of them always competed to see who could catch their dinner the fastest. She smiled, the memory one that lifted her heart even as it brought a tear to her eye. "I'm coming for you both," she whispered to her kin, her promise one given from the depths of her heart. "My life willnae be worth living without you in it."

A sound fact.

She continued setting the trap, hammered twigs into the ground then fashioned the noose and draped it over the top before tossing a smattering of dry leaves as a finishing touch to camouflage it.

"Oh, that's perfect." Cherub rubbed her hands together as she joined her. "I've never been able to set a snare. They're tricky little things."

"It needs one more adornment." She searched within the bushes and grinned as she found exactly what she was after. She plucked a ripe berry from the scrub then set it carefully on top of the trap as bait. "We must leave this now and wait to see if a critter triggers it." She pulled Cherub into a hug. "Thank you for bringing me here, for ensuring this search began."

"You're the one who convinced Alec to join us. Come." Arm hooked through hers, Cherub wandered with her back along the trail toward the stream.

At the edge of the woods, Kirk knelt within the lush grass partially protected by the umbrella of the canopy high above. He dug a small pit, set some river rocks around it then pulled the stringy bark off a log. He struck flint with his dirk and coaxed the sparks to life then as the fire crackled, he added twigs and wood until it blazed.

Cherub plopped down onto the grass next to him, pulled her skin from her bag and sipped.

Annella collected her own pouch, now empty since she'd drunk from it throughout the day. She crouched at the water's edge, filled it up with fresh water and took a swig as the setting sun's golden-red rays glimmered across the sparkling waters before her. There was naught more beautiful than a sunset or sunrise and she adored how the sky flickered with a multitude of colors, from pink to apricot to dusky blue before going completely black. She and Father and Ronan had watched countless days come to an end, as well as new days dawning. Rarely had they spent one apart. Her heart heaved as the pain of her loss intensified. Each day that now passed was another in which they'd been taken even farther from her, another day she couldn't claim back.

Aye, she wished only for a lifetime of sunrises and sunsets with them, a lifetime of laughing, training, and hunting, of never being without her loved ones.

A soft snap dinged from the direction of her snare and she dropped her pouch on top of her bag and strolled along the trail toward it. Dinner was caught and the small moment of joy lightened her heart a touch. She removed the rabbit, returned to the water's edge and skinned and cleaned it, rose and halted as another snap dinged from somewhere deeper within the woods across the other side of stream. Alec too must have caught his prey, although far too late to win their bet.

"It appears we'll eat well this eve." Sitting cross-legged on the grass, Cherub fluffed the navy skirts of her riding habit and raised her hands to the flames, while Kirk continued to build their fire higher.

Smoke wafted all about and the stars high above came out to play, one twinkling bright, then another and another until the sweeping blackness of the night sky glittered with an array of sparkling diamonds. "Even though we're on the enemy's soil, I still cannae halt my love of this land."

"Neither can I." Cherub leaned back, her hands propped on the grass behind her as she tipped her gaze toward the heavens above. "Even though I've traveled far and wide over the centuries, visited almost every land on this Earth, I've still never been able to stay far away from my homeland for long."

"Scotland is in your blood." Kirk sank one hand into Cherub's long golden locks, palmed the back of her head and dropped a kiss on her forehead. "This is the home of our ancestors, land we've spilt blood over, land we've fought for and slaved over."

"And this is the land we were born on, no matter what century that might have been within." She joined Cherub and Kirk, chose some of the sturdy sticks Kirk had set to one side and created a spit for the rabbit, threaded the meat into place and set it to cook over the fire. "This is the land I intend to die on as well. Never will I be taken beyond Scotland's shores."

"Here, here," Kirk murmured with a nod. "As said like a true Matheson."

A cackle of noise sounded from farther downstream then Alec rounded the corner. He splashed through the shallows swinging a goose by its hind legs in one hand, a rabbit in his other. Barefoot and with his pants rolled up to his knees, his boots dangling by their laces over his shoulder, he sat on the bank and cleaned the goose and rabbit, his observant gaze moving from his catch to hers cooking over the fire. Aye, in the depths of the wild, her mate was clearly in his element, just as she was in hers. She loved being out here with him, even though their mission was one that squeezed at her very heart and soul.

She wandered away from Cherub and Kirk, plopped down onto the grassy bank next to him, rubbed a hand along his forearm where he'd rolled the cuffs of his black tunic to his elbows and rested her head against his shoulder.

"How are you feeling? Is your head still sore?"

"You mean from that tiny fall I had this morn?"

"Aye, from when my bear pushed you over."

"Well…" She spread one hand over his leg, gave his upper thigh a gentle squeeze. "You wouldnae even need to ask me that question if we had the merged link of the mind."

"For that we'd need to complete the bond." A gruff answer.

"I'm willing to do so if you are, and my head is fine, any ache I felt at the time now well and truly gone." Reveling in touching him so freely, she tickled her fingers up and down his leg. "I also won the challenge."

He glanced at Cherub and Kirk over his shoulder, their heads close together as they quietly talked, then he eyed the cooking meat again. "I noticed, but I returned with double the catch. Does that make a difference?"

"None whatsoever, and the prize I claim is an easy one for me to choose." She touched a finger to his chin, turned his gaze fully toward hers. "After our mission here is done, I want you to take a day all to yourself and do whatever you most desire, whether that be hiking, fishing, sleeping in a pool of sunshine near your favorite stream, or climbing a mountain. Promise me that you'll do so. I wish for you to relax and set your worries aside, even if only for a short time."

"You make it sound as if I'm the one who just won that challenge."

"Nay, I won, because during that day you do as you please, you must take me with you."

"I see." He leaned in, touched his nose to hers, and murmured, "I vote for lazing in the sunshine."

"I vote for climbing a mountain." Giggling, she rose to her feet, motioned toward the fire. "Come and set your meat to cooking. I'm starving, and I also need my rest. I have much to do this night while everyone else seeks their sleep."

"I'll watch over your body while you're gone." He stood with his skinned catch in one hand and gestured for her to move ahead of him.

"Thank you. I'd like naught more than to have you guarding my body." She returned to the blazing fire, sparks shooting into the air and sizzling bright. Across from Cherub and Kirk, she sat, tucked herself in close to Alec as he skewered his meat onto sturdy sticks and propped them over a metal rack he pulled out of his satchel and set over the flames. He turned her roasting meat over, ensuring the meat cooked evenly on all sides.

As the skies darkened even further overhead and the

coolness of the night descended, she pulled her plaid from her sack and wrapped it around her. She always felt the cold far more than her fellow kinsmen ever did, no doubt because of her smaller size.

Alec fastened the ties of his black leather jerkin together, eased in behind her, his legs either side of hers as he pressed the breadth of his chest to her back and wrapped his arms around her. His heat pulsed through and she gladly leaned back against him, allowed his presence to comfort and soothe her. Being near him, particularly after his bear had been around most of the day and he had not, warmed her deep inside.

"Sometimes, one can be alone even though surrounded by others." She looked at him over her shoulder. "Do you ever feel that way?"

"More often than I should." He tugged the blue silk ribbon from the end of her braid and pocketed it, unraveled her hair then with his hands fisted in her tresses, tipped her head to one side and nuzzled her neck. "We'll always have each other."

"Aye, but in what way exactly?" She stretched her neck, giving him greater access and hoping beyond hope he'd take the bait.

"The only way that counts. I will ensure you remain safe from my beast, and you won't sway me otherwise." He nipped her ear then licked over the mark he'd given her. "Are you hungry?"

"I'm famished and I wouldnae mind some of your chocolate since the meat isnae yet cooked, that's if you're willing to share."

"Sure. Help yourself."

"Thank you." She snagged his satchel from beside him, foraged for the chocolate and grinned as she grasped her prize. Carefully, she broke one square off and held it against his lips. "For you, my mighty bear."

"I can see right through your ploy, Annella." He plucked

the square from her hand and slid it between her own lips. "Your form of temptation isn't going to sway me this time, only my bear's submission to my needs, will."

"His submission to my needs would be even better." She sucked on the chocolate and moaned as its creamy decadence danced on her tongue and slid down her throat. She shuffled around so she sat sideways on his lap, hooked one arm around his neck and burrowed her face deeper into his hair, his silky black locks brushing her nose and cheeks and his deliciously warm and fresh pine scent wrapping around her. Not only did she wish to carry his mark, but also his intoxicating scent deep within her. Aye, mated they were, the man she'd been gifted with the only one she'd ever desire.

"I love holding you close." Alec twirled a lock of her curly hair around one finger then watched it bounce as he released it. "Your hair is so beautiful, so pale it shines like liquid gold in the firelight. I want to see your hair lying across my pillow every night. I need you to know that."

"You truly do?"

"Aye, even if that means I have to sleep on the settee while you're lying between my sheets." He leaned forward, set the sticks of cooked meat to one side to cool. "Not that I just issued an invitation. I simply needed you to know I'll always be here for you."

She sighed, while across from them, Kirk picked up one of the cooled skewers and fed Cherub, the two of them cuddling and chatting with Kirk's plaid wrapped snuggly around them.

The succulent meaty aroma of their dinner wafted all around and Alec selected one of the sticks of cooled meat, tore off a chunk and slipped the morsel between her lips. "When you visit me, I want you to agree to that arrangement."

"On one condition." She plucked a piece of meat from the skewer for him and popped it between his own lips then licked the smear of juice from her fingers.

"What's the condition?"

"You feed me chocolate each night afore I fall asleep in your bed."

"That would be dangerous." He slid another cube of meat into her mouth, then one into his own and they continued to eat until her belly was full and she shook her head when he offered her more.

"I'm done. You eat the rest. I need to rest and see if I can find Father and Ronan within the dream realm." Yawning, she slipped off his lap, wished Cherub and Kirk a good night then curled up in her plaid, the warmth of the blazing fire washing over her.

"I'll take first watch." Kirk clapped Alec on the back then tipped Cherub onto her side and tucked his plaid around her.

Cherub cupped Kirk's cheek, ran her fingers back and forth over his stubbly jaw then yawned and closed her eyes. "I'm exhausted and far more than usual. Good night, all."

"Wake me when you want to swap out." Alec nodded at Kirk then shuffled in behind Annella, his chest to her back as he wrapped his plaid around them both. He doubled her layer of warmth then gently, he slid her hair over her shoulder and dropped a soft kiss on her neck. "Don't travel too far from me this night, my annoying sprite."

"I never will. Sweet dreams, Alec." Hopefully hers would be sweet too.

* * * *

Alec waited as Annella's breathing slowed, the night sky above blazing with a myriad of stars while across the fire, Cherub lay bundled within Kirk's plaid and Kirk sat next to her, his nose to the air and gaze alert as he scanned their surroundings. Alec would be able to scent any possible intruders too, even as he slept. His bear prowled right under his skin, his fierce need to protect Annella and ensure none of them came under any surprise attack, strong.

No one would harm his chosen one and survive it if they ever tried to touch her.

He rolled her over so she faced him, tightened the plaid wrapped around them both and kissed the tip of her nose and both cheeks in the near dark. She murmured in her relaxed state and wriggled closer, her tiny hand sneaking in under his tunic and fanning out over his chest. Even though she'd made her position clear, that she wanted to complete the bond and for them to join together in all ways, he couldn't, not unless he was assured of her safety around his aggressive bear.

Her eyelids fluttered and her body went suddenly limp, her hand slumping within his tunic. Tendrils of wispy-white swirled around him, glided over his lips then dissolved into nothingness. She was gone, now far from him within the dream realm and he sensed her leaving to the depths of his soul.

Holding perfectly still, he waited as her breath blew softly over his neck, her heartbeat slowing under his palm pressed between her breasts. Gently, he stroked her leather-clad backside, tucked one of her legs in between both of his and fully aligned their bodies until not one inch of them remained apart. They touched from head to toe and nothing had ever soothed his bear more than being able to hold her this close.

With his nose buried against the soft skin of her neck, he licked the mark he'd given her, one that had already begun to fade. How he longed to bite her again, to stamp his mark on her flesh and ensure she held his brand. Both he and his bear wanted her, needed her, longed for her. She was everything they'd ever desired, ever hoped to have but never imagined would be possible.

"Annella." He murmured her name in her ear even though there wasn't a chance she'd hear him. "Never think that I don't want you, because I do. I want to bury myself so deeply within your body that neither of us will know where I end and you begin. I wish I had the courage that you do, the trust, faith and belief that joining together is the right thing, only there is nothing that would pain me more than if I ever hurt you."

For a month she'd been visiting him in his dreams and he'd come to know her well during that time, had shared his thoughts and who he was even though he'd grumped and grizzled as well. She'd done the same with him in little ways, not that he'd ever believed she was real. Now, being with her this day, had brought such comfort and joy to his very soul. What if he took that next step, which she clearly wished him to do and gave himself over to their bond and all that it entailed? She'd chosen him, told him very bluntly that she had. His bear might have knocked her to the ground this morning but he'd quickly taken a strong position and maintained his guard over her. Then she'd left her physical body and come to him, forgiven his bear and brought him such hope by her actions. His bear had rolled over onto his back and pleaded for her touch. None of that he could deny.

If only he could trust himself as greatly as she trusted him.

If only…

Chapter 8

Annella drifted amid the twinkling stars as the night sky fully enclosed her. She breezed higher toward the place where Father and Ronan's essence always blazed and gasped as a tiny spark flared. Ronan's. As she circled him, his star glowed more brightly and she latched ahold and sank into his mind. Connected to him, she infiltrated his dreams, found him searching for her. Within his mind, she sensed his need to warn her of all that had happened and she allowed her full form to emerge and grasped his bearded face in her hands. "I'm right here, Ronan. Wake up."

"Annella?" Groggily, he lifted his head and opened his eyes, her name no more than a rasp between his dry lips.

"Aye, 'tis me."

"I'm rarely permitted any sleep." He glanced over her shoulder and she followed his move. A single candle burned in a holder in the corner, its glow flickering over the metal bars of his cell, a darkened passageway leading away and the overpowering stench of urine and damp earth clogging the air. "The guard never wanders far, always keeps me awake."

"Let me see if I can free you." She gripped his wrists clamped and chained to the blackened stone wall behind him and rattled the steel. No good. She'd need a key to unlock the braces.

Bruises marred his cheeks and arms, while dark circles lay heavy around his eyes. His tunic was wet with sweat, his pants torn down one leg, and his feet lay bare and bloody. Oh hell. Was that a rat nibbling on one of his toes? She kicked the rodent and it screeched and scuttled into the darkened corner of the cell. Not far enough away for her liking. After it, she went and swiped at it again. It fled through the bars and darted away, thankfully now gone. "I'll make Duncan MacKenzie pay for taking you. I promise I will."

"Duncan MacKenzie is with Father. We parted ways in a meadow beside a stream. Something with Duncan isnae quite right. During our trek across MacKenzie land, he kept insisting Father and I needed to embrace our destiny, that even our fae princess would understand our capture was meant to be. 'Tis like he's the enemy, yet also no'." He shook his head as if trying to clear it, his gaze roaming her body. "How is it I can see all of you, as if—have you fully evolved?"

"Aye. The moment I connected with you within the dream realm, I allowed my spiritual body to solidify. I can remain right here with you until I force a return."

"Incredible." He shook his head. "You were naught but five when Mother left us, barely old enough to remember all she could do, but I was older and always in awe of how she could be there one moment, completely touchable afore she dissolved and disappeared. I hope a mated bond takes between you and another within our clan, that you'll be tied to this Earth in a way Mother never was with Father. I cannae lose you, little sister."

"I cannae lose you either, and I bring good news. I've met my mate and his name is Alec, although he isnae from our fae village but from Kirk's future bear shifter clan. He's a strong and honorable warrior, is with me right now, back where we stopped for the night to rest in the very meadow you've spoken about." She hugged him tight, her heart heaving. He was solid and right here. Alive even though beaten and bruised. "Where did Duncan take you, Ronan? You must give me directions so I can inform Alec. Cherub and Kirk are with us as well and we're all coming for you."

"I was taken across the stream to the northeast, Father to the northwest. I've been trying to find out his location from the guardsmen and managed to catch the odd thing or two."

"Alec and Kirk have been tracking you both thus far. Give me more on the location of these dungeons. Where are they and how did you get here?"

"From the meadow, we journeyed another half day then left the forest behind. In the valley before the hills, the inner channel of a loch winds inland. At the very innermost point is a MacKenzie holding that now belongs to Coll, Duncan's twin brother, although I've yet to meet Coll. Apparently he's away securing more men for some kind of battle to come. Coll's the firstborn of the two and the Chief of MacKenzie's eldest son. Word is Duncan's holding is close."

"Do you believe Father might have been taken to Duncan's stronghold?"

"From what I've heard, I believe so, although I'm unsure exactly which loch this stronghold of Coll's sits alongside. The warriors who brought me here covered my head with a sack when I caught sight of the waterway. At a guess, I'd say this castle is either somewhere along the length of Loch Kishorn or Loch Carron. 'Twould be no farther north than that. I also have no idea where the entrance to the dungeons lies, but every now and again I catch a trace of salt in the air. Mostly though, 'tis just the reek of urine and the grittiness of the underground tunnels all around."

"I cannae scent any salt in the air, but I'll take a look around. I can do so in this solidified form. I'll search for the key to this cell, take down the guards if I need to." Now she was here, she would do everything she could to free her brother. If only Cherub was here too and could open a portal. Ronan could be freed within a matter of seconds. Still, she was here and would do all she could while she was. "I willnae be gone—"

Heavy footsteps pounded toward her.

A key clicked within the lock and she dissolved her form, wisped up to the ceiling and floated there unseen as a guardsman wearing a darkened nasal helm, chainmail and black boots, marched in. His eyes, so dark in shade that they appeared almost black, glinted through the metal slits as he scrutinized Ronan. "You need to eat. Duncan left implicit instructions, that I'm to keep you alive, to make certain we can use you to ensure your father's compliance with Muirin. Then 'tis time for you to accept your destiny."

Muirin again. If only she knew more about the fae sorceress who'd clearly formed some kind of alliance with Duncan, and in doing so, against her own people no less.

"How do I even know my father's still alive?" Ronan rattled his chains as he got his feet more solidly under him.

"You must trust I speak the truth." The guard removed his helm, his oily dark hair lying slick against his scalp as he leaned in and Ronan moved fast, swept one foot out, hit the guard's shin and the warrior grunted and spat at Ronan's feet. "'Tis just as well we've restrained you."

"Stand aside, Gordon." A lass wearing a sleeveless teal gown and a cream under-tunic with rucked sleeves and a heavy silver-chained girdle clasped around her waist, swished into the cell with a bowl of steaming stew and a tankard of water. She scraped a wooden crate from the corner forward and set the food and drink on top of it.

"Kyla, are you well?" Her brother eyed the young woman from head to toe as if confirming she remained unharmed.

"You need never fear for me, Ronan. I am amongst my own kin here." She shot a look at the guard. "Leave. He willnae eat with you present."

"You pander to him and shouldnae. I shall give you five

minutes and no more. Ensure he does no' fall asleep. His sister is a spirit-walker and can travel to him within his dreams." The guard snorted as he walked out the door, closed it after himself and marched down the corridor.

"You must eat and drink if you wish to maintain your strength, Ronan." The lass picked up the chipped tankard she'd brought and held it to Ronan's chapped lips. "Now, afore I am forced to leave and you miss the chance to do so."

"Cease using force against me." Ronan took a hearty swallow of the water, then muttered, "I can sense your fae skill, your subtle yet clear push within my mind to make me obey your orders."

"I have no idea what you speak of. I hold no fae skill. I am a MacKenzie, the foster daughter of the Chief of MacKenzie and sister to Duncan and Coll, a fact you'd best no' forget."

"Trust me, you hold a fae skill whether you wish to acknowledge it or no', although it likely lays buried somewhat since you have no' had the chance to be guided by our people in the use of it. I too am part fae and can sense your ability."

Kyla touched her head, confusion swirling within her gaze.

"Listen to me well, Kyla. Twenty years ago a young lass of only three summers was taken from the fae village farther along the loch from the House of Clan Matheson. Her name was Christina and she was the first child born to Isaiah and Grace. In the middle of the night, under the cover of darkness, she disappeared without a trace. Kidnapped, the elders of the village said, although they couldnae find her. I remember the lass well even though I was only a lad of eight at the time. The wee one always intrigued me with her mass of golden-red curls and blue eyes."

"I cannae possibly be this lass you speak of," Kyla hushed back as she glanced over her shoulder toward the passageway. "I know who my kin are, and 'tis no clan Matheson." She dipped the spoon in the stew and held the mouthful to Ronan's lips, her blue gaze searing into his. "Eat. Now."

"You're doing it again, using your skill against me. Touch your mind to mine with more strength then issue the command you wish obeyed. It'll force me to your hand far faster than how you are currently making your demands."

"All right. I can touch my mind to another's, have always known I could, but I've never forced another to my will, and no one has ever discovered my touch within their mind. You are the first. Please, you must promise me that you'll not tell another." Gaze narrowed, she prodded the spoon against his closed lips. "Open your mouth. I wish for you to eat. You need the nourishment, and to maintain your strength."

"You'll learn soon enough how to use your skill if you return to your true people, and only those of fae blood can sense your touch." Ronan opened his mouth and slurped the stew down. "Even as young as Christina was when she was taken, her very soul still cried out to mine."

Annella gasped, her heartbeat racing. Ronan had never joined with another from their clan, always sensed a restlessness within him for someone being held beyond his reach. He'd known his mate awaited him, although he knew not where, only that she would remain lost until he'd found her.

"I said open your mouth." Kyla jammed another spoonful of stew between Ronan's lips.

"Look inside your heart and tell me you dinnae feel something toward me."

"I feel plenty, including frustration and annoyance." She continued to feed him, not allowing her brother another moment to speak until the bowl was empty and the spoon clattered against the base. "Now," she bit out, "when the guard brings you a meal, you'll eat it."

"Come closer, Kyla."

"I certainly willnae." She slammed her hands on her hips.

"Aye, you will." Ronan hooked one leg around the back of

Kyla's legs and she toppled forward, palms flattened against his chest and her breath whooshing out.

"You have no right to touch me, Ronan Matheson."

"I have every right." Ronan buried his nose in her hair, his voice a smooth whisper as he said, "It feels so good to have you close, to have your hands upon me. Many of our fae-blooded kind are soul bound to another, and when they come of age and find their chosen ones, they join together in all ways, the silken strands between their souls weaving together into one."

Goodness. Was Ronan saying he was mated to the Chief of MacKenzie's daughter? Surely not. Mayhap his thoughts were all askew from his lack of rest, only he'd given her the details of his location as clear as a day. He was also awake and very aware right in this moment.

"I sense naught between us." Kyla squeezed her eyes shut then pushed herself away from him. With a deep breath, she straightened her shoulders and glared. "You are my brother's prisoner and he intends to use you to ensure your father's compliance. We need Niall battling on our side."

"Where is my father being kept?" Ronan pushed forward, his chains rattling.

"Somewhere safe. You must no' fear for him." Kyla brushed her teal skirts, collected the bowl and tankard and swished to the cell door. "Gordon, I'm done," she called out.

The guardsman's footsteps echoed toward them then he appeared, swung a key from amongst a circlet of keys hooked on his belt and opened the door. The scrape of iron against stone grated in Annella's ears as he motioned Kyla through then banged the door shut and clicked the lock in place.

Once they'd gone, she wisped down and took her solidified form. "Do you think Kyla's truly Christina, Isaiah and Grace's daughter?" She'd heard of the young child who'd disappeared in the middle of the night, no trace of her being found during their extensive search for her. "Is she truly your mate?"

"Aye, she's my chosen one. I can sense the bonds between us strengthening with each visit she makes. I must remain here, Annella, to be given the time to convince her I speak the truth. Go to Father first. Free him, then return for me."

The last thing she wished to do was leave him. She could affect his rescue right now, go and knock the guard out and retrieve the keys. Unlock her brother's cell then find a way out of this place. "What if you cannae convince her? Even if she holds fae blood, she's still Colin MacKenzie's daughter, has been raised at his hand."

"At least then I'll know I've done all I could to ensure she's heard the truth, that she knows I will always be here for her." Ronan closed his eyes and when he opened them again, determination flared strongly within his gaze. He nodded at her. "I love you, little sister. Search this place and discover exactly where I am so you can bring aid with ease, but also search for Father and ascertain his release. I shall be ready to leave with you when you return with Father."

* * * *

Within the meadow, dark clouds moved in overhead, covered the stars and obliterated the moon. A chilly wind rose and Alec held Annella close within the warmth of his plaid, her body aligned with every inch of his as he shared his heat. The fire flickered and he nuzzled her neck. How much longer would she be gone? It had been so long and he'd already switched watch with Kirk, his fellow clansman now asleep.

"Come back to me," he muttered in her ear, only she didn't move, not one inch. She remained far away and he couldn't abide the distance any longer. He clamped his mouth on the sensitive skin of her neck and sucked her creamy flesh deep between his lips then bit down, stamped his mark on her before laving the spot and traveling lower. His chin brushed the upper swells of her breasts where the V neckline of her cream tunic sagged a little. He nabbed one tie and played with it, loosened her tunic some more, then nibbled along the tops of her luscious breasts. She tasted magical, as if her flesh had been touched by the night sky she moved within. He licked her skin, his tongue so close to her beading nipples. Damn, he needed to halt. Ravishing her while she was gone wasn't right. He lifted his head, sucked her lower lip into his mouth and moaned as her warm breath whispered between her sweet lips and touched his. This was both sheer heaven and sheer hell, being so close to her but not being able to speak or allow his passion for her to fully rise.

He lifted her limp hand to his mouth and pressed her palm against his cheek. His mate. Always his. Damn it. Who was he kidding? He couldn't keep his distance from her another moment, not when both he and his bear needed her so desperately. She wanted to complete the bond with him and he'd love nothing more right now than to have the merged link of the mind so he could reach her along that link, particularly for when she traveled so far from him within the dream realm. He'd be able to do so when she did. Aye, surely one single night of being together wouldn't hurt. He could join them together, gain the benefit of the merged link then leave her be until he was assured his bear would bring no more harm down upon her head. 'Twas a sound plan, one that would accommodate both of them.

Along her jaw, he nibbled, kissed her rosy cheeks, her closed eyelids and dainty nose sprinkled with freckles. More. He grasped her bottom, snug within the buttery-soft tan leather of her breeches and held onto her as if his very life depended on it. It likely did. She was his everything, his one and all, and he was currently a mess without her.

In her ear, his words came out all ragged, "You're stealing my will to be anywhere but here with you. I need you, Annella, more than I need my next breath. Come back to me. I demand it."

Except she didn't return, completely ignored his summons. Enough. He crushed her in his arms, covered her mouth with his and kissed her with all the longing contained deep inside him. His need roared hot and hungry as he kissed her wildly, passionately, his and his bear's dual need for her taking over. His desire to protect her, to keep her safe, to make her his thundered through him and he plunged his tongue deeper inside her mouth and captured her sweet essence all for himself. Never would he hurt her, not this night and if his bear tried such a thing, he'd simply take a blade to himself. Day by day. They'd take things slowly, that's if she was willing to do so with him.

He shoved to his feet, slung their bags over one shoulder, scooped her into his arms and crouching next to Kirk, tapped his kinsman on the arm.

Kirk stirred, took one look at him and Annella and grinned. "I'll keep a watchful eye out."

"We'll remain within calling distance, although we won't be returning until dawn."

"She needs you, your strength and protection. There is nothing more beautiful than the mated bond."

"I can't keep holding myself back from her, but I'm not promising her forever. I just need to make her mine for now."

"It's only a short jump from 'now' to forever. You'll never regret taking that jump when you do." Kirk tucked his plaid tighter around both him and Cherub, dropped a kiss on the top of his sleeping mate's head and nodded at him. "I'll see you in the morning."

"That you will." He marched off, carried his woman a furlong or two farther downstream of the meadow, to a place where he was assured not one scent of another lay and they'd have all the privacy he right now needed. With great care, he laid her down next to the stream, set their bags on the grass and ducked under the bower of a bush, one which would provide them with a cozy amount of secluded area. He cleared the ground of any small twigs and the odd bit of debris then assured only the lush grass would be their bed, spread out his plaid, gently lifted her up and laid her down inside the warm cocoon he'd created.

Overhead the dark clouds separated and moonlight sprinkled through the bushy canopy of the bower. Weapons unstrapped and boots kicked off, he settled on his knees between her spread legs, his hands planted on the ground either side of her head as he gave himself up to his mate and the depth of their mated bond. She'd come to him a month ago in his dreams, visited him each and every night since and in doing so, swiftly weaved her way right into his heart. Unable to hold back, he kissed her again, this time a sweetly soft caress over her plump lips. "I want forever with you, my annoying sprite, only I've spent my entire lifetime protecting others by maintaining a certain distance from them. You keep hammering right through that distance and my defenses as well. I can't keep holding those walls in place against you forever. Come back to me now. Give me tonight, and I'll try to give you tomorrow too."

With a sudden gasp, her back arching off his plaid, she returned. "What did you say?" She blinked her sooty lashes open, her bewitching blue eyes with those mesmerizing sparks of gold at the edges glinting as she glanced about the bower. "I found Ronan, tried to leave his cell and discover all I needed to, but I heard your call and returned first. What's wrong and where are we?"

He desperately wanted to hear of her trip away, but so too he needed to explain his current actions. "We're within calling distance of Cherub and Kirk, but still far enough away to ensure our absolute privacy."

"Privacy?" She arched a brow. "What for?"

"I want to complete the bond with you, to have the merged link of the mind and be able to reach you at any moment, only I can't promise anything beyond that point." He loosened the ties of his leather jerkin, shrugged it over his shoulders then hauled his tunic over his head and tossed it aside. "I also have an admission to make, but first, tell me about Ronan."

"He's alive, although restrained within Duncan's brother's stronghold, deep within the dungeons. There is so much I have to tell you, but I also want to hear this admission you want to make."

"You're everything I could ever desire in a mate, ever hope to have and I'm clearly hurting you by withholding who I am. Are you willing to take small steps? I need to make certain I don't pose a threat to you before we go any further than this one night."

"I can accept small steps even though I know you'll never pose a threat to me." She spread one hand over his heart, drew a slow circle around it with her fingers. "I also clearly need to leave you more often if this is what it takes to make sure you hear my plea for more."

"You're truly willing to accept the bond with the proviso I've offered?" He'd give her only one more chance to back out.

"I'm beyond ready, and if you kiss me, then you'll find out exactly how ready."

Euphoria rose within him and he seized her mouth with his. Nay, Ronan. Did her brother need her to return? He had to let her go again if he did. "Your brother. Tell me more."

"I awoke him and I was about to search farther afield from the dungeons and locate the entrance, but there is no way for me to return to him now until he once again sleeps. The guardsman keeps him from his rest. I am all yours at this moment."

"As I am all yours." He kissed her again, with all the desperate need he'd held back. Wildly, fervently, he got lost in the intense emotions rushing through him. She tasted so sweet, and he'd missed her, in the worst possible way. He had to make her his, to complete the bond and tie her to him in all ways. He'd have the right to touch her, as freely as any man did with his woman, and he couldn't wait. Didn't have to wait any longer. He tore her buttery-soft tan vest over her head.

"All I ask is that we take this slowly." She grasped his hands as he reached for the hem of her tunic. "I'm no' going anywhere at present. My body is yours, whether you wish to take small steps or no'. You are my mighty bear, always mine."

"Then we'll go slow." He gentled his touch, lifted her tunic over her head with far more care than he had her vest. Her breasts bobbed free, her pink nipples beading tight and making his mouth water for a taste. "I want you, more than I could ever express with words."

"I dinnae need the words, only your touch."

Trailing one finger down her neck and between the valley of her breasts, he tried hard to give her the "slowly" she'd asked for. Only as she arched her back and thrust her breasts out farther, his thoughts completely scattered. He cupped the creamy fullness of both mounds then dived onto one sweet tip and sucked the luscious treasure deep inside his mouth. He ravaged the tip, flicked it with his tongue until it was wet and shiny and hard then he tortured her other nipple just as he'd done the first.

She whimpered and grasped his face, pulled his head up to her lips. "I feel so much."

"I need to feel even more." He kissed her, plundering the intoxicating recesses of her mouth. Touching her, having her body pressed against his was sheer heaven, a sensation he never wanted to be without. Hell, he couldn't wait to strip the rest of her clothes from her, for them to be skin on skin. He stroked over her leather-clad hips, ripped the laces of her breeches open and hauled the tan leather down her legs and shucked them to one side. Golden curls covered the juncture between her thighs and he groaned at the mouth-watering sight. "You are the only one I want, always and forever, within my time and yours."

"Slowly, remember?"

"Going slowly is about to kill me." Although he'd try, or die trying. More kisses as he ravaged her mouth, his fingers sliding along the wet seam of her lower entrance. Her honey scent rose and smothered him and he lifted his head high and roared, his beast pushing for dominance. Fur rippled across his chest and down his arms, the dark pelt there one moment then gone the next as he shoved his bear back down. No more slowly. He shucked his pants and sensations stormed through him, his blood rushing hot and heavy straight to his painfully hard cock.

"Oh goodness." Her breath whooshed out as she eyed his shaft standing at full attention.

"Got to have you." He needed her, desperately, wasn't sure how much longer he could wait. Aye, taking her and making her his right now was imperative.

Chapter 9

Annella lost her breath as Alec all but ripped his clothes off in his eagerness to join them together. She hadn't lain with a man before and they needed to take things slowly and carefully, otherwise he'd hurt her when they joined together for the first time and if that happened, he'd blame himself and then she'd never get the chance to come together with him again in this way.

She pressed one palm to his bare chest where fur had rippled across his flesh only moments before, giving proof of just how very close his bear was to rising and taking over. "I've never been with a man and I want to experience only pleasure at your touch."

"Help me." He panted, chest heaving and his claws slicing out and back in.

"Mayhap you need to shift first." She tried to push him back but he shook his head and closed the distance between them.

"No, what I need to do is kiss you again." He growled under his breath, snatched his wrist dagger and pressed it into her hands. "Use this on me if you need to."

She'd never be able to take a blade to him. She dropped it

down beside her then gently, she stroked his shoulders and arms, the breadth of him so thick and strong and below the planes of his wide chest, his abs rippled, layer upon tight layer. Itching to touch more of him, she tiptoed her fingers along the delicious trail of dark hair narrowing down his rigid belly then halted where it thickened around his manhood. Sweet heaven. He was far bigger than any man should be, although she'd find a way to fit all of him inside of her. She looked deep into his eyes, ran her thumbs across his warm lips and a whole lot breathless, murmured, "Be gentle with me."

"Cut me or kick me in the balls if I'm not. That should at least get a response out of me that I won't be able to miss." He caught her hands, pressed them back against the plaid behind her head then rubbed his chest against her breasts. "You feel so good, your skin so soft and smooth."

"Let me touch you, to try and calm your other half." She drew in a deep breath, tugged on her trapped hands to free them but made not one dent in securing her release. "Let me free my hands or else I'll kick you in the balls right now." Something she'd never be able to do, but telling him so, would hopefully be enough.

"One moment." He lifted up a touch, let her hands go then dug his claws into the ground to keep himself from trapping her again. "Done."

"I have an admission I'd like to make too since we're being brutally honest." Looking deep into his eyes, she cupped his hips and stroked over his backside. "Having lived amongst so many warriors there have been times I've accidentally stumbled across them coupling with maids in the woods. Once, I wasnae nearly quick enough to leave and I witnessed far more than I should have."

"What did you see?" He dipped his head and kissed her, with breathless urgency, his desire still clearly beating at him even though she'd tried to distract him a touch with their conversation.

A whole lot breathless, she broke their kiss and murmured, "The warrior dived in under the lass's skirts and she fairly screamed with the pleasure he bestowed upon her."

"Even though I've never slept with a woman, not when our shifter kind always waits for our chosen one, I'm not unaware of what happens either. I can't wait to dive under your skirts, that's if you ever wore them, which I'm not asking you to, and by the way, if you're trying to slow me down with this kind of talk, then I can tell you right now it's not working. I have to touch you, Annella. All of you."

"I'll find a way to tame your other half. I want this joining to be the first of many between us, for you to never fear hurting me, and I promise I'll wear skirts for you at some point in time, just so you can dive under them."

"For now you're not wearing anything at all and I say let the diving begin." Claws extracted from the ground, he stroked down her body, caressed her arms and her sides before he scooped her bottom and licked along her inner thighs. He rumbled his pleasure, his eyes ablaze with the shifter gold as he locked gazes with her. He separated her folds below, appeared ready to devour her, as if he intended to leave not one inch of her body untouched and liquid heat rushed through her and pooled in her core. She arched into him and he moaned and licked his lips. "There is a feast awaiting me right here and I'm about to lose my mind at just the sight of you."

"Then feast as you please." Clearly there was no slowing him or his other half down. Longing, desire, and a complete and utter need for him consumed her as well, a myriad of intense emotions that tumbled one over the other within her. No more would she live centuries apart from him. No more would she visit him within the dream realm when she'd rather be standing at his side each and every day, whether that be in her time or his. Alec was hers and tonight, she intended to forge a new future, one in which they lived only at each other's sides. She wouldn't tell him yet though, not when he'd asked only for small steps, but she would share her hopes and dreams with him when the right time presented itself.

"Thank you, my sprite." Fingers firm on her legs, he hooked them over his shoulders until her bottom lifted right off the plaid and she lay completely and fully exposed to him, his silky midnight-black hair brushing sensually against her skin as he bent his head between her open thighs. "There is nothing more tempting and beautiful than what lies before me. You're so pink and lush, and weeping. It's all for me, only me. Are you ready?"

"Always."

"Good answer." He eased one finger inside her folds then went deep, his delicious, carnal touch making her wriggle down against him for more and he obliged, stroking inside her channel then rubbing his thumb across her nub. He touched his tongue to the place where her mounting pleasure stemmed from and she grasped his head and moaned as he sucked her nub between his lips and devoured her.

Such intense sensations stormed through her as her chosen one knelt between her legs, his balls drawing tighter and higher into a thatch of black curls covering the apex of his groin. He was beautiful, big and sexy, sinfully scary and all hers. Feasting her gaze on every inch of him, she took in his very large cock, the plump head darkening and a drop of his essence leaking from the tip. She reached down, gently palmed his balls then stroked his length.

"You taste incredible." With one low growl, he lifted up a little, pushed her knees farther apart then dived back and consumed her. He thrust his tongue inside, rumbled as more of her heat pooled at her core then lapped, greedily. He devoured her and she wouldn't have been able to stop him for the world, didn't wish to either.

She bucked as he stroked harder and faster and she clutched his head as he spread her legs even wider and continued to take and take. He licked her flesh in the most intimate way, increasing her pleasure with every swipe of his tongue. 'Twas such exquisite torture, her desire for more rising to a staggering height. He sucked and she arched, could no longer hold on to the here and now.

"Alec." She cried out his name as she flew, her core pulsing as wave after wave of wild pleasure barreled through her. She soared and a stunning display of vivid colors burst behind her closed eyelids. Her body thrummed until she slowly came back down.

"That was beautiful to see." He kissed her mound, nibbled upward, over her belly until his nose brushed the underside of her breasts. He cupped both mounds, thumbed the peaking tips then sucked one nipple before moving languorously to the other.

"You seem to have calmed a touch."

"Feeling you come around my tongue helped tremendously." He caught her hand, nuzzled her palm then bit the center and soothed the bite with his tongue. With his gaze lifted to hers, he smiled. "I feel less on edge, would feel even less so if I could make you come on my tongue all over again."

"I'm no' sure if I could move if you did that a second time." Her limbs had turned to jelly.

"Please?" He twined their fingers together. "You're mine to make love with, mine to devour, mine to consume. Heart, body and soul, I want all of you."

"What happened to your small steps?"

"Try and walk away from me right now and I'll tackle you to the ground."

"I see." Tears misted her gaze and she sniffed. "Try and walk away from me right now, and I'll tackle you to the ground as well."

"I need to embed my scent into you, and for yours to be

embedded in me." He licked higher, over the tops of her breasts, her neck then along her lower lip. "Your intoxicating aroma is settling my bear."

"There's no stopping this bond or what is to come." She rubbed her breasts against the wicked heat of his chest then traced one finger over the mark she'd placed earlier on his neck. The need to bite him again, to ensure her mark was brought back to vivid and blazing life, rolled fiercely through her.

She stroked his bulging biceps then down his sides and back up again over the solid breadth of his back. His body, all superbly honed muscle and rippling strength, was all hers to touch and adore. Gently, she cupped his face in her hands, his delicious mouth and fevered gaze drawing her ever deeper into him. This was the most beautiful place, right here under this bower, the moon shining high above and the stream trickling only a few feet away. The lush grass underneath her made the softest bed and the man on top of her, the most heart-melting covering. Never would she relinquish him or their bond. "I love being here with you."

"I need to bite you again, to stamp my mark on you so everyone knows you're mine." He tipped her head to one side and licked her neck, sucked her skin deep inside his mouth then with his teeth firm on her flesh, he bit down and marked her.

Her core rippled with pleasure and she opened her heart fully to him, her need to meld their lives together consuming her. "Bite me again," she whispered as she sank her fingers into his hair. "Now."

"I will, over and over until you tell me to stop. Bite me the same time as I bite you." He palmed the back of her head and drew her mouth toward his neck while he settled his own mouth once more against her flesh. He licked over her skin and she nibbled the sensitive hollow where his shoulder and neck met. His pulse throbbed under her tongue and she scraped her teeth back and forth. She needed to brand him completely and fully as hers.

"Alec, I wish to be yours, to hold you deep within me, to be a part of you, just as you will be a part of me. Forge the merged link of the mind and ensure we need never be parted again. Take me now."

"I can't take away the initial pain of our joining." He stroked down her sides, nudged her legs farther apart with his knees. With his shaft in hand, he rubbed the thick head against her wet folds below. Hot and slick, he continued to caress her tingling flesh with his cock alone and she rocked, her hips moving of their own accord.

"Then you'll need to make it up to me later." Hungry for more, she sucked on his neck, clamped down on him and bit him and as she did, he bucked and moaned against her. A low rumble vibrated in his chest and she hooked her legs around the backs of his legs and gripped his butt. "Make us one."

"Aye, no more shall we be apart." Determination flared in his gaze and he grasped her hips, thrust deep inside her and tore through her barrier below in one fast move.

"Oh goodness." His mind surged into hers, tunneled deep and she panted as he created the private pathway that would only ever be theirs. Such a stunning connection. She grabbed ahold of it, cemented it within her own mind then along their link, whispered into his mind, *"Naught has ever felt so right, as if you're now exactly where you belong, deep within me."*

"You're my chosen one, the other half of my soul, the only one I shall ever live for." He seized her mouth with his and liquid heat surged through her core. With breathtaking reverence, he deepened their kiss, showing her with his body alone just how very deep their connection ran.

"I cannae believe we actually fit together. I must admit worry flittered through me for a moment, but now I feel only incredibly full and completely at peace." The sheer depth of her feelings for him rose and keeping them from him was

impossible. "*Your essence is the very purest I've seen, your star within the dream realm shining the brightest.*"

"*Being inside you feels incredible, phenomenal. Every inch of me is ablaze where we touch. My bear is also in heaven, has calmed right down now that I've claimed you and made you ours. This is what he wanted, what I wanted and needed too. I wish I'd seen it sooner.*" On the ground either side of her head, he pressed his hands then he rocked over top of her, pulled back and heaved all the way back in again. Moving harder and deeper, he increased his pace and her lashes fluttered down, her heart singing with joy and her body on fire for more. "*Look at me, my sprite. Tell me you feel pleasure, that I'm not hurting you.*"

"*I promise you, there is only pleasure.*" He lunged in, until she almost couldn't take any more of him yet still craved whatever he could give her. Desperately craved. "*Go deeper. Please, go deeper.*"

Clinging to him, her arms wrapped tightly around his neck and her legs hooked around his backside as he thrust with such a heavenly drive, she accepted all of him, over and over.

"*I cannae hold on any longer. Forgive me.*" He latched onto her neck, bit down and sent a fiery blast of unadulterated pleasure through her.

She cried out at their raw and primitive joining, clasped him tightly to her and as she bit him in return, he roared his pleasure, dived even deeper inside her, his thoughts a blustery storm of pure heat and lightning that swarmed in and around her own.

* * * *

Alec bellowed and sank balls-deep inside his woman, clamped down on the other side of her neck and marked her again. He bit her hard and then she did the same to him in return and cried out at their fiercely intense joining. Her bite had him soaring to the edge of no return. More, he needed even more. He surged, pumping into her as her inner muscles squeezed and dragged his cock right to her core then together, they careened over a high ridge and soared to the heavens, his essence pulsing into her in one long, hot stream. Carnal thoughts consumed him. He wanted her connected to him in the ultimate way, for his seed to take root and for her to carry his child. *"You're my lover, my chosen one, my everything and all."* Never would he be able to accept anything less than her complete and utter surrender to their bond and all that he was. *"Want me, the same way that I want you."*

As he kissed his woman, he locked his mind tightly around hers and laved each of the marks he'd stamped on her neck, nibbled on her tiny earlobe, all of her a heady and intoxicating mix that made his spine tingle and the pressure in his shaft once again build. Hell, he'd only just come, but soon he'd need to come all over again. With his need riding him hard, he gave into his body's demand and kissed her, cherished the luscious recesses of her mouth as he plunged his cock ever deeper inside her, her fiery heat bathing him below as she clutched his butt and pulled him in.

"Take whatever you need from me. You are where you now belong, my warrior, my ravenous bear, the other half of my soul."

He moved deeper inside her, and she met each of his thrusts with one of her own, her teeth scraping back and forth over his neck. *"Do it. I need every mark you're prepared to give me."*

"There is naught more beautiful and all-encompassing as this bond." She clamped her teeth down on him and he roared and whipped his teeth into her neck in return. Her inner channel tightened like a fist around him and she lapped the new mark, inched along his neck and bit him again, her arousal flying down their link and swamping him in it. *"Can't hold on—must—please—"*

"I've got you." With her channel contracting, pulsing and sucking him in, he bucked into her, his essence jetting from him a second time, thick and heavy to her core. No one would ever

be able to separate them again, not now their connection had been forged like steel into his very heart and soul. She was his, always his, and his bear gripped him tight, clawed then saturated himself in all that she'd so willingly given them.

Damn, if anyone ever attempted to come between him and his chosen one, he'd kill them. He and his bear had stated their claim and he'd never allow another to impinge upon it.

"*Dinnae go anywhere.*" Her beautiful long lashes fluttered down and she softly sighed. "*Stay right inside me where you belong. No separation. I cannae abide the thought yet.*"

"*You'll be lucky if I ever leave the sanctuary of your body. You're my mate, my destiny, my past, present, and future. Where you go, I now go.*"

"*That's the most perfect, smallest step I've ever heard of. I look forward to seeing what a big step is for you.*" She smiled and yawned then succumbed to sleep and he did exactly as he'd promised he would and remained right where he was, his woman tucked tightly within his arms as he carefully wrapped his plaid around them both.

Aye, it appeared he couldn't take small steps, didn't even have a chance of doing so. Glad he was too. As a gentle breeze blew and rustled the bower of leaves over their sacred place, he finally allowed the pull of the night to tug him under, or as much as his bear would allow with him still being so deeply entrenched within their enemy's land.

Chapter 10

An owl hooted and Alec, resting in his light state, opened his eyes, the night skies still dark, although he sensed dawn neared. Annella lay snuggled against him, her mind and soul drifting toward the dream realm even as she tried to hold onto their connection. He followed her thoughts, joined her as she soared higher amongst an array of twinkling stars, her body going limp within his arms.

She circled a particular place as if waiting for something to appear and anxiety ate at her. Needing to comfort her, he stroked her back within the warmth of his plaid, their merged link of the mind a gift beyond measure. 'Twas a connection he'd never give up, wished he'd claimed the very first night when she'd solidified her spiritual form. Never would he ever be able to take one simple small step with her, not when all his heart and soul desired, was forever.

He wanted her in his bed each and every night, her hair a tangle of gold on his pillow and his shaft captured firmly inside her snug channel as it currently was. His balls tightened something fierce and he couldn't halt his body's need. Down between them, he fondled her nub then thrust his cock even deeper. Her inner channel contracted around him and he came, so swiftly, his ragged grunt muffled into her neck as his essence shot into her. "I'm so sorry, Annella. I didn't mean to come that fast and while you traveled so far away from me."

Before his greedy other half could command him again, to wake her and force her return from the dream realm, he pulled out.

His bear rose up and rumbled his displeasure at the separation. He didn't care for it either, but so too he couldn't take his mate again without her being fully present, nor could he allow her to go unattended any longer. She must hurt. He'd taken her maidenhead and she'd cried out with the initial pain of it. He spread her legs and touched the smear of blood along her inner thighs lit by a trace of the sprinkling moonlight. She'd given herself to him, in every way and he'd ensure she never regretted doing so.

He slid out of their bower, stepped into the stream, splashed his cock and cleaned himself before scooping a handful of cool water and returning to her. Gently, he washed the blood from her thighs and once assured he'd done all he could, he touched his lips to hers, his mind still entrenched within hers as she traveled through the night sky so far away. She waited, for either her father or brother's stars to glow, but neither did.

"Wake up, love. Return to me." He urged her back to him with soft kisses. Last night he'd demanded her return then barely caught how her search had gone. She'd found Ronan alive although restrained within Duncan's brother's stronghold, deep within his dungeons. Only he'd awoken her just as she was about to search farther afield from the underground cells and locate the entrance. She hadn't been able to return to her brother then, and she still couldn't connect with him or her father now."

"Mmm, Alec." She murmured his name in her sleep, her thoughts infused with his then slowly, she blinked her eyes open, wrapped one arm around his neck and drew him down on top of her deliciously curved body, the most sinful smile on her face.

"I'm back."

He rubbed himself against her and a fiery burn invaded his limbs and stiffened his cock. His bear demanded he take her again and with her folds spread, he gripped his aching shaft and rubbed the head of himself against her wet entrance. Groaning, he tried to hold back, but couldn't. He pushed his length deep into the heart of her intense heat and slid home.

She gasped underneath him, her eyes now wide open as she panted. "Oooh, that was fast."

"Did I hurt you?"

"You could never truly hurt me."

"I have a confession to make." He rocked his hips and she hooked her legs around him and kissed him, so possessively his cock throbbed on the verge of release. He had to calm this fever he had for her, only he had no idea how to do so. "I woke up a few minutes ago, still inside you and I'm sorry. I couldn't help myself. I touched you down below and you contracted around me and made me come so fast."

"I'm sorry I missed the moment." Panting, she moved with him as he lunged inside her, the tight, heated slickness of her channel making his eyes nearly roll to the back of his head. "Come again as you please. I've no intention of missing this joining."

"The next time I come it'll be when you come, and not before." He plundered her mouth, thrust his tongue between her lips just as he thrust his cock into her below. Filling her in every way, pumping deep inside her, he'd never stop loving her until she too couldn't take any more.

"Mmm, I'm so close," she whispered against his lips.

Buried deep within her, he rubbed one finger over her clit and she cried out and came, so swiftly, her channel snagging him deep within and making him fly right along with her. He coated her womb with his seed, jet after jet until she'd milked him completely dry.

"Well," she murmured as she softly sighed, her eyelids fluttering down. "Dinnae ever let me miss a joining again. They are too precious, and rather addictive."

"Then don't fall back asleep and we should be just fine." He wrapped his arms around her and held her close, his heartbeat a thumping mess against hers. "I need to apologize a second time. Tell me more about Ronan."

"One moment." She covered his mouth with hers and kissed him, a gentle teasing of tiny licks and nips that made his bear roar for more, only 'twas time for her kin to come first, not him.

Carefully, he pulled out of her then touched the marks he'd made during the night either side of her neck and across the top rise of her full breasts. She was the only woman who could ever tame both him and his beast, and loving her from this moment forth would be a journey filled with promise and the ultimate adventure. Aye, he wanted everything, all of her, and for them to always be together. Never would he miss even one more day without her by his side. "Begin."

"I found Ronan and spoke to him, although Father still remains beyond my touch and I searched for him as often as I could after our joining when I once again slept." She pushed against his chest and he let her roll them over until she came up on top. "Ronan and Father were separated at the meadow, Father taken in one direction and Ronan the other. Just as you and Kirk discovered from their tracks. Ronan gave me the directions to where he's being held. From the meadow, we journey another half day then when we leave the forest behind in the valley before the hills, we'll find the inner channel of a loch winding inland. At the very innermost point is a MacKenzie holding that now belongs to Coll. He's unsure which loch exactly since they covered his head with a sack when he caught sight of the waterway, but the stronghold is either somewhere along the length of Loch Kishorn or Loch Carron. He also has no idea where the entrance to the dungeons lie, but every now and again he catches a trace of salt in the air, although all I caught while I was with him was the grittiness of the earth and the overpowering reek of urine and sweat. I wish I'd gotten the chance to look around, but 'twas no' to be."

"I'm sorry. I shouldn't have called you back, only I couldn't help myself. Patience isn't one of my virtues."

"You didnae know I'd found him." She cupped his face in her hands, gently stroked her fingers back and forth along his jaw. "There is more. There's also a lass with Ronan by the name of Kyla and she's the Chief of MacKenzie's daughter and Duncan's sister, but more than that she holds a fae skill and even though she initially said she knew naught of it, she finally admitted to Ronan that she did. She's hiding her skill, even asked Ronan no' to tell another soul about it. She cared for him, brought him a meal and ensured he ate it as well."

"How can she be a MacKenzie and of fae blood too?"

"She and Ronan spoke while I listened in. Ronan told her twenty years ago a young lass of only three summers was taken from the fae village farther along the loch from the House of Clan Matheson. Her name was Christina and she was the first child born to Grace and Isaiah, two of our highly skilled fae. In the middle of the night, under the cover of darkness, Christina disappeared and the elders of the village believed she'd been kidnapped, although in the search for her afterward, none could find her."

"Your brother remembers her?"

"Aye, he does. He was a lad of eight at the time, said the wee lass had always intrigued him with her golden-red curls and blue eyes. He told Kyla she was his mate, that he sensed the threads of their bond taking form, although she is in denial, said there wasnae a chance they were soul bound."

"A man knows when he's soul bound." Even though he'd denied the truth during the times Annella had come to him in his dreams, deep in his heart, he'd known all along she was his chosen one. He's just been too stubborn to admit the truth, even to himself.

"Ronan pleaded with me, told me to go to Father first and free him. Once that is done, we're to return for him. My brother wishes for more time to convince Kyla that they're soul bound."

"She's been raised by the MacKenzies. Her loyalty to them will be strong."

"Aye, that I fear too." She glanced skyward at the lightening sky, the stars slowly disappearing as red speared through the dark blue, the sun slowly breaching the horizon. The rising sun sent a flare of gold through the foliage overhead and sprinkled over them.

"I told Kirk we'd be back at dawn." Even though leaving this magical place with her was the last thing he wished to do, he rose and collected his scattered belongings. Taking care not to look at her for fear he'd tumble her back to the ground, he donned his billowy sleeved white tunic, sheathed his daggers at each wrist, then hauled on his black leather pants and shrugged on his steel-studded gray jacket. Needing to keep something of hers on him, he swiped her blue hair ribbon from where he'd pocketed it the night before in his now discarded pants and tucked it inside his shirt pocket, right over his heart. Sword belt strapped on and boots laced up, he knelt next to the stream and dunked his head fully in the water. He lifted up and shook the drops free, scented the air and slid his claymore from its sheath. All still remained clear. Swiftly, he stabbed a wild brown trout darting through the water and pierced another swimming right along behind it then holding his catch up, grinned at his woman as she sat on his tartan, her mass of golden tresses tumbling around her shoulders and swaying over her full breasts.

"Nice catch." She smiled, pushed the tartan pooled in her lap away and stretched, her arms raised high and her breasts bobbing beyond the curtaining of her hair.

He was beside her in less than a second and on his knees, he flicked her locks back and ensured he didn't lose the glorious sight of her nipples beading tight in the cool morning air. "You need to dress."

"Aye, I do, my mighty bear." One finger hooked into the front V of his buttoned jacket, she tugged him closer and touched her lips to his. She kissed him, so sensually soft yet with a hungry undercurrent of simmering need, the same as what roared through him. "We need to spend some time alone, and the moment we've freed my kin, I'm going to demand you take me somewhere where 'twill be only the two of us together."

"I'm going to lock you in my bedroom and feast on you until you're screaming my name."

"Aye, your chamber it shall be then." She jiggled, her breasts bouncing. "I cannae wait."

"Hold still, lass, otherwise we'll never leave this place when it's truly time for us to be away." Head dipped, he fastened his mouth on one rosy nipple and moaned. He would crave her for the rest of his life, an addiction he intended to get lost within. Gently, he lapped the beaded tip, moved to the other peak and plumped it up with the same dedicated attention as he'd done the other, until it shone all wet and red from his mouth.

"Mmm, I love the way you kiss me." She caught his face in her hands, drew his mouth to hers and seized his lips. Her kiss had his cock filling and straining for release within his pants. Hell, he needed to cease touching her, and right this second.

Breathing heavily, he pulled back and stood, fisted his hands behind his back and bit out, "We have a busy day of tracking ahead of us. Get up and get dressed. That's an order."

"Aye, Captain." With a sly smile, she rose to her feet, so gracefully then rubbed her body against his and whispered in his ear, "Thank you for last night, this morn and all the hours in between."

"Get dressed, now. Orders are meant to be followed."

"Some orders are also meant to be broken, although this one

I'll agree with following." She blew out a long breath, hauled her traveling sack closer and tugged on black breeches then pulled on a loose-sleeved tunic of rich red, the hem fluttering over the snug black leather molding her bottom. Her tunic's laces swayed at the neckline and his reddened marks dotting her skin made his bear preen deep inside him. He bore the same marks from her and gladly did so. With one hand held out, she eyed him. "I need my hair ribbon."

"Pardon?" He picked up her knee-high black boots that curved gloriously around her calves and tugged them on her feet.

"You pocketed my hair ribbon last night, then mere minutes ago switched it from your discarded pants pocket to your shirt pocket. I need it back."

"I like your hair down."

"'Tis more easy to control when braided." She belted her sword at her waist and her jeweled dagger at her wrist then held out her hand once more. "I'm still waiting. Pass it to me."

"You're not getting it back." He twined one of her long locks around his finger.

"When I leave my hair unbound, it flutters all about my face and draws too much attention to me when I'm amongst my fellow clansmen. I prefer to blend in, or at least as well as I can." She braided her hair, held out her hand yet again. "Give it to me, please."

"Having something of yours that holds your scent is important to my bear, and by the way, you could never blend in."

"You are impossible." She tsked under her breath then released her braid and it unraveled as she bent over and stuffed her discarded clothes into her bag. "I shall give into your request to keep it, but you owe me a favor for doing so."

"Name your favor and I'll grant it." He smoothed his hands under her tunic's long hem and cupped both firm cheeks of her pert bottom. "I want to bite your backside as well."

"You arena biting my bottom." She swatted his hands,

tossed him her bag and pinched his butt as he caught it. "Let's move out. I'll claim that favor later, as soon as I can think of a worthy one."

"Aye, my annoying sprite, let's move out." Tartan folded, her scent entrenched within his plaid, he stuffed it inside his satchel and with his catch in hand, marched back toward camp while his chosen one skipped along the bush-lined trail ahead of him.

Birds twittered within their nests high above in the leafy green canopy, the sun peeking through and spreading its warmth all around. His chosen one now held his very heart in her hands and he intended to make certain she understood exactly where he now stood. No more small steps. There would only be forever from now on.

As she bounded into the meadow dotted with white flowers and lavender bushes, she nabbed Cherub's hands and twirled her about. "I have the best news. Alec and I completed the bond last eve and formed the merged link of the mind."

"That's wonderful news. I'm so excited for you." Cherub giggled, her olive gown cinched at her waist with a golden-chained girdle, the thinly chained ends flaring as she spun about.

"I am beyond excited." His mate touched her mind to his, sent an explosion of love and warmth surging down their link and he almost tripped over at the fierce intensity of her feelings. He certainly clutched his chest, his heart heaving. It was a love he too held for her, a powerful emotion he wished to tell her about only now wasn't the right time, not when they had such company.

"Congratulations on accepting your destiny." Kirk grasped his shoulder, his grin lighting up his face. "Having another mated pair in the clan is the best news."

"My bear's been roaming within me with far less aggression since we completed the bond. He's more content, less on edge and demanding." If he'd known joining with her would calm his other half, he'd have done so far sooner. Aye, his love for her expanded, became almost too much for him to hold within his heart, his next words slipping free along their link. *"Don't ever leave me, because if you do, I'll never survive it."*

"I promise I'll be here to annoy you, today, tomorrow, and throughout all of time. There shall be no ascending for me." She danced around the blazing fire and sprang into his arms, barely giving him time to toss the fish to Kirk. She nibbled his ear and his bear prowled to the surface, demanded he sweep her away and take a few more hearty bites out of her once more. "You have one very territorial-sounding bear. I can hear him inside you, sense his thoughts exactly as I can sense yours. You two are a very close blend."

"He's a part of me so I'm not surprised his thoughts mirror mine. Come and eat." He guided her to the fire, motioned for her to sit then passed her an oatcake from the stash Cherub had brought and set out for them on a blue and white checked square of thick fabric. Seated on the grass beside his woman, he munched on an oatcake himself, his nose lifted to the air as he breathed deep and searched through each and every scent. Lavender swirled within the earthy mix of the damp ground and dewy grass. The freshness of the stream's gurgling water blended with the clear aroma of pine, although Annella's enchanting fragrance, that of the very stars she moved amongst when within the dream realm, imprinted its unique and magical scent over it all.

"Did you have any luck finding your father or brother in the dream realm last eve?" Cherub plopped down beside Annella, her fae skin sparkling in the rising sunshine, the glimmer a physical attribute held only by the eldest child born within the ancient royal line of the fae. Their princess had been born to lead, and did so with such dedicated attention to her earthbound kind.

"I shall tell you everything I can. Even though I had no luck finding Father, I did find Ronan and spoke to him." Grinning, Annella slid one hand over his upper thigh and rubbed, her touch so soothing even as her fingers came perilously close to his hardening cock. "Ronan confirmed that they were separated right here at this meadow and that there is more afoot."

"Where's Ronan being kept?" Cherub plucked an apple from her bag and bit into it with a juicy crunch.

"He's locked within the dungeons of the holding belonging to Duncan's elder twin brother, Coll." She rattled off all she'd learnt, not missing even one tiny detail then with a long breath, rolled her shoulders.

"So you're saying this lass named Kyla used a fae skill against Ronan?" Cherub's eyes opened wide with clear wonder. "It certainly sounds as if she is Isaiah and Grace's lost child. I remember the night the wee bairn was taken. Christina held the mind-walker skill, could touch her mind to another's as she so wished, listen to their thoughts or could even speak to them. Those with her ability can also form merged links of the mind with their chosen one and hold that link open so both can speak back and forth, much as Gilleoin's shifter line can. At any time following her disappearance, she could have reconnected with her mother and father through her skill, but never did, and unfortunately, none of our other mind-walkers could reach her. She'd either closed her mind off to them, or had been taken too far for them to reach her. To discover she is alive is incredible news."

"Ronan believes Kyla is his mate, even sensed the threads of their mated bond taking form and asked her if she did too. She said she sensed naught between them, but Ronan wishes for some time to convince her. He asked me to find Father first, ensure he was freed then to come for him.

"Then that is what we must do." Cherub eyed Kirk as he set the fish to cook over the fire. "We'll follow Niall's tracks this morn and see where they lead us."

"That sounds good to me." Kirk eased in behind Cherub then pulled her back until her back rested against his chest.

"I cannae believe I must leave Ronan behind, but I understand my brother's need for more time with his mate." Annella snuggled deeper into his mind. *"Certainly if our positions were reversed, I too would wish for the same additional time in convincing my mighty bear that he was all mine."*

"You've already convinced me." Hell, he'd been such a fool to believe he could have ever ignored his mated bond with her. No longer would he deprive himself of all they could be together. His chosen one came first, each and every day from this moment forth. He dipped his head in reverence toward Cherub. "I've been remiss in thanking you for bringing my mate to me through a portal and for being here now. I've seen the error of my ways."

"I knew you would." With a soft smile, Cherub plucked some cooked fish from the fire. "You and Annella will also find yourselves living in two separate times now that you've got kin in both. You need only call out and I'll ensure I bring you back and forth as needed. I've already given Annella my word I'd do so."

"Aye, the writing was on the wall, so to speak." With the same smile as Cherub, Kirk passed him some fish and munched on his own. "Turning our chosen one away is impossible. Even Cherub tried such a tactic with me to begin with, a tactic that lasted all of a single day."

"'Twas more like half a day." Cherub popped a kiss on Kirk's cheek. "'Twould have been even less if you'd been a whole lot less proper with me during our first meeting."

"What?" Shock coursed across Kirk's face. "Don't you remember that I had you on your back and underneath me within a half hour of when we met? I couldn't have been less proper if I'd tried, or perhaps you need a reminder of that night, my imp?"

"Aye, please, a reminder would be lovely." She giggled and rubbed her cheek against Kirk's cheek. "Or are you just all talk?"

"Now you're asking for trouble." With a low growl, Kirk bounded to his feet, tossed Cherub over his shoulder then marched off through the trees. A giggle floated toward them then disappeared on the breeze as the two moved farther away.

"'Tis wonderful to see them so in love." Annella scooped dirt and extinguished the flames.

"I'd say we've got some time now before they return." He caught her hands in his, kissed the tip of her nose. "I need to speak to you about something incredibly important."

"I'm listening."

"I love you."

"Pardon?" She arched one shocked brow and he chuckled.

"I love you, Annella, with all my heart. Will you marry me?"

"Pardon?" Still dazed.

"I asked you to marry me. Remain with me for every day that's to come and I'll make certain you never regret doing so."

"I cannae believe you just asked for my hand. Are you certain you wish to wed, that I haven't in some way forced you into asking the question?"

"There's been no force or coercion."

"I'm sure there has been. You're inside my mind, know how very much I desire you, would never let you get away. What happened to your small steps?"

"They disintegrated."

"Truly?"

"Annella." He growled her name, pressed one hand over her belly, and muttered, "You could be carrying my child right now, and I damn well hope you are. My bear loves you. I love you. Don't make me live without you. Small steps are out. Only firm and certain ones remain."

"Release your bear. I would like to speak to him afore I

give you my answer."

"Of course." If that's what she wished to do, to seek more acceptance of his change of heart and mind, he'd gladly do so. He stripped off his boots, weapons and clothes, bagged his belongings and standing naked before her, made the Change. On all fours, the pain of his shifting receding and just as quickly as it had come, he ambled around his woman, brushed against her sides and butted his muzzle into her belly.

"You need a pat, my mighty bear?" She bent over him, stroked down the length of his back, her nails raking through his fur and across his skin. "If you truly wish to marry me, then give yourself over to me right now. Lie down and roll over. Show me your full and complete submission."

He clawed the ground to keep from rearing up onto his hind legs and taking her down to the lush grass with him. To keep her pinned right here in this place rode him hard.

"Your bear is purring so loud and so fast." She knelt, wrapped her arms around his neck and rubbed her soft cheek against his furry one. "I knew you'd never fully submit, but please try."

With one gentle push, he toppled her onto her back, plodded in over top of her and buried his wet snout in her hair. He'd submit his way. He licked her, from her ear to her chin and back again.

"All right. Let me up." She giggled, pushed against his belly and tried to roll out from underneath him, only he planted one paw in her way and kept her completely contained within the safe protection of his legs.

"*I love you.*" He licked her neck, right over his mark and she laughed and covered her face with her hands. "*Marry me. Be my wife and I promise to lick you all over.*"

"*I love you too, and aye, I'll marry you, my mighty bear. Your current form of submission is perfect for me.*"

"*Thank you.*" He rose up onto his hind legs and roared, his bear stating loud and clear that he guarded his mate and none would ever be permitted to harm her. His woman loved him, had agreed to marry him and he couldn't ask for anything more. He went to shift back only the murmur of voices, Kirk and Cherub's, floated toward him. Bright lights burst beyond the trees, the odd spark flaring high as Kirk shifted. *"Kirk and Cherub are returning."*

"Then 'tis time for us all to go." She clambered to her feet and swung her sack over her shoulders. *"Do you need my father's woolen cap and my brother's plaid to sniff?"*

"No, their scent is now embedded in my mind, exactly as yours is." Snout high, he sniffed, her father's scent curling around his senses, along with that of the warriors who'd captured him.

Kirk plodded out of the trees and into the meadow with Cherub, his bag strapped to his back, the magnetized straps holding firm around his belly.

Annella plucked a leaf from her hair and dusted her hands. Pink suffused her cheeks and highlighted the adorable smattering of freckles across her tiny nose. His heart pumped out with pleasure. Aye, he was desperately, completely, and irretrievably in love with his mate.

"Let me get your bag for you." She picked up his satchel and slotted his weapons into the side of it, sat the pack on his back and reached around his middle and clicked the straps into place. With her mouth near his ear, she blew a soft breath across his cheek. *"I cannae wait to find Father."*

"Duncan can't keep him hidden from us forever, not when our bears can track so very well."

"Aye, that is so very true." She patted his rump and his bear reveled in her touch. *"Find my Father and I'll forever be in your debt."*

"I am already forever in yours." She'd agreed to marry him and he couldn't be more elated, although right now he had work

to do. He gave his bear his head, prowled across the meadow and joined Kirk as he waited for him. Alongside the stream, they trod and followed the booted tracks and the scent of Annella's father. Find Niall, they would, this very day. Not another night would pass in which he had to watch his chosen one become distressed as they searched for her loved ones.

* * * *

With her traveling sack heavy on her back, the straps digging into her shoulders, Annella kept pace with Cherub as the morning wore on and the sun passed high overhead. They trekked alongside their mates through the thick underbrush of the forest, the river weaving through the woods on their right until it joined another river and widened. The crashing tumble of a waterfall ricocheted toward her from somewhere up ahead and she stroked down the silky pelt of Alec's back as the ominous sound intensified and beat inside her head.

She halted as they emerged from the woods and stood on the edge of a cliff, white water cascading over slick black boulders and careening down the rocky cliff face into a ravine a hundred feet below.

On the craggy rise overlooking the heart of MacKenzie land far below, she crouched and pressed one hand to the slick black rock. A steep trail led down the left side while in the distance beyond, Scotland's rugged coastline sat and across the choppy sea, the Isle of Skye rose like a long line of lush green amongst the roiling waves of the ocean. Dark and ominous clouds gusted in, a pall of bubbling gray that made her shiver. *"We'll lose Father's scent and any possible tracks if it rains."*

"Cherub can send those clouds back to where they came from." Alec's bear nudged her side, his touch reassuring. *"We won't lose their scent."*

Of course. Cherub commanded the very air itself, could whip up a storm or send one fleeing if she so desired. Her worry had her on edge, her thoughts askew. In the valley below, the inner channels of both Loch Carron and Loch Kishorn wound their way inland, the odd wattle-and-daub longhouse nestled along the pebbly shoreline. Cattle grazed within the lower pastures surrounding a village of thatch-roofed houses cloistered tightly together on the northern shores of one of the lochs, while mountainous land rose in all directions, a range that spread for as far as the eye could see. Sheep dotted the craggy hills in the distance, and she raised a hand to her brow and squinted. A stronghold sat at the far end of the inner channel of Loch Carron several miles distant. Excited, she jumped to her feet. "Do you see that, Cherub?"

"I do." Cherub peered at the castle, her white fur cloak flapping back from her shoulders in the brisk mountain breeze. "'Tis an older holding and its position matches Ronan's description to perfection. He's imprisoned right there and even though we didnae follow his trail, we've found where he's been taken all the same."

"Which means we willnae have to traipse all the way back to the meadow and follow my brother's tracks to reach where he's being contained."

"Aye, I can easily take us through the skies once we've found your father. Let's stop here for a short rest. You should attempt to locate your father again in the dream realm. Duncan cannae keep him awake forever. Meanwhile, I'll disperse those rain clouds." Cherub raised her hands to the sky and with a flick of her fingers, called forth her ability to control her element. Her olive skirts beat against her legs and her pale hair whipped back and the brewing clouds swept higher then swished back out toward the sea. Cherub brushed her hands against her sides. "There, that should do for a wee bit."

"Thank you. I'll go and find a quiet place where I can rest."

"Kirk and I will keep guard here while you do."

Leaving Kirk and Cherub behind, she backtracked into the woods with Alec lumbering along beside her, his bear ever watchful of their surroundings.

"*This spot should do well.*" Alec halted a furlong in where the grass grew thick between the trees and the canopy opened up overhead, the breeze stirring the leaves and making them rustle, the vibrant colors of dark green and warm yellow, relaxing her.

"*This is perfect.*" She dropped her sack next to the tree, laid down and patted the space beside her. "*Shift.*"

"*I'm coming.*" With a hungry growl, he made the Change in a blaze of red and orange sparks, his bear gone and her man now standing before her, his beautiful body thick with muscle and rippling with strength. Satchel and weapons in hand, he placed them on the ground then eased down next to her, flipped the top leather flap open and pulled his black leather pants, white tunic and steel-studded gray jacket out.

"Wait." She caught his hands before he could don his clothes and shook her head.

"What's wrong?"

"Naught is wrong." She wrapped her arms around his neck and drew him down on top of her, his delicious scent floating all around. "Rub against me."

"If I rub against you, I'll likely want far more." Yet he did exactly as she'd asked, his warm and fresh pine scent swirling around and embedding itself deeply within her. Aye, naught could satisfy her more, of being held within his strong embrace.

She slid her fingers into his silky black hair, palmed the back of his head and brought his mouth to hers. Need rose strongly within her and she kissed him, tasted his passion and shared her own. "There is nowhere I wish to be right now than right here with you."

"I can't believe I ever thought I could turn you away." He tangled his fingers in her hair, brought the golden mass to his nose and breathed deep. "My life won't be worth living without you by my side. I give you my oath, Annella, that I'll keep you safe, never bring harm down upon your head. I'll only ever cherish and adore you."

"'Tis about time you believed in the bond, and right now, I'm in a fierce mood to cherish and adore every inch of you. I also wish to request my favor now. I want to be loved by you, afore I go, but in my own way. Are you prepared to trust me?"

"You'll always have my trust."

"Thank you." Feeling a whole lot naughty and glad they currently had sufficient privacy, she slowly closed her eyes, allowed herself to drift toward the dark of the dream realm, set her spiritual body free of her physical one and floated overtop of her and Alec, her physical body slumping beside his and her head tipping to one side.

"Where did you go, my annoying sprite? I can't love you if you disappear." Alec sat up and swept his hands through the air as she swirled around him.

"My way, remember?" Gently, she touched her wispy lips to his, no more than a light brush of her inner essence streaming over him then she swirled against his bare chest, traced her tongue over each of his tiny and hard male nipples before licking down over each rigid band of tight flesh covering his stomach.

"Annella." He groaned her name as he fell back on the grass and patted the air in search of her. "I can feel you all over me but I can't hold onto you. Solidify your spiritual body."

"Brace yourself, my mighty bear. I'm about to have my wicked way with you." She stroked his hips with her essence alone, his cock rising high and firm from within the lush black curls at the V of his groin, and too tempted not to take what was on offer, she solidified herself, wrapped her lips around his full length and gasped at the deliciousness of having his cock in her mouth. With her hands on him, she softly caressed his balls as she tickled her tongue over the head of his shaft and sucked him deep.

"Ah, hell." He clutched fistfuls of grass, his breath coming harder and faster. "That feels incredible."

Taking his length even deeper into her throat, she bobbed up and down on him until a hot burn sizzled through her. No more could she wait. She wished to give him the ultimate pleasure, as he'd only ever experience at her hand.

"You're a minx. I want to be inside you, now." Raspy words as he shoved his elbows behind him, heaved her tunic up and suctioned onto one of her nipples.

"Me too." She shoved her black rawhide pants off, straddled his hips then sank down on top of him. Impaled on his cock, she kissed him as she rode him hard and fast. "I'm going to come."

"I'm right here. Come as you please." With one flick of his finger over her nub, her channel tightened something fierce and she pulsed around him, over and over and he held onto her firmly with his hands on her hips.

As she slowed her pace, he grasped her physical body's hand which lay limp next to them then rolled her onto her side and trapped her between him and her physical body. "I have to bite you, where I know the mark will remain."

"Do whatever you wish to either of us. Both are me, just as both you and your bear are you."

"Thank you." He leaned over and past her, sank his teeth into the sensitive skin at the hollow of her true body's neck and bit down, the connection remaining in place between both her forms making her gasp with pleasure as his bite sent her flying once more to the stars, her channel sucking greedily at his length and making him lurch.

"I've got to come, can't wait any longer, but within the other you." He pulled himself from her, whipped her physical body's pants down to her knees and grinning at her spiritual body still convulsing next to him, moved over top of her limp form and thrust deep inside her once more. He grunted and shuddered and so did she, his orgasm coming swift and fast, his seed spurting deep inside her true form where it could take.

"Woman," he muttered as he pulled both of her into his arms and squished the three of them so deliciously together, "I can't believe I get two of you."

"Well, I get two of you, man and beast, so I believe we're even."

"I get the far better deal." He kissed her and she kissed him back, then he nuzzled the neck of her limp body, his shaft still embedded deep inside her true self, the thickness of him something she sensed dually even though in her spiritual form.

"Are you going to come again?" She wriggled to her feet even though sensations still stormed through her, straightened her tunic and stood over her chosen one as he thrust inside her body below him again and again, every fierce push making both of her contract around him. What he did to either of her, she sensed and while he continued to pound, she gasped and tried to pull her breeches back on. Dressed, she stood over her mate and her naked limp self, stroked down his back and cupped his balls from behind as he thrust heavy and fast, his passion flaring strongly, his need for her intense.

He bellowed and sank even deeper inside her, then he came, shooting his essence within her before he rolled to his side and onto the grass. A wide grin lifted his lips as she stepped in between his spread legs and crouched. Even her limp self somehow had a smile curving her lips.

"You are making both of me very happy."

"I'm beyond happy right now."

"Aye, you appear so." Gently, she wrapped one hand around her chosen one's spent cock and raised a brow. "Might I recommend that you have some more fun with me while I'm gone. Even though I'll no' be here in spirit and soul, I shall clearly be here in body." She swiped her thumb over his slippery head.

"You're going to make the perfect wife, but I'll wait to do that again for when you return." He picked up her limp body's hand and nibbled on her fingertips and as he did, she blew him a kiss and returned to a wisp before allowing the dream realm to take her. She soared through the dark of the heavenly skies and breezed in and around the twinkling stars.

Aye, theirs would be a most heavenly loving each time they came together, with twice the fun it seemed.

Chapter 11

Within the dream realm, Annella flew through the darkened skies, although barely any stars blazed being that so very few slept this early in the afternoon. She spied the smallest, littlest twinkle, one single soul, not Father's by any means, but that of a newborn babe whose essence flickered so very close to where Father, Ronan, and Alec's stars usually glowed when they rested. The star's essence called to her and she clutched ahold of it, drew inward and blinked within the sweetly innocent dreams of a heavenly new life. The newborn babe, only a few days old, held a soul that shone like a beacon of hope. Beautiful. Peaceful. Fully at rest.

She allowed her solidified body to emerge and touched a hand to her chest as she crouched next to the wee babe swaddled in white cloths and lying in a crude wooden crate on the dusty floor of a small thatch-roofed house with walls of brown mud. A fire burned in a pit in the center, smoke curling from it and drifting through the vented cone-shaped roof above. A young lass of mayhap eight and ten lay asleep on a straw pallet beside the babe, her MacKenzie tartan covering her and her damp brown locks tangled about her face.

"Ariel, Muirin sent some healing herbs to aid you in your

birthing recovery." An older woman with an ample bust and wide hips hustled through the door, her kirtle's russet skirts swishing about her legs and a basket hooked over one arm.

Annella dissolved her form and wisped upward before the woman could see her.

"Och, child." The woman smiled at the sleeping lass and in a whisper continued, "'Tis good to see you're finally resting. The herbs can wait until after you've awoken."

Muirin again, and this woman knew the fae sorceress. "*I'm getting closer to where I need to be, Alec.*"

"*You've found your Father?*"

"*He does no' rest at the moment, although a wee babe's essence drew me toward the child. Muirin's name has been mentioned here in this hut. I need to take a look around.*"

"*Be careful, and keep your mind fully open to mine. I'll follow your every move, and ensure I see what you see.*"

"*Aye, of course.*" A mere wisp of white, she breezed out the door and drifted over the village of houses cloistered so tightly together. On the forested mountain across the loch, a waterfall cascaded over a high ledge and crashed into a stony ravine a hundred feet below. "*I have no' traveled far, just to the village across the other side of the loch. I'm near the junction where Loch Carron meets Loch Kishorn. I can see the waterfall from here.*"

"*Don't draw any attention to yourself as you look around.*"

"*Aye, Captain.*" She kept her mind fully open to his, withholding naught as she glided over the thatched rooftops while below a central fire blazed in the middle of the village and two flush-faced women in brown kirtles and aprons tended blackened pots bubbling over the flames. The heavenly scent of seafood stew wafted upward and several villagers ambled toward the fire as they gathered together in chattering groups for the coming evening meal. 'Twould be dark soon, although as yet, the sun still hovered above the far horizon.

Farther she coasted, past goats baying and munching on the thistly grass sprouting alongside a short stone wall near the shoreline. Two lively children squealed as they tore barefoot under a hemp rope strung between two trees, drying clothes and several lengths of the MacKenzie plaid flapping in the breeze. The children's giggles made the corralled horses within a wooden-beamed enclosure near them, whinny and stomp. Dust floated into the air and she breezed through it toward a lad with a woolen cap, his grass-stained tunic's sleeves rolled to his elbows as he brushed one of the animals tethered to a post.

She soared along the sandy shoreline of the loch, searching for even the minutest sign of Duncan and his men. Such a group of warriors would be hard to miss if they were somewhere here.

Out in the loch's bay, an elderly fisherman in his skiff tossed his nets out, while perched on a boulder along the grassy embankment, a lad of mayhap six and ten wearing brown breeches and a frayed shirt whittled away on a long length of yew as he fashioned a bow. He picked up a length of cord lying across his lap and slotted it between the notches he'd made at each end of the wood, then he stood and with his bow in hand and a pouch of arrows slung over one shoulder, cupped his hands to his mouth and yelled, "Papa, I'll go join the laird's warriors as they hunt."

"Take care and obey Duncan MacKenzie's orders."

"I shall." With a jaunty whistle the lad followed the worn pathway running alongside the shoreline and disappeared into the forest beyond the grazing cattle.

"Did you catch that, Alec?"

"I did. Stay on the lad's tail. The laird he speaks of is clearly Duncan." He shared his movements with her as he scooped her physical body up, now fully clothed, and cradling her in his arms, he jogged back to the waterfall where Cherub and Kirk watched over the trail weaving downward toward the village. To Kirk, he called out, "Annella's at the village, is

following a lad who's on his way to see Duncan."

"Then we follow the lad too." Kirk, dressed in a faded blue shirt and brown pants with his black war coat donned overtop and claymore fastened at his side, nabbed Cherub's hand. "Take us to the skies."

Alec nabbed Cherub's arm. "As fast as you can."

"Wait, Alec. You need to leave my physical body somewhere safe if we're heading directly toward Duncan's lair." She whizzed after the lad, weaved through the towering trees in fast pursuit. *"Should there be a battle to get Father back, then I'm safest remaining like this in my spiritual form."*

"There is no safer place for your true body than in my arms."

"I agree, but we are only four compared to however many warriors Duncan has and you will need both your arms free if there's to be a fight." She pursued the boy with his dark hair flopping forward over his brow. *"Take me somewhere safe."*

"Not yet. We're following you first."

She streamed higher, broke free of the treetops just as the lad too dashed out of the woods and hurried along the winding upward cliff side trail overlooking the rocky shoreline. The waves rolled in and hit the rock wall, splashed high and sprayed the blackened surface. She breezed alongside the boy as he climbed the silt and stone pathway then soared ahead of him, made the top of the cliff's peak and gasped. Down the other side within a secluded bay at the base sat a protected garrison with a powerful war galley bobbing in the water from its mooring at the end of a stone landing. A second MacKenzie stronghold, this one sitting on Loch Kishorn and also hidden well out of sight. *"Duncan and his brother appear to be amassing an army along these shores."*

"Along with procuring a battle-skilled fae, your father."

"They'll not have him for long, although something still bothers me. When I visited Ronan, he said he sensed something

was amiss, that 'twas as if Duncan was his enemy, yet also no'."

"*Things definitely aren't quite as they seem. We must be prepared for anything.*"

"*Cherub also told me she understood only what she'd sensed that night I'd been taken, that like me, my father and brother too had a journey ahead of them, one that she was forbidden to halt. Her exact words, 'The mated bond is a very sacred union and I'm no' permitted to breach its creation or completion.'*"

"*And now we've discovered Ronan has found his mate, just as you and I have found each other.*"

"*Duncan's also aligned himself with a fae sorceress, and I've never known any of the fae to make a stand against their own kind. Ask Cherub what she thinks about all of this.*" She streaked down the shingled side of the cliff, wisped over the curtain wall and into the bailey. A good thirty men trained in battle leathers, gritty dust pluming at their feet in the waning afternoon light, their claymores clashing and each strike ringing loud in her ears. Slowly, she circled the main tower as she searched for an open window or door.

"*Cherub has Kirk and I cloaked and we're not far behind. She said Muirin must be from beyond the veil, one of the full-blooded fae. She's never come across her before. She's also unsure what we'll find within Duncan's lair, but to be prepared for anything.*"

"*If Father is here in this stronghold, then he's being kept only a mere hour or two's ride from Ronan.*"

"We ride out now for Carron Castle." Duncan stepped out from under the eaves of the front door with two warriors at his side. He slapped both men on the shoulders. "I have a proposition to put to Ronan and it cannae wait any longer." He clomped toward a stone shack tucked against the curtain wall, an iron rod in one hand and his short dark hair glinting blue on the ends. Wearing his battle leathers, he bellowed to a lad at the stables. "Ready my horse."

"Duncan is leaving for Carron Castle, said he had a proposition to put to Ronan. At least we now know the name of his brother's holding."

"I caught what he said through our link. Keep sharing, love."

In his thick black boots, Duncan entered the shack and she waited with bated breath. Moments later, he stepped back out, the iron rod he'd been carrying dispensed with. He bounded onto his war horse, snatched the reins being held by the stable-hand, the two warriors who'd been with him already mounted on their own destriers. Heavily armed, the three men rode out the main gate under the arch, their horses galloping hard.

"I dinnae know if this proposition he has for Ronan is good or bad, but regardless, we're running out of time, and I've still yet to find Father."

"I'm coming. I'll help you search for him."

"No' until after you've taken my body somewhere safe." Underneath the chunky wooden door of the shack, she snuck and into the gloomy recesses lit only by a fire burning in one corner, the hot coals glowing and the iron rod Duncan had been carrying now protruding from one side. The fire's glow flickered over the blackened walls of mud and stone as well as the unclothed back of a seasoned warrior standing in his kilt in the center of the room, his feet planted wide and his blond-haired head with its streak of silver on one side, bowed in supplication. Her heart clenched in on itself. Father. She streamed down and glided around him, brushed a kiss across his cheek, her heartbeat a thumping mess as she whispered in his ear, "I'm here, Father."

"I can sense your presence," he breathed back as he lifted his head a notch, tipped it toward a woman dressed in an exquisite silver gown with long draping sleeves who stood near the far wall. She'd not noticed the woman before, but now the elegantly clothed woman crossed the room, a torque necklace of fine gold encircling her neck and her iridescent eyes shimmering as she scrutinized Father.

"My father is here, in the shack." She floated toward the ceiling. *"There's a woman with him, and by her unusual eyes, I'd say one of the fae. She must be Muirin."*

"Stay hidden, and that's an order."

"You've gone quiet all of a sudden, Niall." The woman's eyes reflected the colors of the rainbow, her gaze both breathtaking and fearsome to behold, her beauty undeniable. Flawless skin, high cheeks and rich red hair. Her locks were twisted high upon her head, the odd strand clinging to the long column of her neck. The woman's face remained untouched by age yet her gaze held centuries of knowledge.

"She's definitely full-blooded, an immortal for certain." The half-blooded fae of the village lived longer lives than mere humans alone, but they weren't immortals as the full-blooded fae beyond the veil usually were.

"What do you wish for me to say, Muirin?" Father's bare torso gleamed with sweat from the intense heat churning from the fire, his Matheson plaid fastened at his waist with a leather girdle and his sword sheathed at his side.

"Father remains armed, Alec."

"Then he remains there willingly."

"Aye, it appears so." With a blade in his hand, her father could so easily have left.

"I have sworn my allegiance to you and Duncan in order to ensure my son's freedom." Father glared at Muirin. "Now Duncan leaves and it better damn well be to free my son as we agreed upon."

"Father would never swear his allegiance to another, not when doing so would break his oath to our chief and our clan. There is far more than just a little amiss here. There's a damn lot."

"I agree."

Gently, Muirin touched her fingertips to Father's cheek then swished down to his neck. She brushed against him, her breasts pressed to his chest.

"*Oh goodness. Father allows her touch, as if they are far better acquainted than they should be.*" They had a problem, a very big problem.

"I completed the bond with you, Muirin. Honor your word to me, just as I've honored mine to you." Father grasped Muirin's trailing fingers, pressed her palm firm over his chest and leaned in. "Allow me to go to Carron Castle and ensure Duncan does as he has promised me he'll do."

"You need to show Duncan more trust. His proposition for Ronan is one that expresses his coming intentions, of accepting the fae to the deepest degree."

"*Father completed the bond with her.*" Shock coursed through her. "*They're mated, soul bound as you and I are.*"

"*Keep sharing with me.*"

"*My parents, even though they loved each other, were never soul bound. They chose to wed when neither sensed a bond forming with another. That is why Mother ascended. She loved Father dearly, but 'twas no' enough to keep her to this Earth. Neither believed they'd ever find their chosen ones. I cannae believe Father now has.*"

"*It's more like Muirin has found him. We're passing over the forest now.*"

"*The tension in this shack is so thick and even though Father and Muirin are soul bound, she clearly willnae allow him to leave, no' even to ride to Ronan.*"

"*We're coming down the shingled cliff side. I see the stronghold and the war galley moored at the landing.*" He opened his mind further to her, her physical body held tight within his arms as he soared, cloaked and unseen, through the skies with Cherub and Kirk.

"When two are soul bound, Niall, neither can leave the

other for long, and I've no wish to travel to Carron Castle at this moment." The sorceress dug her fingers into Father's arm, lightened her touch then scraped downward. "You also hold the battle skill, my mate, an ability coveted by our fae kind, an ability you have yet to fully utilize. Your half-blooded kind within the fae village hold such a wealth of skills, yet there is more you can do to grow your abilities to their complete fullness and I shall be the one to show you how, particularly now I've spelled your soul to mine and you too are now an immortal as I am." She stepped back, bent before the hearth, grasped the iron rod and returned to him. "Should your son agree to Duncan's proposition, then I shall train him too so he might fight at your side and mine as well. Are you ready to accept your destiny?"

"My destiny has always been set, to protect Ronan, Annella, and my people. I will never allow any harm to come to them, which means if I must remain at your side to see that done, then so be it. Certainly if my children were here, then they'd understand and accept my decision to remain." He raised his arm, slapped his bulging bicep. "Brand me and be done with it, woman."

"As it is my destiny to protect those who are mine, which now includes you and your son and daughter. We are in quite the quandary, my chosen one, for you dinnae believe I have only the best intentions toward you and yours. Hopefully you will learn that is so within time, of which we now have a great deal ahead of us." Muirin raised the rod, the iron burning red and hot as she shoved it hard into Father's bicep. Skin sizzled and the acrid odor of burning flesh pervaded the air. Muirin pulled the rod away and the brand blazed bright on Father's arm, an insignia depicting the ancient Celtic woven circle for infinity. The symbol of their Matheson fae village. "We are of fae blood, Niall, and from this moment forth, the fae village you are one of the leaders of is now one I too shall guard, whether you wish to fully believe me or no'."

Muirin lifted her sleeve and exposed her own arm. The same brand that now lay upon Father's skin also lay stamped upon Muirin's flesh. "The fae have lived for thousands of years beyond the veil, but I intend to remain here and walk this Earth with you. I am no' asking you to fight alongside the Chief of MacKenzie or his youngest son, Jeremiah, who are both menaces, but alongside Duncan and Coll who have now both successfully broken away from their father and intend to fight the good fight. 'Tis time for the fae to live."

* * * *

Alec cradled Annella's physical body to his chest as Cherub swept them toward a small copse of trees near the shoreline just beyond the guardsmen's sight and set them down. He'd repeated all he'd seen and heard within Annella's mind with both Cherub and Kirk and now he turned all the new information over in his mind, tried to process it all. "Niall has now been placed in a very unique position."

"Most definitely." Arms folded, Cherub paced back and forth. "Not only is he now mated to Muirin, but he has also agreed to fight alongside Duncan, yet from what they've said, on the side of the fae. That better be the truth."

"Yet what on earth would suddenly cause Duncan and his brother to align themselves with the fae? I've never known a MacKenzie to do anything that didn't benefit themselves in some way." Kirk shoved a hand through his hair. "At least Niall is here."

"Aye, Niall's loyalty to his people will never sway and since he's here, he can most definitely keep an eye on things." Alec brushed his lips across Annella's forehead, tucked her limp hand between them and murmured in her mind, *"You understand, don't you? We can't take your father from this place, not now we're aware he's soul bound to Muirin."*

"Aye, 'tis as Cherub said, the mated bond is a very sacred union and neither her or any of us are permitted to breach its

creation or completion. Clearly my father has completed the bond with her, and chosen his path in doing so. I dinnae wish to say farewell to him. He is my only parent."

"*You'll never be far from him, not with your skill.*" Alec let out a long breath as he eyed Cherub and Kirk. "We leave Niall here."

"Aye, Niall can oversee all Duncan does, until we too discover why he and his brother have chosen to side with the fae." Cherub pressed two fingers to Annella's neck. "Her pulse is strong. Ask her if she'd like me to take her to her chamber at the House of Clan Matheson where her kin can guard her body, or somewhere else?"

"*Not my chamber. Tell Cherub to take me to your chamber at Ivanson. That is the only place where I wish to be.*" Her desire to remain with her father for a few more minutes barreled through to him, time he'd never deny her.

"*Will do. Be waiting for me when we return. I won't be long.*" He sent a blast of warmth and love down their merged link and she sent the same wave of love and devotion right back. To Cherub, he murmured, "Annella wishes to be taken to my chamber at Ivanson." He'd place her safely in his bed and ensure Megan, his chief's wife, watched over her. Not only would Megan be able to ensure Annella's physical body came to no harm, but so too she was a highly qualified nurse and would be able to offer a level of care none other could. "Megan can guard her."

"Megan is the perfect choice." Cherub linked her arm through his and Annella's floppy arm as Kirk wrapped his hands around Cherub's waist from behind. With a swish of her fingers, Cherub opened a portal and the four of them fell away into the dark abyss.

Through the endless streams of time, they traveled and mere minutes later arrived in his chamber.

Gently, he set Annella down on his bed and tucked his fur

bedcover over her, sat next to her and leaned in, nuzzled her neck and nibbled on her ear. Leaving her here would be difficult, particularly now they'd finally joined together as one. All he wished to do was remain right by her side.

"I'll go and fetch Megan." Cherub opened the door then dashed out in a flurry of olive skirts.

"I'll be but a moment too." Kirk swung his satchel and Cherub's from his shoulders. "I'll just drop these off in my chamber, give you a little more time with your chosen one."

"Thank you." Any time was appreciated.

Kirk disappeared down the hallway.

Holding Annella's hand, he kissed her fingertips. "From the first night you visited me in my dreams, you enthralled me, made me crave each following visit, and far more than I was prepared to admit at the time. I won't accept anything less than forever with you." He now lived and breathed for his chosen one and always would. With one hand pressed over her heart, he counted several strong and steady beats. With a soft sigh, he dropped a kiss on her lips and savored the soft breaths she emitted against his own. "No getting into any trouble while I'm gone," he whispered to the one woman he could never survive without. "Or I'll hunt you down, no matter where you might go."

He rose, eased his satchel and hers from his shoulders, pulled the remainder of his chocolate bar from his bag and set it on the pillow beside his wife-to-be. He ached to remain with her, to shake her and demand her spiritual form's return, to keep her safely locked away right here in his room, only he'd been gifted with a warrior mate, a lass who'd always be in the thick of things, just as he always was. A smile lifted his lips. Aye, he'd been given the perfect woman, his chosen one matching him in every single way, and he'd never wish to change that about her, or anything else.

"I'm here." Megan rushed into the room in a wine-colored woolen skirt and white blouse with a ruffled neckline, her dark wavy hair bobbing on her shoulders and Cherub and Kirk one step behind her. "Cherub updated me."

"Don't leave my woman alone." He gripped Megan's shoulders, pulled her into a hug. "Not even for one moment. She holds my very heart and soul in her hands."

"I understand and I promise I'll remain right here until you return." Megan hugged him then swept Cherub and Kirk into her arms. "Be safe, all of you."

"Always." Cherub held out her arms for him and Kirk to take. "Let's leave."

They still had such a perilous mission ahead of them, of finding and freeing Ronan. Even though Duncan had aligned himself with the fae, he'd still kept Ronan heavily restrained within his dungeons, which meant stealth would be needed this night in order to free his mate's brother.

He grasped Cherub's arm and she opened a portal with one flick of her fingers then with them all connected together as one, they fell away and soared back through time.

Chapter 12

Annella remained no more than a wisp of white as she floated near the ceiling of the shack, Father and Muirin standing below her as Father hunkered down next to a pail of cold water in the corner and scooped water.

Glaring at Muirin, he splashed his arm. "Leave me be for a while."

"I must see to your healing first." She touched her palm over the brand she'd burned into his flesh and murmured,

"With this mark, seal and heal.
No festering wound may be revealed."

Sparks flared under her palm and she lifted her hand. The mark, now fully sealed, appeared as if it had been imprinted into his skin many moons ago. "There, 'tis done."

"Thank you." Father rose and tipped his head toward the door. "Now please, go. I wish some time alone."

"In the days and weeks to come, your skill will rise in strength under my tutelage, until the point where even the dust I'd spelled and given Duncan wouldnae have slowed you down during your battle with him."

"'Twas as if my legs had turned to lead. Ronan too couldnae fight the compulsion within your concoction." Father crossed to the door and opened it. "Leave, Muirin."

"I will give you this time you've asked for, but remember this." She halted next to him, the wind whistling in from outside and fluttering her silver skirts. "You have spent your entire life here on this Earth without me, but now that I too am here and no longer residing beyond the veil, you need to accept your heritage as one of the fae, as well as your place at my side."

"You also need to accept your place at mine." Father pulled the pins from her hair and her long red locks slid free and swayed down to her waist. He dug one hand into the thick mass, wrapped it around his fist and gently brought her mouth closer to his. A breath from her lips, he whispered, "We may be mated, our souls calling to each other's and making me unable to deny you very much, but never forget this. I love my children, and if you ever wish to one day hold my love as well, then you will need to stand behind your word given to me, that it is in fact time for the fae to live."

"Of course. I would have it no other way." She reached up on her toes and kissed him then sashayed out the door and closed it, the heavy clunk resounding firmly as she did.

"I love you too, Father." She wisped down and solidified her spiritual form, clutched her only parent to her and held him tight. "I wish you didnae have to stay."

"You can see why I have no choice. Muirin is my mate and I've accepted the bond, couldnae deny it even if I wished to. She may have ensured my capture and Ronan's, but she did so because her soul cries out for mine. I shall embrace the challenge she poses and ensure our fae people from the village continue to grow from strength to strength. Tell Ronan that will be so." He cupped her face in his hands, such a well of love filling his gaze. "Go to your brother and ensure he is freed. He shouldnae be forced into accepting any proposition Duncan gives him unless 'tis a proposition he wishes to accept."

"I shall, but afore I go, I have news I must share with you."

"I can see your skill has evolved, and glad I am that it has. You'll be able to visit me with far more ease, of which I expect. To begin with though, dinnae allow another to see you here at Ardan House. Only me."

"I shall, but you need to know I've also met my own soul bound mate and completed the bond with him. His name is Alec Matheson and he's a shifter from Kirk's future clan. Cherub has promised to bring us back and forth as needed through time, and I've spoken to Ronan. He too has discovered his chosen one and she lives at the castle where he's being restrained."

"What do you mean?"

"Ronan's chosen one is Duncan's sister. But more than that, Kyla holds fae blood and the mind-walker skill, although she isnae fully aware of how to use her ability since she has never been trained by our people."

"Hell." Father clenched his teeth, shook his head. "Ronan always sensed his mate resided somewhere beyond his reach, has never been able to find her in all these years, but I never would have imagined he'd find her here, in the heart of MacKenzie land."

"Ronan told her a story which I overheard while floating above him. Twenty years ago, a young lass of only three summers was taken from the fae village farther along the loch from the House of Clan Matheson."

"Aye, the lass was Isaiah and Grace's daughter, Christina. She was taken in the middle of the night, under the cover of darkness and although we searched high and low for her at the time, we never found her. Ronan was mayhap eight, and she'd always intrigued him, although I didnae know they were soul bound. One cannae usually tell until they come of age, although a few have sensed tendrils of the bond forming afore that time. Still, 'tis most rare."

"Ronan told Kyla they're mated, although she is in denial."

"Then it appears Ronan too will have a battle ahead of him to ensure he catches her." Father rolled his shoulders and quirked a brow. "From here, I will do all I can to aid Ronan in his chase. There will certainly be some interesting days ahead of us."

"There shall." Tears misted her gaze, her time with him disappearing fast when the last thing she wished to do was say farewell to her most beloved parent. Nay, she would never say farewell. He would be close, not unreachable, not considering her skill. Through the dream realm, she'd visit him. "I too will offer Ronan my aid in his chase should he need it, and when you rest, I will come to you as often as I can."

"I will always be here, for you and for Ronan both. Never think that I willnae, but for now I have a mate who needs me possibly even more than both my children currently do. I must remain here and do all I can to ensure Muirin speaks the truth and remains on the side of the fae. If danger lurks, I'll deal with it."

"I'll miss you."

"As I will miss you." Father kissed her cheek, squeezed her tight in his arms before he released her. "Travel safely, and return soon. I demand it."

"Aye, Father, I shall." She dissolved her form, slipped underneath the door and soared high into the darkening sky. Night would soon fall, the sun a heavy orb of golden-orange sitting low along the horizon.

Unseen, she whizzed over the curtain wall, right between two kilted guardsmen then flew down along the rocky shoreline toward the copse of trees where Alec had last been. In the wide bow of an ancient elm tree, she settled then tried to open her link with her chosen one, only nothing but a black hole gaped where he should have been. "*Where are you, Alec?*"

No answer.

The setting sun sank lower, sent a final flare of brilliant red through the skies then disappeared. Within the dark of night, a mountain mist streamed down the hill and through the trees, an eerie cloud of ghostly white that suddenly swirled and churned. The air rushed all around her and signified only one thing. Cherub's cloaked return through a portal.

She allowed her spiritual body to solidify then with one hand on her sword hilt to keep it from banging against her side, she dropped down and landed with a soft clunk on the ground.

"There you are." Alec hauled her up against him, appearing right out of thin air as he smothered her in his heat, a radiant warmth she completely adored. "Did you have enough time to speak to your father?"

"Aye, I updated him on all that has happened, about you and that Ronan has discovered he is soul bound to another. He's promised to always be here for Ronan and I. He also demanded I return, and I shall through the dream realm, as often as I can." She kissed him, with all the love she held for him overflowing her heart. "I've missed you."

"I hated having to leave you behind in my chamber, and I also hated having to leave you here to start with, if that makes any sense."

"Completely."

"'Tis so good to see you're safe and well, Annella." Cherub squeezed her arm. "We delivered your physical body to Alec's chamber and the chief's wife, Megan, watches over you. You'll come to no harm under her care, that I can assure you."

"Thank you."

"Are you ready to find and free your brother?" Kirk, standing behind Cherub, rubbed his chin over the top of her blond-haired head.

"I'm beyond ready, and we must do so afore Duncan reaches him. I dinnae wish for my brother to hear any proposition Duncan might have to offer him. Ronan needs to return home, to heal and regain his strength, and I'll accept naught less." She leaned against Alec and he hooked his arms around her waist as she snuggled deeper inside his mind. How had she been so lucky to have been gifted with such a wonderful mate? "*Thank you for allowing me to see my father and to spend a few more precious minutes with him.*"

"*I would never keep you from your loved ones.*" He rubbed against her, embedding her in his deliciously warm and fresh pine scent, his presence calming and settling her deep inside.

She curled her fingers into his steel-studded gray jacket, and held onto him as if her life depended on it, which it likely did. "*I wish to be with you, joined as one, as we were earlier this day.*"

"*I wish for that too, and I'll demand such a joining right after we've rescued your brother and returned you to your physical body. But at least for now, I know you can't come to any true harm in this spiritual form during our coming mission.*" He buried his nose in her hair and breathed deep. "Grab ahold of Cherub. It's time we were away."

"Aye, we must move, with all haste." Cherub held out her arms.

Annella grasped Cherub, just as Alec and Kirk took a firm hold of her too, then Cherub extended her cloaking over them all. "We'll travel through the air rather than use a portal. No' only do I need to conserve what strength I have for the coming mission, but the stronghold where Ronan is being contained is so very close, only a few miles at most. I can us take us there just as swiftly this way, and still beat Duncan and his men along the way."

Cherub lifted them up and whizzed them through the air. Moonlight shimmered through the dark layer of cloud drifting in overhead as she took them higher, breezed them across the darkened, craggy mountains and silver-tinged forested hills toward the stronghold at the end of the inner channel of Loch Carron.

Carron Castle loomed. Candlelight lit the windows of the main tower house and armed guardsmen stood in their MacKenzie plaids and leather jerkins along the battlements, two at each corner with several standing at attention within the arched two-story gatehouse as they searched the waterway and surrounding land. *"I didnae see Duncan and his men riding along the way. Did you?"*

"Not a glimpse. He would've had to ride farther inland and around the hills." From behind her and unseen, Alec scraped his teeth back and forth over the sensitive skin of her neck. *"I can barely hold back this hunger I have for you."*

"Bite me if you need to." She stretched her neck. Nothing would settle her quite like his gloriously possessive bite would. *"I would never turn you away."*

"I wouldn't let you either." He sank his teeth into her flesh and she gasped then whimpered for more and he didn't disappoint. He slid one hand underneath the hem of her loose-sleeved red tunic and spread his warm palm over her breast, his voice a deep purr in her mind. *"I want to nibble away on every inch of you, suck your nipples into my mouth and thrust my—"*

"You're making me extremely hot with your naughty words."

"Expect a full and complete ravishment the moment I get you back to Ivanson. I intend to allow my bear his release and ensure he doesn't hold back."

"I love your bear." She wriggled around in his embrace, inched up and sucked on his neck. His pounding pulse point throbbed under her tongue and she licked his skin and bit down, allowed her fierce desire for him to surge along their link and saturate him. Goodness. She needed to bite him again, only Cherub began her descent and soared over the ramparts.

"We're here, everyone." A whisper as Cherub set them gently down inside the inner bailey within the shadows of the curtain wall. She maintained her cloaking over them and murmured, "Now, 'tis time to find these dungeons then—"

"Gordon, you must allow me to see the prisoner." Kyla rushed out the front door of the keep in fast pursuit of a warrior wearing leather chausses, a plaid and a blackened nasal helm tucked under his arm. Her golden-red curls bounced down her back and the silk folds of her violet gown swished about her legs. "He's to be kept alive and no' beaten. The maid who took him his last meal reported to me that he bled, badly."

"He infuriated the guards with his continual demands to see you. The two of you seem to have formed an unusually strong attachment to each other." The warrior turned on her and snarled under his breath. "Why would that be?"

"I have no' formed any such unusually strong attachment to him. I simply seek to do as Duncan requested of us. Even though Ronan's been restrained within our dungeons, we're still to ensure his wellbeing. That was my brother's order."

"Then return to the keep and I'll ensure his wellbeing for you, right after he's had sufficient time to repent from those aggravating demands he keeps making. Seek your rest this night. You arena permitted into the dungeons again until the morn." He stormed away, took the steep stone steps along the curtain wall up to the battlements and joined the guards on duty at the gatehouse.

"We must hurry. Ronan has immediate need of us." She squeezed Cherub's arm as she maintained her hold on her, her tone whisper-quiet. "Where should we begin?"

"The entrance leading to the dungeons could be anywhere. In Colin MacKenzie's castle on Loch Alsh, the entrance to his cells is through a trapdoor in a lower storage room near the kitchens. At his keep to the far north of here at Loch Broom, 'tis by way of a stairwell leading upward to the highest point of the tower. We'll begin our search inside the castle and if we have no luck there then we'll spread out and take in the bailey, the outbuildings, and finally scour the cliffs overlooking the loch and surrounding land itself. We also need to remain hidden while we do so, which means you'll all need to maintain your hold on me until 'tis safe to let go. We search together."

Yet she could remain unseen by dissolving her form. She opened her mouth to say so, only Alec nipped her ear, his teeth sharp as his mind moved through hers.

"We remain together, and that's an order."

"Aye, Captain." How frustrating.

* * * *

Alec held Annella tightly within his arms as Cherub swept the four of them unseen through the side door of the keep, down a darkened passageway and directly into the kitchens, which were thankfully devoid of even one soul. He wouldn't allow another separation from his chosen one, not while they searched this keep.

"'Tis just as well the evening meal is done." Cherub uncloaked them all within the quietness of the kitchens. "Let's scour this area first, including the storage rooms leading from it."

Annella walked toward the fire still burning in the ovens, her gaze on him. "Our dungeons at the House of Clan Matheson lie directly underneath our castle's kitchens and the scent of the cooking food often drifts down and torments those who are restrained far below, although I never scented anything other than foul and musty air when I visited Ronan." She peered into the blackened pots sitting over the hot coals, which bubbled with water. "Someone has requested a bath and even though the cook isnae here, one of the maids might no' be far away."

"We'll be careful." He shuffled the wooden pails stacked neatly next to the fire aside, crouched and swept his hand over the ground as he searched for a trap door. "You mentioned Ronan picked up a trace of salt in the air."

"Aye, but I never did while I was with him and I saw naught more than his cell and the darkened passageway leading from it through the bars." She leaned over him from behind, her full breasts brushing his back and her enchanting scent flowing all around him. "The floor appears clear."

"It does."

"All appears clear on this side of the kitchens too." Kirk closed the door of a large pantry then walked through a side door and into the storage room beyond, Cherub following close on his heels.

"We'll search high and low, not take any place for granted." He rose, caught Annella's hands and buried his nose in her long golden tresses. Breathing deep, he pushed her back against the wall. "You're distracting me in our search."

"How is that?" She touched her lips to his with the lightest of kisses.

"Just by being so damn touchable."

"That I can rectify." With a smile, she dissolved her form and streamed under his arm and into the storage room.

"I wasn't asking you to rectify the matter." He clomped after her into the darkened recesses of the side room where a trace of firelight penetrated through from the kitchens. Head bent to keep from knocking it on the low ceiling strung with herbs and medicinal plants, he scented the air as he wandered around the large space. Bags of oats lay stacked against one wall, bags of dried beef and pork too, while salt permeated the air from a thick saline bath Annella stood over and inspected.

"'Tis fresh meat being brine-cured and would provide a touch of the salty smell Ronan picked up if he were directly below." Annella traced one finger along the bath's rim and glanced at him. "Look for a trap door here."

He set to work doing so. Spices infused the air, pepper, cinnamon, cloves, nutmeg, ginger, and garlic. His bear caught each and every one of the scents as he searched the storeroom, turned each aroma over until he'd discarded them all, Ronan's scent not amongst any from within the heady mix. No trap doors either. He moved anything that appeared moveable and searched underneath.

"I can't catch even a whiff of Ronan in here." Kirk stood next to a tall chest propped against the far wall. He hunkered down, wiped one finger through the dust at the base then wriggled the chest forward and searched behind it. "There's nothing here at all. We should continue on."

"I agree." Cherub held out her arms, the golden girdle fastened around her waist glinting overtop of her olive gown. "We'll search the great hall and surrounding antechambers next."

"We also need to pick up our pace." Kirk wrapped his arms around Cherub from behind, stuck his nose against her neck and took one deep breath. After a heartfelt sigh, he murmured, "You smell so good compared to the dust clogging my airways at the moment."

"Well, I thank you for the compliment." Grinning, Cherub plucked a cobweb from his hair. "Hold tight, everyone. I need to extend my cloaking over us all as we head out."

Annella brushed up against him and murmured in his ear, "I'll race you to the great hall."

"Wait." He grabbed her hand, but she dissolved and flowed out the door before he could pull her into his arms. "Come back here, woman." He stalked into the kitchens and around the perimeter of the room, his increased shifter hearing attuned to any noise that might alert him to the arrival of another, particularly when someone would need to attend to the boiling water soon. Ahead of him and no more than a wisp, his woman breezed out the door and he set out after her in fast pursuit.

"Hold onto me, Alec." Cherub caught up to him, arm extended. "There is naught more intriguing than the chase. Am I right?"

"Aye, although this is the last place I want to be chasing her." He nabbed ahold of Cherub, Kirk already gripping her other arm, and they left the scents of coriander, cumin, and mustard behind as they weaved through the darkened back passageways toward the great hall, all invisible to the other.

Moments later, they entered the hall and moved around the perimeter. Massive wooden-beamed rafters rose to an impressive height with several tall, narrow windows holding stained glass within. Trestle tables and benches filled the central area along with a fireplace large enough for a man to walk within. *"Where are you, sprite?"*

"I'm leaving the great hall for you to search. I can remain unseen in this form and I'm already upstairs and have whipped through the chief's solar and am now scouring the upper bedchambers. We cannae discard the entrance to the dungeons being up here and winding downward through a secret tunnel perhaps."

He should order her to return, only in all truth, it made sense for her take the upper floors when she could move about so swiftly and surely, without alerting the maids or any others who might be about. *"Be careful,"* he gritted. *"Go no farther than you have."*

"Aye, Captain."

* * * *

Annella wisped through the rooms above-stairs, alert and watchful, then whizzed up the stairwell to the uppermost level of the main tower. Even though 'twas doubtful Ronan would have been moved from the underground dungeon where he'd been placed to a high-tower cell, 'twas still possible and she'd leave no stone unturned.

Down a darkened corridor lit only by a single candle burning in an iron wall sconce, she hurried then halted before a thickly paneled wooden door with a bolted lock. No circlet of keys lay in sight, not that she'd expected they would so she glided underneath the door and emerged within the cell holding a musty odor with dust motes floating through the air. A straw pallet sat on the ground and chains bolted to the wall over it held heavy cuffs dangling from the end. *"I found an upper cell, but no prisoner within. They clearly like to keep prisoners restrained at this keep."*

"We've come up with nothing in the great hall as well. We're moving onto the lower antechambers."

A dirt-encrusted window overlooked the courtyard below and she emerged her form enough to shove the iron-barred window open then became unseen again and swept out into the cool night air. Breaking Alec's order to go no farther made her shiver with unease although she continued on. Every minute that passed was another minute her brother remained in danger and she desperately needed to find him.

Through the inner courtyard, she flew then slipped underneath the doorway of the armory and into the pitch black. She'd begin the outer search here. Without anything to light her way, she solidified her form and patted the closest wall in the hope of finding another wall sconce with a candle. She bumped her hip into a high wooden workbench and traced across the top of it, her fingers knocking into a candle holder. Wonderful. Light. From her wrist sheath, she slid her dagger and flint free, struck the flint with her blade and sighed with relief as the sparks caught the candle's wick and light flared.

Along one side of the armory, sacks lined the stone wall and crates sat stacked next to them, while on the other side, battle axes, shields, pikes and various weaponry hung on hooks. She picked the candle up, the melted wax dripping onto the metal saucer and its light flaring across the blade of a massive two-handed claymore lying on top of the workbench, a weapon with precious stones encrusted into the hilt. The blade gleamed under the candlelight and the words *Luceo non uro* etched into the blade on one side, flashed at her.

"We've still got nothing. What about you?" Alec's words resounded in her mind and she clutched ahold of them.

"I've left the upper floors and I'm now outside in the

armory." Candle set back down, she ran one finger over the motto of the MacKenzie clan, this exact blade one she'd seen before. Within Duncan's very hand when he'd fought with Father in the forest near their warrior encampment. *"Duncan might be here. I've just found his sword."*

A creak sounded from behind and the armory door slammed shut. She whipped around, clutched a hand to her chest.

"I've been waiting for you to arrive, lass." Duncan scraped the bolt across and biceps bulging, he heaved a wooden crate in front of the door and blocked the gap underneath the doorway. A very strategic move, one to keep her contained, although 'twas truly impossible to keep a spirit-walker captured for long, a fact he'd soon learn.

"I was hoping to have come and gone with my brother afore you returned from your holding farther along the loch." She planted her hands on her hips. "How did you know where to find me?" To Alec, she whispered in his mind, *"Duncan's definitely here."*

"In the armory?"

"Aye, and he's bolted and blocked the door, the gap underneath it as well. I cannae stream out."

"I'm coming."

"Muirin's brother holds the sight and during our ride from Ardan House, he caught an intriguing image of you, right here in this very outbuilding." With one hand extended, he muttered, "Hand my blade across, if you will."

"Puh-lease." She scoffed and tossed it behind the benchtop. It clattered onto the floor where it would remain completely out of his reach, then she became naught more than a wisp of white, swept around him and reemerged. "Your weapon is useless against me in my spiritual form, and from what I've learnt of late, you've aligned yourself with the fae. Raising arms against me would go against your promise to my father."

"Aye, I have no intention of ever harming you, or one of the fae." He stepped closer and slowly lifted a hand and she held perfectly still as he gently touched his palm to her cheek.

"You had me bound and gagged in a tree. I call that harming." She remained on edge, prepared for his attack in case it came. If he truly had no intention of harming one of her kind, she'd soon see it.

"All for a good cause I can assure you, and even though I instructed my guards to keep Ronan contained within Coll's dungeons, I did so because Muirin needed time with Niall first, and your brother does hold the battle skill, could so easily have left if I allowed him his freedom to roam this keep." His gaze traveled down her body, over her loose-sleeved red tunic and sword fastened at her side. "On the night of your capture, you impressed me greatly with your feisty nature, although you left far too soon."

"I recall your words well. You wished for a wife."

"I've never raised a hand against a lass in my life, never intend to either."

"You stole my loved ones from me. That is raising a hand against me in the worst possible way." She dissolved her form, swept in behind him, reemerged and tripped over a sack of grain. It spilled over and grain scattered, pinged and echoed underneath her, as if the pellets had slid through a crack in the ground and toppled down something hard. Heartbeat racing, she hauled the sack out of the way. A trap door. She grabbed the iron handle protruding from the ground and heaved the lid up.

Metal clanged and candlelight flickered over the thick stone steps leading downward into the darkened depths of an underground tunnel. *"Alec, I've found the entrance to the dungeons."*

"We're almost there. No one keeps my mate from me, particularly a MacKenzie. Step back from the door." An animalist roar rumbled from outside. Something hit the door and it shuddered and rattled on its hinges.

"Hold up!" Duncan rushed toward the door and she grabbed a shovel propped against the wall, swung and hit him hard on the head. His eyes rolled, the whites showing as he toppled and crashed to the floor.

With two fingers pressed to his neck, she checked his pulse, found it steady. *"Alec, please, no more noise. You'll alert the guards and then we'll have a hundred men to fight. Duncan is down. I knocked him out, although he did naught to harm me. Give me a second to move the crate."*

"It's too late."

"It's never too late." She hauled weapon after weapon from the crate to lighten the load, steel crashing and clanging on the floor.

"The guards have already been alerted. Stand clear." Another thunderous roar reverberated.

Oh hell. She moved out of the way, fast.

Chapter 13

In the gloomy dark of the inner courtyard, shouts boomed as warriors swarmed down the side stairs from the battlements and tore from the gatehouse toward Alec. He reared back and with Kirk beside him, they heaved forward together and rammed their shoulders into the armory door. Wood creaked and the door split down the center.

"I'll ensure these warriors dinnae reach us," Cherub yelled as she raised her hands to the skies. With one flick of her fingers, clouds brewed into a swirling mass overhead and the wind rose and whipped all about.

"Let's get this door down now," Alec bellowed to Kirk.

"I'm right beside you." Kirk gritted his teeth and dipped one shoulder.

"Now." Alec hurtled forward and they plowed into the door together. Wood splintered and the door broke apart. He bounded inside over the scattered debris, his sword raised.

"I said Duncan's down." Annella jumped over the spill of weapons and bounded into his arms.

"I heard you. Where is he?" He crushed her against him, his heartbeat a raging mess.

"In the corner, and he's not getting up anytime soon.

Muirin's brother has the sight and warned Duncan I'd be here. He's well and truly out of it. He also never tried to harm me."

"He's lucky. Let me make certain he's down." He picked up a shovel, tossed it aside then crouched next to Duncan where he lay slumped on the floor. He lifted the man's eyelids and nodded. All was as Annella had said. Sword sheathed, he returned to his woman and cupping her bottom in his hands, shoved her against the wall and captured her mouth with his. He kissed her, his need wild and untamed and rising fiercely from deep within his soul. Even though in her spiritual form and unable to be harmed, he'd still been beside himself with fear. Through good times or bad, no matter what difficulties lay ahead of them, he'd always guard and protect her, never allow another to bring any harm down upon her head, either her true or ethereal forms. "Where's the trapdoor?" he murmured against her lips as he pulled back an inch.

"You sent the crate flying over it." She dropped out of his arms and pushed the crate out of the way where it had wedged itself over the entrance leading downward.

"You two go on ahead." Kirk slapped him on the back. "I'll remain outside guarding Cherub while she keeps the warriors at bay. Be careful down there."

"Will do." Outside, Duncan's warriors surged toward Cherub, their swords and battle axes raised and Cherub sent a wall of wind at them. Their enemy skidded backward, toppled head over heels across the stony yard and slammed into the curtain wall.

Dazed, a few stumbled to their feet and Cherub sent another blast of wind their way then glanced over her shoulder at him and Annella. "Go, both of you," she hollered. "And be quick. I can only keep these warriors at bay for so long."

"Thank you, and be careful." He jumped through the trap door and bounded down the steep stairs winding downward into the darkened passageway below, Annella one step behind him with a candle in her hand. "Stay behind me at all times. Are we clear on that?"

"There's no time to delay." She snuck past him and raced down into the chilly depths of the stony-walled tunnel.

Damn it. She'd disobeyed a direct order, again. No more would she do so. He pounded after her, the air holding the cloying odor of dirt and grit, her candle's flame casting its flickering glow partially down the length of the passageway ahead. Water dripped from overhead and splashed his booted feet, the mucky dirt underfoot squelching with each step he took.

"There's a divide in the tunnel up ahead." Frosty air puffed from her mouth.

"I see it." He nabbed her hand, pulled her to a halt at the junction which divided into three separate passageways, breathed deep of the air in the first corridor, then the second and lastly the third.

Annella waited, her blue eyes wide and the sparks of gold glittering bright at the edges. "What have you found?"

"The first passageway is drier, with chunks of rock on the ground and within the walls. I'd say it veers away inland toward the hills. The second has fresher air and a hint of pine, possibly leads to the forest, and the third is musty and holds the reek of urine."

"Then it appears these tunnels dinnae just hold the dungeons, but escape passages for those who reside within the keep."

"Exactly, which means we need to be quick and ensure we don't get trapped down here. Our enemy could come at us through any of the other underground entry points."

"We'll hurry." She dashed past him and down the third passageway.

"You're supposed to stay behind me," he growled as he shot off, ducked around her then halted as up ahead, voices traveled to him. With one finger to his lips, he gave her the silent command to remain quiet.

She blew out her candle, crouched and left it against the wall and stood.

Around the bend, he crept, the light from another lantern flickering somewhere up ahead, and the iron-rich taste of blood in the air coating his tongue. Hell. The scent made his bear rise and there wasn't a chance he could hold his beast back when blood had clearly been spilt. *"I need to shift."*

"Now?"

"Aye, hold onto my belongings." He shucked his clothes as quick as he could without making a noise and dumped them in her hands along with his weapons then dragged her against him and kissed her before he made the Change. In a blaze, his beast burst from him and on all fours, he pounded down the tunnel, claws slicing into the gritty floor.

Two mail-clad warriors stood outside a cell lined with iron bars, both with whips in hand, the dozen barbed tails of leather from both dripping with blood. He pawed the ground and the warriors whipped around and heaved their claymores free.

Teeth snapping, he growled. They'd harmed his mate's brother. Unacceptable.

"I'm here." Annella hunkered down behind him, spread one hand over his rump, her fingers sinking into his pelt. *"What's the plan?"*

Thick brush clogged the end of the tunnel and booming shouts swept through the scrub.

"We're about to have company, and far more than I'd like. You remain here, and I'll go and dispatch these MacKenzies. I have to take care not to kill any of them since your father has now aligned himself with this clan."

He rose up on his hind legs and roared. Forward, he charged, the two warriors both releasing a fierce battle cry. They slashed their swords as he sailed through the air and came down on top of them, blood spurting, his claws razor sharp and as precise and deadly as any blade could be. Bellowing, he sank his teeth into the wrist of one warrior and his weapon clattered to the ground, stamped on the other's body and his bones snapped. He reared back, ready to hit them again but both lay motionless on the ground, their breath rasping out. They were injured, and neither would be getting up anytime soon. Perfect.

Head down, he snorted as three more warriors surged forward through the slashed brush at the end of the tunnel, their weapons drawn, the scent of salt now stronger and the crashing of waves echoing toward him. This tunnel exited out high over the loch. He roared and tumbled all three men into each other with his fierce momentum. Blood ran, his beast raging at him as they all soared through the brush as one. Nothing but cool night air swished past him as he fell away over the side of a sheer rock wall and dropped down into the darkened depths of the ocean thirty feet below.

* * * *

Annella screamed as Alec's bear barreled through the warriors who'd slashed through the brush, their weapons coming down on him as he sent them all flying over the edge and into the dark abyss of the night-shrouded sea far below. She jumped the first two warriors he'd downed then teetered at the edge of the tunnel. The wind rushed all around, the storm Cherub had set in motion thrashing all about.

"*Alec, where are you?*" She searched the crashing swell.

"*I'm coming.*" A grunt as he shifted in the water, lights flashing, then he was there against the wall, hauling himself up using whatever hand-and-foot holds he could within the craggy rock wall. Water sluiced down his body, running in a river of red. Cuts everywhere, his pain fierce and storming down their link and saturating her. He made the top and rolled onto the ledge on his back and stared up at her. "I'm fine."

"There's so much blood. You arena fine." She fell to her knees, heart heaving as she checked each and every wound and only when she was assured he hadn't actually sustained any life-threatening injuries, did she burst into tears and thump him.

"Hey." He caught her fisted hands against his chest, his golden eyes shifter bright. "I'm truly fine."

"I'm not. Losing you would kill me."

"Shifters heal far faster than mere humans alone can, and I've always healed even swifter than any of my kin. A few changes back and forth and I'll be back to my usual self."

"Annella!" Chains rattled from one of the cells.

"Oh goodness. Ronan, I'm coming." She fled down the passageway, skidded in beside the two downed warriors, swiped the keys still jangling from the belt of one while Alec checked on both fallen men and nodded at her.

"We're clear for now, but if either of these warriors move or the other three I took with me into the sea return, then I'll tear their heads from their shoulders." He snagged his clothing which she'd dropped in her mad dash, dressed and fastened his weapons. "Give me the keys."

Hands shaking, she passed them across and he jimmied the first key in the lock. It didn't turn. He tried the second while she gripped the door's bars, the metal cold against her palms.

Ronan dangled from a chain strung over an iron hook hammered into the rocky ceiling above, his ravaged body swaying and turning, his black tunic hanging in shreds over his leather pants and his back bleeding from deep welts slashed into his skin. So much blood. It coursed down his legs and bare feet and splashed the ground.

One click and the lock popped open. Alec shoved the door and iron grated over stone.

She stumbled inside, snagged the wooden crate from the corner and hauled it across and set it firmly under Ronan's dangling body. "Feet down."

"Got it." Ronan found his footing, rolled his shoulders as he tried to ease the ache in his raised arms. Voice raspy and dry, he mumbled, "Is there another key to unlock this chain and cuffs?"

"It'll be one of these." Alec jumped up onto the crate next to Ronan, slid another key that looked like the right fit into the cuffs and turned it. The clamps swung open and fell to the ground, the chain coiling down like a snake and clattering in beside them.

Ronan swayed and Alec slid one shoulder under his arm to support him then helped him down. "Come here, little sister."

Still shaking, she grasped her brother around the waist and clung to him.

Gently, Ronan stroked the back of her head. "Are you going to introduce me to your mate? You said he was from Kirk's future bear shifter clan."

"Ronan, meet Alec, the man who holds the other half of my soul, the man I intend to wed." She rubbed her cheek against Ronan's chest, tears flowing down her cheeks. Goodness. He'd been strung up then so badly beaten, and for what reason?

"'Tis good to meet you, Alec. I enjoyed seeing your bear storming through that passageway. Those warriors deserve their broken bones." Ronan spoke over the top of her head, gave her hair a tug as he did.

"I'm sorry we couldn't get here sooner." Alec slipped a finger under her chin, tipped her gaze toward his. "Do you want me to explain about what's happened with your father?"

"Nay, I shall." She squeezed her eyes shut then opened them again and looked into Ronan's eyes. "Father has found his mate, or I should say Muirin, the fae sorceress who has allied herself with Duncan, is his mate and he's accepted their bond. Father and I spoke and he intends to fight alongside Duncan and his brother who've both apparently broken away from their father. Muirin said 'tis time for the fae to live."

"I see." Yet clear confusion swirled in his gaze.

"Are you all right?"

"I'm still a little groggy, not quite of sound mind and body as I usually am."

Aye, he needed to be tended to then allowed to rest. Following that, she'd speak some more to him. "Father won't allow any harm to come to our people. Why the beating?"

"Apparently I infuriated my guards when I demanded to see Kyla more times than they appreciated."

"This is all such a mess." She shook her head, worry consuming her.

"Aye, but we'll deal with it as we always do." Ronan hugged her. "My mate is Duncan's sister, and her soul cries out for mine, just as mine cries out for hers. Once I've healed, I'll return to this place, just however I can manage it, although preferably without being seen."

"I'll come with you when you do."

"We'll see." Ronan grimaced, arched his shoulders back then with a small smile, he popped a kiss on her forehead. "I love you. You have my immense thanks for the timely rescue."

"I love you too." She smiled at Alec, the one man she could never live without. "*Thank you for protecting me, for saving my brother and most of all, for being my chosen one.*"

"*You've accepted my beast, even tamed him as I thought none other ever could. Without you by my side, I would never survive.*"

"*I would never survive without you either.*" He was her life, and always would be.

A breeze rustled through the tunnel and swept all around then Cherub appeared out of thin air with Kirk and dashed into the cell, her golden hair a wind-tossed mess and her olive skirts flaring. She grasped Ronan's hand. "Glad I am to see you're alive."

"Thank you for coming to my aid, Cherub. It appears we still have some trialing times ahead of us, but for now we need to leave." Ronan nodded at Kirk. "How quick can we be gone from here?"

"There's a storm of warriors on our tail, warriors we need to divert and we'll do so through one of Cherub's portals." Kirk sheathed his sword. "This very moment."

Shouts and thundering footsteps ricocheted down the passageway.

"One second." Cherub glanced at each one of them. "Who has the key to this cell?"

"I do. Here." Alec tossed the keys to her as he kept Ronan propped up and on his feet.

"We need to lock ourselves inside since I dinnae wish for these warriors to jump into the portal I open. Our trip through time will be for those of Matheson blood alone. No other will be permitted through." Cherub slammed the door shut and through the bars, twisted the key in the lock then tossed the keys into the far darkened corner and held out her arms. "Grab ahold, everyone. We're about to return to Ivanson Castle and the twenty-first century."

They held on and once all connected to her, the Fae Angel of Love did as she was born to do, to protect and guard her people. With a flick of her fingers, she swirled the air blowing in and sent them all falling away into the dark abyss of time. They soared amongst the stars, thunder and lightning crashing and blazing all around. Aye, 'twas the most blessed portal Annella had ever traveled through, her brother now once again at her side and her mate so very close.

She caught Alec's hand in the churning darkness as she aided him in keeping Ronan upright, his fingers curling warm and firmly around hers. Then a minute or two later, they bumped down inside a large room holding white-painted walls and a bed on wheels that sat in the middle of it. So much white. The ceiling glowed white, as did the cupboards lining one side of the room, the steel benchtop the only concession to it all as it reflected the brightness of the lights overhead.

"Hell." Ronan jerked, his gaze wide on the lights above.

"How is there is light without fire?"

"The glass bulbs are run from electricity, and you'll find there will be a million and one other new and amazing things to discover in this time." Cherub patted Ronan's hand. "Now you're here for a visit, Kirk and I will be sure to show you around until you've healed well enough to return to your chase of Kyla."

"Aye, that is one chase I look forward to, provided I can remain out of those dungeons. I've no intention of visiting them a second time." A sparkle lit Ronan's eyes, his lips lifting. There was naught her brother adored more than fighting the good fight. Father too. Trialing days might lie ahead of them, but they'd also be days filled with a vibrant and soul-soaring hope. Ronan's mate awaited him, not lost to him as he'd always believed, and although currently beyond his reach, not for very long. Her brother would never give up his chase of Kyla, and of that she had no doubt.

"Here, let's get you sitting down." Alec aided Ronan to the white-sheeted medical bed and her brother shucked off the tattered remains of his black tunic and sat in the middle, a fluffy pillow at one end and a white folded blanket at the other.

"I'll go and fetch Tavish. He's our clan doctor and an excellent healer." Kirk strode out the door, his black war coat flapping at his sides and his sword gleaming.

Never more glad to be back on Matheson land, Annella twirled around, caught Cherub's hands and whirled her about too, such happiness overflowing her heart. "You've done so much for me, Cherub, stood right by my side during this perilous journey and never faltered with your aid. You have my immense thanks."

"I will always be wherever my fae kind need me, no matter what time or place that draws me toward."

"'Tis so wonderful to be back." She released Cherub and bounced to the window. Palms on the windowsill, she took in the moonlit inner courtyard of Ivanson Castle, the curtain wall rising high and the forest's treetops beyond swaying in the distance. Aye, she was back in Alec's time and where he'd brought her physical body. Eyes closed, she reached out with her senses and found herself lying in her mate's chamber one floor higher up and farther down the hallway, exactly where she wished to be, snuggled in his—

Her chest tightened.

"Annella." Alec moved in behind her, slid his hands over her shoulders then turned her around to face him. "Do you wish to return to your true form?"

"I must stay with Ronan until—"

"Nay," Ronan grumbled from across the room. "Time is marching on and you're still in your spiritual form. Return, little sister. I'll speak to you again once I'm done with the healer."

"Are you certain you wish for me to go?"

"Aye, too much time spent away from your true self isnae good for you. Do you no' remember how Mother was toward the end?"

"I remember and you're right." The tightening in her chest was her true body's warning to her, and that tightening would spike into fierce pain should she not take care and return. She filled a tumbler with water from the sink and handed it to Ronan, gave him a gentle hug as she made certain not to touch an open wound. "Be good while I'm gone, and do exactly as the healer says."

"Aren't I always good?" With a teasing smile, he sipped the water.

"No' that I've ever seen." Giggling, she twirled back to Alec and twined her arms around his neck, slid her fingers deep into his silky black hair and looking into his golden shifter eyes, got lost, her very heart and soul now held within his hands. "Without you I'd have no reason to live."

"Then it's time to live."

"My thoughts exactly." On her toes, she reached up to touch her lips to his but her true form pulled more strongly at her. Her heart skipped a beat, her breath coming harder. Her physical body would wait no longer.

"What's wrong?" He gripped her arms.

"I must leave. There is no more time." She dissolved her form, shimmered away through the starlit expanse of dark and breezed back to her body, her heart throbbing at having left her chosen one.

She gasped, flung her eyes open and dragged in a deep breath and rubbed her aching chest.

"Are you all right, my dear?" A woman in her mid-forties wearing a wine-colored woolen skirt and white blouse with a ruffled neckline, her dark wavy hair bobbing on her shoulders, leaned over her in the bed, two fingers pressed to her wrist. "Your pulse stopped then started then skittered right out of time. I'm Megan, Kirk's mother and the chief's wife. Alec requested I guard your body."

"'I'm fine now that I'm back, and 'tis lovely to meet you Megan. When I'm gone too long from my body, it sends me a warning, one I must always heed if I'm to ensure I remain right here on this Earth. Thank you for watching over me while I was gone."

"I shall always do so if you need the aid."

"Annella!" The door banged open and Alec was there, his chest pumping out and almost popping the buttons on his steel-studded gray jacket. He rushed toward the bed, hauled her out from underneath the black fur cover and crushed her in his arms. "Don't you ever leave me like that again."

The door clicked shut, Megan having quietly left.

"I'm sorry. I didnae mean to worry you so." She brushed her lips across his then snuggled her cheek against his chest and—was that chocolate on the pillow? Smiling, she snatched it up, broke off a piece and popped it in her mouth. Mmm, delicious. Her belly rumbled for more and she broke off another square, waved it in front of her mate's nose. "Are you hungry?"

"I'm famished, but for far more than mere chocolate alone." With his teeth, he nipped the square from between her fingers then he scooped her into his arms and strode with her into his bathroom, hit the light switch with his elbow and knocked the door shut with his hip.

Gently, he set her down on her feet on the white tiled floor in the center of the room, unstrapped her sword belt from her waist and her dagger from her wrist, placed her weapons on top of the black marble vanity and removed his own weapons and added them to the pile of armory.

Hands on the hem of her dusty red tunic, he lifted it over her head and tossed it into the corner wicker basket then gazed at her breasts, all full and pink-tipped and now bobbing free. "Beautiful. I want to eat you."

"Make sure you take your time when you do." She popped another square of chocolate into her mouth.

"Now we finally have all the time in the world, I shall." He dipped his head and laved each beaded nipple, his tongue rasping over the tips and making them pinch even tighter. Exquisite. Her legs trembled and she dropped the chocolate bar, her chosen one the only treasure she wished to consume. She wanted each and every inch of him touching each and every inch of her, their bodies unclothed and not a breath of air separating them.

"You are far too overdressed, my mighty bear."

"Then let me get rid of my clothes." He shrugged his steel-studded gray jacket off, stripped his billowy white tunic over his head and sent both items sailing into the basket. His golden skin, broad shoulders, and chest packed with muscle made her fingertips tingle with the need to touch him.

Carefully, she walked around him, inspected a long cut on his shoulder and back, a few on his sides then coming back around in front, she touched a nick along his neck and frowned at the grazes slashing his chest. Red, each and every one of them, but also partially sealed over, the healing process having already begun. "You said making the Change increases your ability to heal. Shift again."

"Are you certain? My bear might get a little pushy with you being half undressed and in the same room as him."

"I can handle your bear."

"Aye, that you can, and with sheer perfection." Grinning, he kicked off his boots, shoved his black pants to the floor and stepped out of them. His cock rose sure and strong from the thatch of dark curls at the juncture of his groin, the head of his shaft plumping to a deep purple color. "Are you ready?"

"Almost." She leaned in, licked across one cut on his chest then sucked his tight male nipple into her mouth. She moaned at the deliciousness of him.

"I can't shift if you keep doing that, love."

"I'm sorry, I'm getting greedy, and you're still injured."

"I've been injured far worse than this over the years, but I'll make the Change and show you my injuries never last long." He stepped back, shook his dark mane of hair that brushed his shoulders then in a lightning bright display, shifted and lumbered around her, his beast's silky black pelt the same stunning color as the hair on his head. He brushed against her legs then pushed her back toward the shower until her back knocked into the glass door.

On his hind legs, he rose up, slammed his paws down either side of her head, the shower door rattling as he growled, all low and throaty, and just the way she loved.

"I dinnae believe I'll ever tire of seeing you shift." Her magnificent bear, so fierce and demanding, completely enthralled her. She wrapped her arms around his neck as he loomed over her, his hot breath pulsing from between his sharp teeth. "I would like to thank you for guarding me so well these past few days."

His growl tapered away, turned into a hungry rumble as he swiped his tongue across her cheek then he pushed his chest toward her and she giggled and scratched his belly until one long purr vibrated from him.

"Do you feel better?"

A low moan as he stretched, pushed off the glass door and plopped down onto the tiled floor and flopped onto his back, paws extended and his belly on full display.

"Oooh, I finally get full submission." She knelt, spread her hands over his belly and gave him a tummy rub until he closed his eyes, his purr so loud it made her sigh with delight. Such a magical moment, one she wanted to experience each and every day of her life. Just the two of them like this, both together and his big bossy bear showing her exactly how very docile he could be. "Will your cuts have healed sufficiently by now? I want my chosen one in the flesh, returned to me and showing me exactly how very well we come together as one."

In a bright sizzle of lights, he made the Change and she gasped as he lay on the floor, the cuts scattered across his body now barely visible.

"That's incredible." She caressed his skin, smoothed one finger down the center of his wide chest and along the dusting of hair narrowing between his impressively defined abs. Along his trim waist, she swept her finger back and forth, his cock lengthening and thickening even further and her desire to touch more of him swarmed through her. Leaning over him, she swished her breasts across his chest, her nipples tightening at the decadent touch then with her lips a mere whisper from his, she murmured, "I wish for you to make me yours."

"You're already mine, fully and completely." He wrapped his arms around her, rolled them both over and pressed her back into a plush white bathroom rug in the center of the room, his glorious body spread perfectly over hers.

She gripped his bulging biceps, roamed down his arms,

over his sides and cupped his backside. "I cannae wait to hold your body deep inside mine."

"I can't wait to wed you and call you my wife." He eased down her body then on his knees, knelt between her spread legs, bent and with his teeth, gnawed on the ties of her black rawhide breeches. His warm breath feathered across her skin and sent a bolt of heat straight to her core.

"And when shall we wed?" Mmm, his touch, so sinfully delicious, made her ravenous for more and she raked her nails over his scalp until he growled. He nabbed one knee-high leather boot, tugged it off then tossed the other aside as well before gripping her waistband and hauling her breeches down her legs. With his hands on her hips, he nipped her belly button and nuzzled her mound.

"The first moment we can." He blew a soft breath across her mound, his teasing touch drifting over her entrance. "You're so beautiful, every single inch of you. I need to taste you and it can't wait any longer, but if I go too fast right now, tell me to slow down." He spread her legs even wider. "Both me and my other half are roaring for more of you."

"I have no need to be anywhere else but right here with you. Take all the time you need, fast or slow. It matters not to me."

"I love it when you get all agreeable." Pure need laced his tone as he rubbed his cheeks against the insides of her thighs, his nose bumping her nub. He breathed deep, slid one finger along her seam then pushed inside her and touched a spot that had her arching into him.

"I can be this agreeable whenever you wish." Her breath came harder and she gripped the rug underneath her. "Give me more."

"More you shall have." Licking her most private place, he plunged a second finger inside her and caressed her, so wickedly, so deliciously, his rhythm making her rise toward a peak she only wished to fly from. Every flick of his tongue and stroke of his fingers built her desire higher and higher, until it rose to such a swift and thunderous level she could no longer hold on to.

She rocked, her breasts thrust high and her need for him consuming her. "Alec." She cried out his name. "I cannae hold on any longer. Come inside me."

"Are you certain?"

"Very."

"I love how very much you need me." He flipped her over onto her belly, lifted her onto her knees and crawled in over top of her. Completely covering her body with his, he teased her with the caress of his skin across hers.

"I will always need you, to the depths of my soul." Over her shoulder, she smiled back at him, her hair sliding over her side and swishing onto the floor. "Take me."

"I intend to take you over and over until this night has passed and a new day dawns." Folds opened with his fingers, he gazed at her, stroked along her slit and scraped his teeth back and forth along her neck. "Are you ready?"

"Aye, mark me so well that there will be none who could ever say I am no' yours."

"Good answer." With her hips clasped in his hands, he pushed his cock between her legs and before she could draw her next breath, he plunged deep inside her with one fast and sure stroke, his mind tunneling deep inside hers and locking around tight. He shared his fierce pleasure and she shared her own.

More. She still needed more.

"I've got you." He sank his teeth into her neck and a wild surge of pleasure barreled through her. Her inner muscles contracted and as he thrust, she urged him deeper, pushed her backside back into his groin and met each and every one of his hard and fast moves. His possession was everything she needed and desired, their bodies joined so completely together as he sent her soaring to the stars.

Such indescribable pleasure roared through her. She'd been

gifted with such a wonderful mate and an incredibly deep soul bond that sent her heart lifting high. "I love you, Alec, your fierce bear and your complete and utter devotion and possession. I will always want you, only you."

"As I love you. You're my match in every way, my every hope and dream. We'll stand at each other's sides for the rest of our lives." He plunged balls-deep inside her, his seed shooting to her core and caressing her with its warmth. "This day, I give you all of me."

"As I do with you." Flying over the edge, she soared and joined him in heaven amongst the brilliance of the stars, her body clamping tightly around his and their souls now forever entwined. Aye, she was his for all time, just as he was hers and together, they'd journey to where their souls would always remain united, until the end of time.

* * * *

Such pleasure ricocheted through Alec's body as Annella pulsed around his cock. His hunger for her increased even though he'd just come. Aye, he needed her with a thirst his bear would never relinquish and he only hoped his mate was prepared for the depth his hunger would rage this night. He stroked deep inside her, her breathy little moans making him stiffen and go excruciatingly hard all over again. Grazing her neck with his teeth, he scraped over the mark he'd made then soothed it with a lick or two before he pulled out of her. Not for long though. He turned her over onto her back on the white rug, pushed her inner thighs wider with his knees and thrust his cock back through her lower folds and into the heart of her welcoming heat.

She stirred, her eyelids fluttering open. "You're insatiable."

"Which is something that'll never change. I want your bite. Have you enough energy to oblige?" He longed for her mark of claim and always would, intended to shower her with his own brand before he took her to his bed and lavished even more attention on her. Head dipped to hers, he swept his tongue inside her mouth and kissed her, until her breath became as ragged as his and their joint desire flared to a staggering height.

"Harder." Deep panting from his chosen one. "I want it harder, Alec."

So did he, only her full breasts captured his attention and he had no desire to neglect them a moment more. He rolled his tongue around one exquisite nipple, sucked the treasure deep inside his mouth and groaned as his need for her escalated to an excruciating level. No holding back. He surged into her below as he lavished her breasts, nipping, licking, kissing and devouring them. Hell. She tasted so delicious, and her pure womanly scent rose and swirled all around him. 'Twas pure torture, but in the most divine way. He'd need another taste of her down there, and soon if he was going to survive this day.

Half insane with need, he razzed his teeth over the sensitive flesh on the other side of her neck. "When I bite you, I want you to bite me in return. That's an order."

"Aye, Captain."

"Thank you." He slid his palm around the back of her head and drew her mouth to his neck, and as she stretched and offered her neck more fully to him, he suctioned his mouth over her flesh and drew it deep between his lips.

Licking and sucking her neck, he trailed one hand down her belly and over the golden curls covering her entrance. He caressed her clit and she reached down and palmed his balls, her soft touch making his bear roar for dominance and buck into her. He growled and bit down and she thrashed underneath him and bit him in return, her channel clamping fiercely tight around his cock and squeezing with sheer perfection. Over and over, he came, in one long hot rush that sent his essence streaming thick and full straight to her womb and she bathed him in her sensual heat, her body clenching so perfectly around him and together, their minds deeply entrenched within each other's, they flew to the heavens then soared far beyond.

"Oh goodness." She went limp underneath him and he slowed his rocking as he gently brought them both back down.

"Are you all right?"

Dreamily, she sighed. "I dinnae know where you begin and I end."

"Which is as it should be." He cupped her face in his hands and kissed her, moved his mouth slowly over hers and cherished her lips. The shower. He needed to at least get her into the shower then he'd take her to his bed. The hot water would refresh her, ease any discomfort he'd caused by taking her on the floor and before his bear reared up and made even more demands, he pulled out of her, scooped her up and opened the shower door. Lever flicked on, he stuck his hand under the water and once it had warmed to the perfect temperature, he swept her inside with him and closed the door.

Hot water pummeled his back and he lowered the pressure, turned her into the spray and smiled as she soaked in the steamy heat that swirled all around them.

"This is wonderful." She wrapped her arms around his neck, fingers gliding through his hair and her nails scraping over his scalp.

"I love it when you do that. Your possessive touch makes my bear roll around for more."

"He's a greedy beast." With her long golden tresses tumbling to her waist, she stroked down his back.

"He always will be." He grasped her pert bottom, locked his gaze with hers and almost drowned in her beautiful blue eyes with their sparks of gold glittering bright at the edges. "Can you handle it?"

"I shall likely be just as greedy."

"Show me." He ached to be deep inside her again, the flare of need burning at the base of his spine and making his cock go rock hard once more.

"As you wish, but just know that I want it hard and fast

again, with you filling me up." She pushed him against the glass side, lifted one knee and rose onto the very tips of her toes. "Lift me over you."

He lifted her up then brought her back down right over his cock, hard and fast and exactly as she'd commanded, the hot shower water sluicing down their bodies and her smooth skin rubbing slickly against his. Ravenous, he captured her mouth with his and kissed her, shared his hunger and soaked up the burning desire she held for him in return. Such an all-consuming need filled him and as she crushed her breasts against his chest and sucked on his neck, his cock throbbed and he pumped into her.

He got lost within her mind, her bite and body, her heart and soul all his and he savored the fierce peak of pleasure which sent them both hurtling to the stars. No more being alone. He'd found his chosen one, a woman who matched him in every single way, from her beautiful, fiery spirit to her ability to battle right alongside him. His heart expanded, drew her in and folded itself around her.

Love, peace, and promise.

She'd gifted him with it all, and never had he ever been more grateful.

She was his, always his.

Chapter 14

On the high grassy peak of Ben Nevis, the late afternoon sunshine flaring overhead and the wilderness surrounding them far below, Annella stood in front of her warrior shifter as he wrapped his arms around her from behind. It had been three weeks since their return to Alec's home at Ivanson and three days following their arrival, they'd spoken vows before his clan's clergyman, her brother and their kin. A more beautiful day she couldn't have asked for.

"Thank you for bringing me here," she murmured as she stroked his muscled arms crossed firmly around her waist, their satchels propped against a rock near a plaque that declared James Robertson's name and the year seventeen-hundred and seventy-one as the date he'd first scaled this tallest mountain in the heart of the Highlands. "I've never been so deliriously happy as I have since I arrived."

A hawk swept the air currents high above then drifted down over the large pines below, the glistening blue-green waters of three lochs zigzagging the lower land and a misty mountain fog flowing up the rise and swirling all around.

"I intend for you to always be this deliriously happy." He slid his hands underneath the fluttering hem of her silver threaded tunic and caressed her hips. "We are also all alone without another soul about."

"Is your bear getting hungry again?" She turned in his arms, tugged his royal blue shirt over his head, skimmed her fingers across his tanned chest and tip-toed down to the ties of his tan leather pants.

"He'll always be ravenous for you, as will I." His golden shifter eyes heated to a smoldering hue, then deftly, he eased her snug black pants down her legs and tumbled her onto the lush grass. "Both here in my time and in yours."

"I cannae wait to see my clansmen when we return." Her brother's chase for his chosen one would soon begin and if he needed her aid then she would be there for him. She certainly longed to see him capture and contain the one who held the other half of his soul, just as she'd captured and contained her chosen one.

"I'd rather see more of you right now." He stripped off her tunic and kissed her with such searing seduction. "Mmm, all mine."

Heavenly tingles raced through her body and across her skin then with heart-pounding need, she gave herself over to her mate and his fierce hunger, hers just as ravenous as his.

Their destiny was set, their souls and spirits united as one.

"Give me your child," she whispered against his lips. "Right now. I wish for my mighty bear to have a son."

"As you wish, although I have a confession."

"And what would that be?" She moaned underneath him as he surged into her.

"We shifters can scent when our mate is at her most fertile and then again when she has conceived, and you my love, are already carrying my child." One wicked grin as he thrust fully home and sent her careening toward the highest heavenly peak.

A more perfect joining she couldn't have asked for, and when she slowly came back down, she grinned as widely as her chosen one did. He was the most precious gift she'd ever been given, a treasure she'd cherish for all time to come, and when their child arrived, she would have yet another part of him to love and adore.

So much love filled her heart, too much to contain. She pushed against his chest and rolled him over, then with her joy overflowing her, she took him deep inside her body and made love to him all over again.

'Twas the most perfect union, one of the heart, body, and soul.

One she'd crave for all time to come.

Always.

Come and join **Ronan and Kyla** in **Highlander's Bride** as their adventure unfolds. Theirs is to be a sweeping journey across the Highlands with red-hot passion.

Author's Note

Clan Matheson descends from a twelfth century man called Gilleoin, a man who was believed to have been from the ancient Royal House of Lorne. The name Matheson has been attributed to the Gaelic words Mic Mhathghamhuim which means "Son of the Bear," and the clan chief's arms carry two bears as supporters. In the twelfth century, clan Matheson settled around the area of Loch Alsh, Loch Carron, and Kintail, and gave their allegiance to clan MacDonald whose chiefs were the Lords of the Isles. Clan Matheson became a large and powerful clan with a force of around two-thousand men, although by the middle of the sixteenth century they'd diminished greatly in size and influence due to the blood feuds raging across the isles at that time. This warring left them to possess less than a third of the original Matheson property on Loch Alsh.

It's also well known in history that clan Matheson also forged an alliance with clan MacKenzie during the middle ages, which meant at times the two clans fought side by side, yet also against each other when clan Matheson found themselves stuck in the middle of the feuding between the MacDonalds and the MacKenzies. Be sure to catch the next book in this series to see where things head in the future and how I've captured the alliance made between both the Mathesons and the MacKenzies to come.

It's time for the whispers to reignite. Clan Matheson are the "Son of the Bear."

This story is woven with as much accuracy to the period and locations as possible, although any mistakes made are mine alone.

Please feel free to search for any of my other works. I simply adore strong heroines, and have a ton of fun matching them with their honorable alpha heroes.

Looking for more sexy Scottish adventure?

Catch a teaser excerpt of the next book in
The Matheson Brothers series.

Highlander's Bride

The Matheson Brothers, Book Seven

by Joanne Wadsworth

Highlander's Bride

The Matheson Brothers, Book Seven

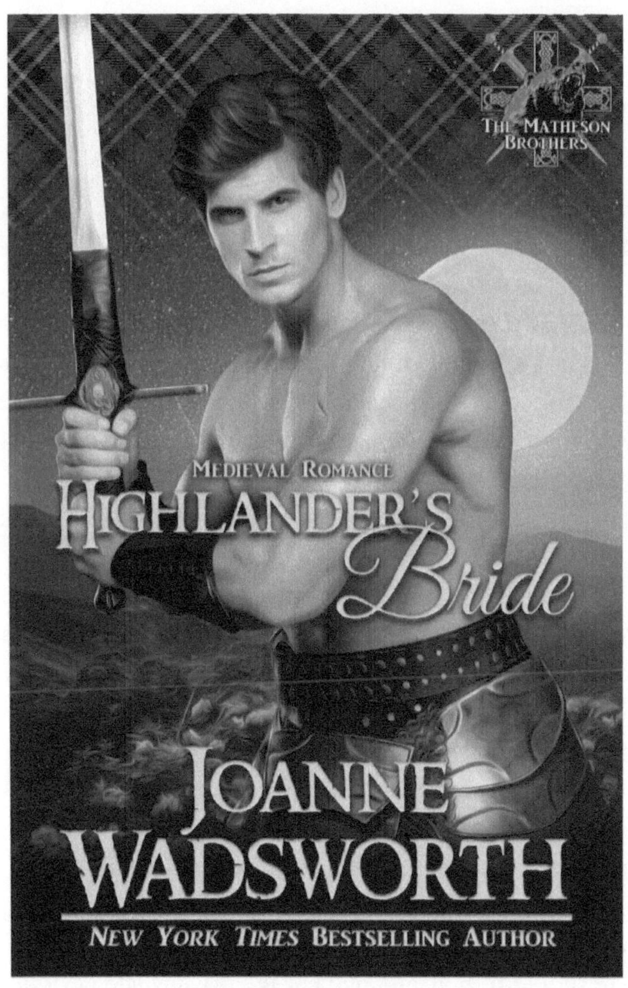

Teaser Excerpt

For the past month since Ronan's escape from Carron Castle's dungeons all he'd wished to do was heal then ensure an adequate disguise so he might return to Kyla without anyone discovering his true identity. He longed to see the fiery spark in her blue eyes. She was spectacular, mesmerizing, a true Scottish lass with the fire of the fae in her blood. Aye, no more would he allow his mate to deny their bond.

Along the trail, he snuck then halted as up ahead splashing trickled toward him.

With nary a noise, he stepped out from amongst the thick trees encircling a clearing. Sunshine rippled across the glistening surface of a perfectly round pool holding his enticing siren within.

Scooping water at her sides, Kyla floated on her back, her waist-length locks splaying out like a lily pad of golden-red, her dainty face upturned and eyes closed. The water swelled around her, cascaded over her bare legs and belly. Her full breasts rose above the surface and—hell. He hadn't expected to find her without a stitch of clothing on.

He should turn away, give her the privacy she desired, only doing so right now was impossible. Her lips, softly parted, drew his gaze even though every curved inch of her remained on glorious display. His chosen one had been raised far away from her true clan, and now his battle to capture and contain his fiery mate had begun, a battle he'd never walk away from.

Today, she'd learn that the fae never gave up on one of their own.

He lowered his satchel to the ground, toed off his boots and unbelted his sword. 'Twas time for his mate to see he was back and wasn't leaving without her, not one more time. At the edge of the pool, he planted his hands on his hips, determination spurring him on. "Kyla."

Water splashed and his enticing siren gasped and dunked under the surface. She came back up spluttering, her beautiful blue eyes alight. "Coll? What are you—" She scrubbed her knuckles into her eyes then blinked. "Nay, you're no' Coll. Who are you?"

"Rand MacKenzie, my lady, at your service."

JOANNE WADSWORTH

The Matheson Brothers

Highlander's Desire, Book One
Highlander's Passion, Book Two
Highlander's Seduction, Book Three

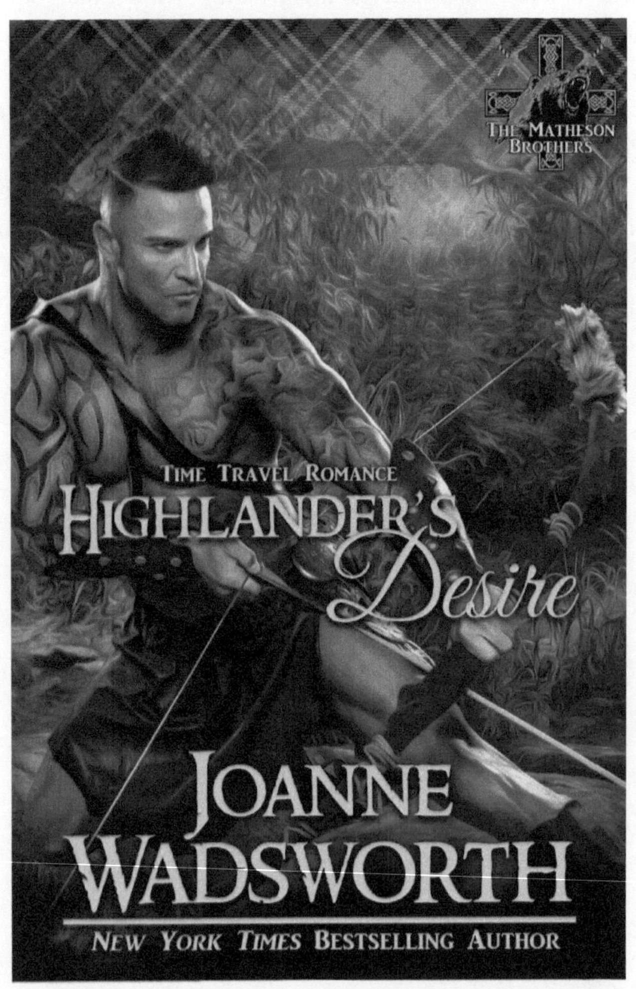

The Matheson Brothers Continued

Highlander's Kiss, Book Four
Highlander's Heart, Book Five
Highlander's Sword, Book Six

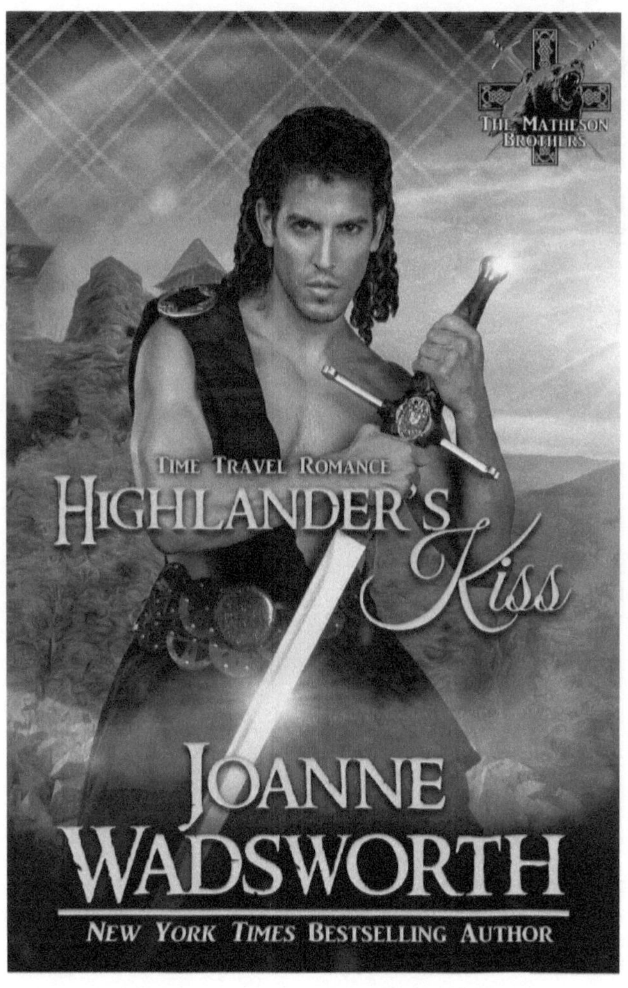

JOANNE WADSWORTH

The Matheson Brothers Continued

Highlander's Bride, Book Seven
Highlander's Caress, Book Eight
Highlander's Touch, Book Nine

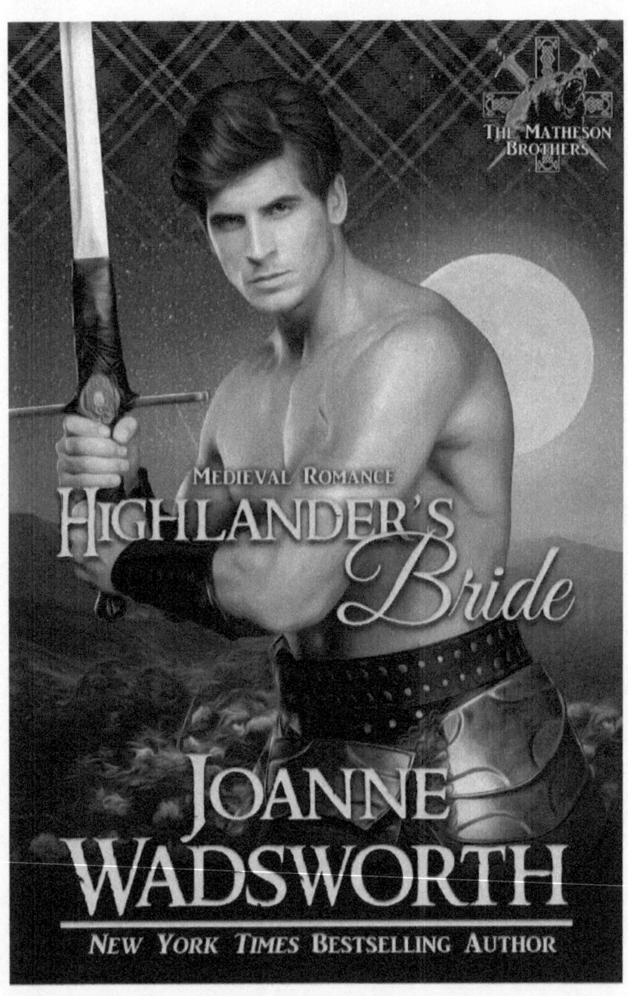

The Matheson Brothers Continued

Highlander's Shifter, Book Ten
Highlander's Claim, Book Eleven
Highlander's Courage, Book Twelve
Highlander's Mermaid, Book Thirteen

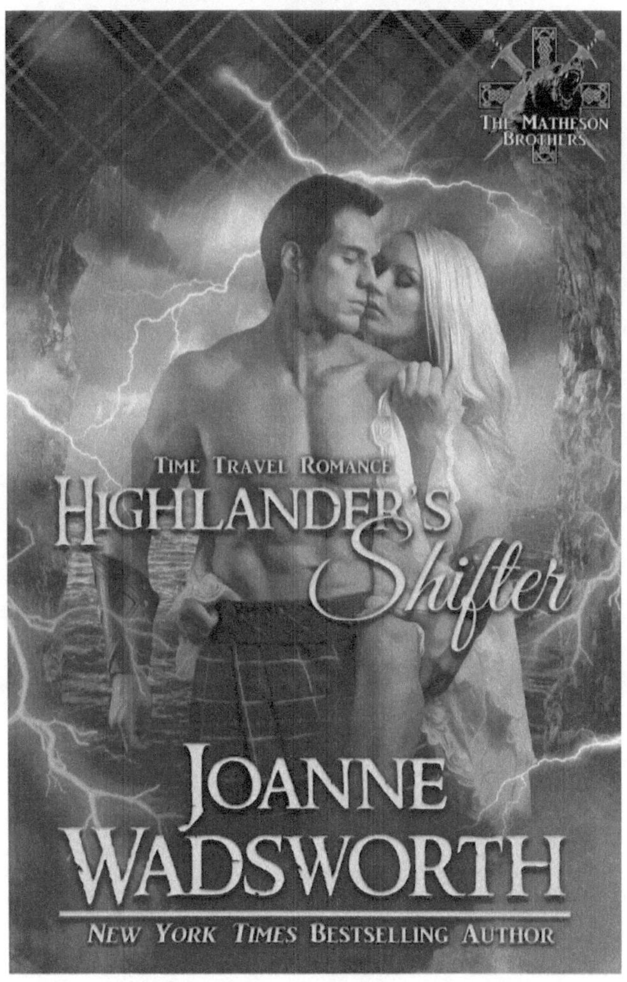

JOANNE WADSWORTH

Highlander Heat

Highlander's Castle, Book One
Highlander's Magic, Book Two
Highlander's Charm, Book Three
Highlander's Guardian, Book Four
Highlander's Faerie, Book Five
Highlander's Champion, Book Six

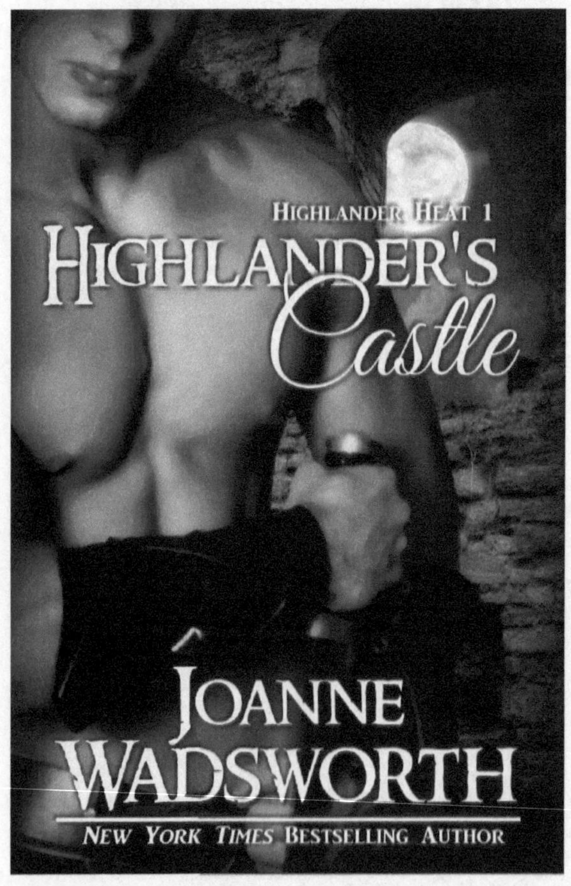

Regency Brides

The Duke's Bride, Book One
The Earl's Bride, Book Two
The Wartime Bride, Book Three
The Earl's Secret Bride, Book Four
The Prince's Bride, Book Five
Her Pirate Prince, Book Six

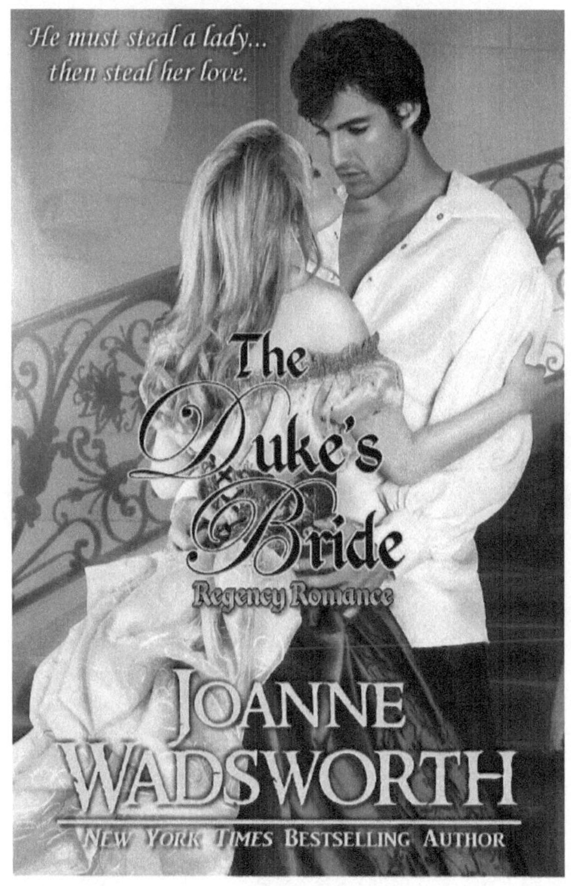

JOANNE WADSWORTH

Princesses of Myth

Protector, Book One
Warrior, Book Two
Hunter (Short Story - Included in Warrior, Book Two)
Enchanter, Book Three
Healer, Book Four
Chaser, Book Five

Billionaire Bodyguards

Billionaire Bodyguard Attraction, Book One
Billionaire Bodyguard Boss, Book Two
Billionaire Bodyguard Fling, Book Three

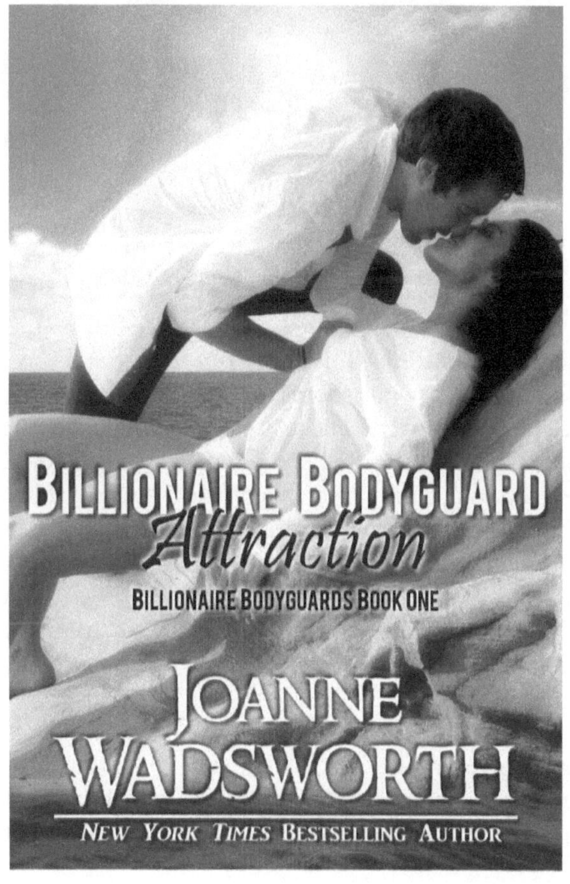

JOANNE WADSWORTH

Joanne Wadsworth is a *New York Times* and *USA Today* Bestselling Author who adores getting lost in the world of romance, no matter what era in time that might be. Hot alpha Highlanders hound her, demanding their stories are told and she's devoted to ensuring they meet their match, whether that be with a feisty lass from the present or far in the past.

Living on a tiny island at the bottom of the world, she calls New Zealand home. Big-dreamer, hoarder of chocolate, and addicted to juicy watermelons since the age of five, she chases after her four energetic children and has her own hunky hubby on the side.

So come and join in all the fun, because this kiwi girl promises to give you her "Hot-Highlander" oath, to bring you a heart-pounding, sexy adventure from the moment you turn the first page. This is where romance meets fantasy and adventure…

To learn more about Joanne and her works, visit
http://www.joannewadsworth.com

www.ingramcontent.com/pod-product-compliance
Lightning Source LLC
Chambersburg PA
CBHW030822210726
48290CB00002B/718